WENDY LOU JONES

I was born and raised in West Sussex and moved to Birmingham to study Medicine at University, where I was lucky enough to meet my husband. We now live in a little village in Herefordshire with our two grubby boys. I discovered a love of writing not long after my youngest son started school. And if you were to ask me what it was that made me make the switch, I'd tell you quite simply, that it started with a dream.

You can follow me on Twitter @WendyLouWriter.

By My Side

WENDY LOU JONES

A division of HarperCollins*Publishers*
www.harpercollins.co.uk

HarperImpulse an imprint of
HarperCollins*Publishers* Ltd
77–85 Fulham Palace Road
Hammersmith, London W6 8JB

www.harpercollins.co.uk

A Paperback Original 2014

First published in Great Britain in ebook format by HarperImpulse 2014

Cover images © Shutterstock.com

Wendy Lou Jones asserts the moral right
to be identified as the author of this work

A catalogue record for this book is
available from the British Library

ISBN: 9780008104405

This novel is entirely a work of fiction.
The names, characters and incidents portrayed in it are
the work of the author's imagination. Any resemblance to
actual persons, living or dead, events or localities is
entirely coincidental.

Automatically produced by Atomik ePublisher from Easypress

For my mum, whose patience and love helped shape me into the person I am today. Blame her!

Chapter 1

The woman had heard the whispering; she had seen the furtive glances and listened to the hushed tones that faltered every time the girl looked up. She had looked into the mother's face and seen the torment hiding there. She knew the story, the hurt that had been caused and the agony of loneliness felt by the girl. She knew, and that was why she was there.

Looking around the room, Lena could see huddles of faces talking quietly together, their eyes speaking loudly in their attempt to convey harsh rumour with subtlety. How could they think she wouldn't have noticed? Their whispering would have been pointless about anything else. She sighed and looked over at the covered windows, deliberately screening the faces within from the harsh light of the bright summer's day.

Cards covered every surface. Flowers poured out their overpowering scent to all around them; oppressive, claustrophobic, smothering.

It had been nearly a month since Lena had tried to take her own life and now she was left empty, trapped under the weight of guilt and loneliness.

She looked at her ragged finger nails, worn down by the loss of her best friend and boyfriend in the same stupid affair. Of course, the two lovers had never stood a chance after she'd found them together. Their guilt had put paid to that. But for Lena it had all been too much, and in losing both of them she had also lost faith in herself and even life. Away at university, she had failed her end of year exams and one afternoon, had taken herself off and quietly swallowed a handful of tablets with a bottle of gin.

Her friend, for her sins, had been the one to find her, lying alone and unconscious in her student house.

Her mother had stuck by her every moment since that day. That was why Lena was there, at a stranger's house, for a funeral of a person she didn't even know. It was a funeral, for heaven's sake; who in their right mind brought a depressed person to a funeral? Whoever it was, meant nothing to her, but her mum seemed to think she wasn't safe to be left on her own. Maybe she wasn't? Not anymore. She didn't resent her mother for her loss of freedom; she had brought it on herself. But still, she would rather not have been there.

The doorbell rang and a friend of the grieving family walked sombrely over to answer it. Faces turned as another huddle, dressed in black, slipped inside to sip tea and join with the others in their attempts to meet the desolation in the family's gaze.

Through the gap in the door, bright light streamed in and Lena caught a quick glimpse of the dozens of beautiful wreaths laid out along the pathway of the small front garden, the vibrant colour basking in the warmth of the summer sun, and then it was gone.

A few minutes passed and the bell rang again. Caterers appeared. They were shown into the dining room and quietly started to set up.

No-one came near her. They were all too scared to try. So she stayed trapped in her cocoon, remote and afraid.

Gloria moved through the void that circled her daughter, her face trying hard not to reflect her despair. "Are you all right, Lee?" she asked laying a gentle hand on the side of Lena's head. Lena nodded. "It shouldn't be too long now," she said. "The cars are meant to be arriving shortly. I'm just helping out with the tea. Would you like to come and help me, or are you all right in here?"

Lena had looked into her mother's eyes and seen the suffering there. "I'm fine," she said. She paused momentarily from picking her fingers to look up and then Gloria nodded and walked back to the kitchen, looking like the weight of the world was resting on her shoulders.

From beside her, a woman began to speak. Lena hadn't even been aware that anyone had sat down there. She turned and looked at her, a young woman, probably in her thirties, dressed unusually for the day in a deep blue top and skirt and smiling warmly at her. Lena was a little unnerved by the woman's arrival in her bubble. She turned back to her lap and continued picking at her fingers.

"You know, I could tell you a story about a woman who met the love of her life at a funeral," the woman said.

Lena looked back at her. "Sorry?"

"I said, I could tell you a story about a woman who met the love of her life at a funeral. If you like? Well, not *at* a funeral, but shortly after."

Lena's face turned back to her lap, she kept her eyes on her fingers, barely muttering an acknowledgement.

"You're Gloria's girl, aren't you? Lena, isn't it?"

Lena nodded and briefly met her gaze again with curiosity.

"We used to work together, your mother and I. A wonderful woman, isn't she? Always ready to help if you need her."

A barely noticeable nod was the only proof Lena was willing to offer that she was actually listening, but the woman did not seem to mind and she carried on.

"She was a bit like you, in a way."

Lena's eyebrows pulled together into a frown.

"The woman in my story. *She'd* lost her faith in love too. Hurt too deeply, I suppose," the woman said.

Wondering how painful this was going to be, Lena looked out around the room for distraction and then returned her gaze to her lap.

"Of course she didn't realise it at the time," the woman continued.

Lena let out a harsh breath, wishing the woman next to her would go away, but then she thought better of it, deciding it would at least pass the time, and so she asked, more politely, "Realise what?"

"That he was the love of her life," she said, infinitely patient with her.

The woman waited for a moment to see if Lena would look up and when she did the woman smiled. "Would you like to hear it?"

Lena weighed this up and then finding nothing better to do, she nodded. "Okay."

The woman laid a soft hand, as light as a feather, on Lena's right arm and began.

"It was a few years ago when it started," she said. "The woman's name was Kate and this story starts with her sat at her grandfather's funeral. She was only a few years older than you are now, and it was near the end of the service. You know? When the curtain comes round and that feeling of complete emptiness finally hits you...

~~~

Kate was looking straight ahead to where the coffin had been standing, daring her to touch it, to throw her arms around the wooden shell and beg her grandfather to stay. Fresh tears began to creep out along well-trodden pathways and she reached again for the handkerchief she'd not long stowed. Kate's father asked her if she was all right. She nodded, composing herself and they walked back outside in quiet procession.

The family had gathered around to look at the flowers and read the fond farewells, but Kate could not. She forced herself to talk politely with aunts and cousins for a short while but then she had to go.

She wasn't sorry to be out of there. Small talk and sandwiches are little comfort on days such as these. So she said her goodbyes to her mum and dad and made her way quickly back to her car, with just enough time to get home and change before her shift started at two.

At work that afternoon, Kate tried to carry on as if it was just another day. She stitched and bandaged and cleared up the mess that life had brought in and then, about half way through the afternoon, she was asked to escort a patient from Accident & Emergency up to Aintree ward.

As they arrived, a nurse walked over to greet them.

"This is Mr Patterson," Kate told her, handing over a rather bulky set of notes. "Right upper quadrant pain. He's been seen and sorted by the doctor in A&E and the bloods have already gone off. We've given him some analgesia so he's a bit more comfortable now. He just needs his drug chart writing up. The doctor said she'd do that when she got to the ward because she had to dash off, so if you give her a bleep when you're ready, she'll be expecting you."

The nurse thanked her and turned to the patient, smiling warmly. "Mr Patterson," she said. "Let's get you settled in then, shall we?" And she turned to the porter, "Bay Four, please, Mike."

Walking back along the ward, Kate passed a bay where one of the teams was busy doing a ward round, but what she heard as she passed made her stop in horror. A rather stern-looking orthopaedic surgeon was standing, towering over a young lad with an injured leg. The lad was lying in bed with a pile of metalwork sticking out of his shin, and cuts and grazes all over his body, and the consultant, whose voice was not unduly loud, but abrasive, was haranguing him about his inconsiderate attitude.

"Who gave you the right to play with other people's lives?" he said. "The woman you crashed into had no say in it at all. She'll be lucky if she gets out of here in any condition resembling her former life, and you get away with little more than a broken leg.

And you're young; you'll heal quickly. Think about that the next time you get behind the wheel of a car. Think about that woman and what you've done to her." The registrar cleared his throat as the rest of the team examined the floor about them. "The only person you've got to blame for this is yourself." He pointed sharply at the patient. "So stop moaning and complaining about your lot and start making an effort."

If his intention had been to intimidate, Kate suspected he had succeeded. The lad was visibly cowering in his bed and had paled to the same colour as his sheets. Kate was incensed. *Cold-hearted bloody surgeons, treading all over people's feelings without a moment's consideration*, she thought. *Who the hell did he think he was?*

~~~

Lena's eyebrows rose. "Nice bloke," she said and the woman smiled.

~~~

The team moved on to another, now very timid, patient and Kate marched off, searching for an outlet to vent her anger.

Two nurses were raiding the linen cupboard near the end of the corridor when Kate stormed in.

"Mim, Becca, you'll never believe what I just saw," she told them. "I was just walking past Bay Three when I came across one of the consultants tearing strips off some young boy. It was awful. The poor thing was lying there stuck in bed with his leg all banged-up and riddled with metalwork and he just laid into him."

"Who?" Miriam asked.

"Elliott, I think."

"Elliott?"

"Yes. I've never seen such outrageous behaviour in all my life, let alone from a consultant," she said.

6

"Well he doesn't take any rubbish from his patients, that's for sure. But he does seem to be very good at what he does."

"Maybe he is," she said, "but he was completely out of order in there. I was embarrassed to be in the same room as him." She paused. "His team looked mortified."

"Oh, I think they're used to him by now," Becca added.

"Well, they shouldn't let him get away with that," Kate said. "*We* wouldn't get away with it. Someone should report him."

Miriam and Rebecca's faces suddenly blanched, but Kate was too het-up to notice.

"One of you two should go back in there and see if that poor lad is all right," she continued, building into a fury by this point. "That stern-faced, self-important, egotistical… bully," her mouth was struggling to keep up with her brain. "Ugh! People like him make me so cross."

A cool, steady voice spoke up from behind her. "Well, I think we're all quite clear about that now."

Chills ran down Kate's spine as she turned round to see the granite face of Mr Elliott staring back at her, his team hovering uncomfortably behind.

"I'm sure you have plenty of work to be getting on with," he said to the two nurses standing either side of her, and Miriam and Rebecca shuffled away as quickly as they could. Kate could feel the ice of anxiety beginning to trickle through her veins.

Mr Elliott fixed his gaze on Kate and without moving he spoke calmly to his team. "I'll meet you on Ascot Ward in five minutes," he said and they looked at each other and quickly left.

Mr Elliott took a step back. "If you wouldn't mind, please, Nurse?" and he gestured that she should move out of the linen cupboard and walk along beside him.

Kate braced herself and stepped out, still a flicker of fire in her belly. Mr Elliott walked a few paces up the ward and then opened the door to Sister's office. He checked it was empty and then indicated that Kate should go in. Kate entered the room and turned to face him. She was definitely in the right and she knew it. Perhaps she shouldn't have been voicing her opinions so loudly on the ward, but that was nothing compared to the ordeal he had put that poor boy through. So she squared up her shoulders and lifted her chin.

Mr Elliott was tall and dark; a striking man, whose features, suffused with even a modicum of warmth, might have been quite good looking on anyone else, but on him, they favoured only his gravitas. Unfortunately, in the serious light of her current situation, Kate couldn't help but quake.

She had to be strong. She had to stand up for the weak and the ill, the people who couldn't fight for themselves. It was going to be down to her to make him see how unfeeling he had been.

Grey-blue eyes bore into her as the silence lingered like a guillotine above her head and the trembling inside her began to grow.

"So you think, Nurse…" he said, deliberately peering closer at her uniform to read the name on her badge. "Excuse me, Staff Nurse Heath, that I should be reported for speaking plainly to one of my patients, do you? Maybe you would be kind enough to enlighten me as to why?"

Kate's jaw clenched. He was patronising her, she was well aware of it, but while the little courage she had left remained, she was going to speak her mind. With the callous words of the surgeon who had recently treated her grandfather so appallingly hurtling to the forefront of her mind, she looked up into his steel-armoured eyes. "It was quite obvious that you were completely out of order in there," she said. "What gave you the right to judge that poor lad? I bet you don't even know the first thing about him; stuck up there in your ivory tower where life is so easy and Armani suits grow on trees. Who's to say it wasn't a genuine accident? But you wouldn't think of that, would you? You just laid into him. He was a quivering wreck by the time you'd finished."

Mr Elliott stood, poised in obvious frustration for a moment and then, when his voice finally broke, it was clenched and steady, as if a great force was being needed to keep it so. "And how should I have addressed the situation instead, may I ask?"

By this time Kate was rapidly running out of fire. She knew how to fight when her opponent shouted back, but this cool, calculated analysis had her on the wrong foot. She searched for something further to say, but came up blank.

"What, no sound advice? No words of wisdom?"

Kate bristled and shot him a glare, cursing her brain for letting her down right when she needed it.

"Maybe I had better remind you of your objections. I think the word 'bully' was in there, and from what I can remember you were attempting to incite mutiny on one of my wards. So would you care to elaborate on any of that? You were very free with your opinions a few minutes ago." He looked at her for a moment as her brain struggled hard to find the right words to say. "Maybe you should try running my team, doing my clinics and operating on my patients for a few days and then come back to me. At least then you might have some idea of what you're talking about."

"I wasn't questioning your abilities as a doctor," she said, suddenly finding the spark she needed and tossing it right back at him, but her conviction was waning.

"Oh? Well, that *is* a relief." His tone had taken on a sarcastic quality that ignited the dying embers of her rage.

"No, it was your lack of compassion that I was questioning," Kate said. "It's not your right to play judge and jury, deciding who should be worthy of treatment and who should not. Are you absolutely certain he was the one to blame for the crash? It's just as likely that he wasn't. In fact we had one, just the other day, where a woman swerved to avoid a cat and crashed head-long into a van coming in the opposite direction."

Elliott's face paled. His stone wall cracked just a little as Kate could see the doubt settling in. For a second she could sense his turmoil and found new strength in his weakness. She looked at him straight in the eyes. "Precisely."

"Do *you* know what happened to bring him in here?" He asked, pausing for a moment to see if Kate would respond, but she didn't. "No, you don't, do you? So I say to you, if someone had been a bit harder on that lad a few years ago, then maybe I wouldn't have another patient fighting for her life on ITU right now." He let out a small breath. "Maybe you should keep your nose out of business that does not concern you from now on and go back to... A&E?" He looked at her for confirmation of her department, "and concentrate on your own job. And the next time you try accusing someone of being 'unprofessional', I suggest you make absolutely sure your own behaviour is beyond reproach, or it might end up being you that gets reported for misconduct and not the poor wretch who finds himself on the sharp end of your malicious and ill-founded gossip."

Kate was defeated. Tears threatened to well up but she was damned if she was going to give him the pleasure of seeing it. She looked at the dull grey floor in front of her, Elliott's crisp black leather shoes firmly blocking her way. He hesitated for a moment, his brow crinkling and then he opened the door and stood back, letting her slip away in silence.

Kate's hands were locked hard at her sides as she escaped the ward and walked as fast as she could, breaking out into the fresh air a few minutes later, in search of a moment's privacy. Away from prying eyes.

~~~

"I know how that feels," Lena mumbled and the woman was relieved to see the girl had been paying attention. Empathy was going to help her now.

~~~

Alone at last, Kate broke down. She leant back against a brick wall, with her palms pressed against the cool hard surface. She closed her eyes and tipped her head to the sky and slowly sank to the ground and wept. All the tension of the past few days had finally come to a head, exploding, quite dramatically, at Mr Elliott.

Footsteps approached and she quickly wiped the tears from her face and pulled herself together. A porter passed by, his thoughts a million miles away from her own. Kate dabbed her eyes with an old tissue she found in her pocket and lifted her chin, ready to face the day again.

In the canteen, she bought a sandwich and two Mars bars and found a quiet corner to sit down in. The first bar disappeared in a matter of seconds. How dare he? she thought as she sat there. Elliott had been the one losing it over one of his patients and he had had the nerve to take it out on her when all she'd done was have the courage to stand up to him. She pulled out her sandwich. He was a bully, but he was a consultant; he would never get his comeuppance. She had half a mind to go right back up to that poor lad and point him in the direction of the complaints procedure.

She wondered at how many times Mr Elliott might have been allowed to get away with this behaviour before. Maybe it was the reason he left his last hospital, she thought. She swigged back her carton of juice and decided to pocket the other bar of chocolate for later, binned the rubbish and then held out her hands. Still trembling.

Mr Elliott had slipped in under the radar when he'd joined the hospital almost six months before. Kate had neither particularly noticed, nor heard much about him, but if a fight had been what he'd wanted that day, then Kate had been in just the right mood to oblige him. She checked her watch. Arrogant bastard, she thought. She took a deep breath, straightened her uniform and walked back down to A&E.

Kate said nothing of the incident to her colleagues that day, if not because she was already questioning her part in it, then for the greater fear that if she began to speak and let go of her control, she might just fall to pieces in the middle of the department. But her reluctance to share did little to quell the undercurrent of anger she felt towards the arrogant, overbearing man, for the rest of that day.

That evening, her housemate, Sophie, realised something was up when she came home from work. She searched round the house only to find Kate in the kitchen, scrubbing the living daylights out of the work surfaces.

"Everything all right?" she asked, looking around quickly for any clues.

The sudden noise made Kate jump. "Grief! Don't do that to me," she said.

"Sorry," Sophie said.

"It was getting dirty in here," Kate told her, not faltering for a moment in her mission.

"You know I think that bit's pretty clean now," Sophie soothed.

Kate continued cleaning, her mind focussed on the task in hand and thereby avoiding everything else. She rubbed hard at the tiles on the wall behind the cooker.

Sophie watched her for a moment and then walked over and laid her hand on Kate's, stopping the movement. Kate paused mid scrub, but did not step back, so Sophie slowly took the cloth and spray out of her hands and put them to one side. Then she led Kate to the living room and sat her down.

Sitting opposite her, Sophie took a deep breath. "Out of ten, where one is lovely and ten is crappiest day ever, what exactly are we talking about here?"

"About a nine and a half," Kate said.

"Do you want to talk about it?" Sophie asked her.

"Not really," Kate said.

"Is it just the funeral - and I'm not saying that isn't *absolutely* enough on its own - but has there been something else as well?" Sophie asked.

Kate nodded.

"Something else as well as the hideousness of having to go through your grandfather's funeral *and* a day's work?"

Kate nodded again and rubbed her face before recoiling rapidly at the overpowering smell of bleach.

Sophie scratched her head. "Are you on in the morning?"

"No. A late," Kate told her.

"Me too. How do you fancy going out and getting plastered?"

Kate looked aghast. "What, now?"

"Yes."

"Oh, no, Soph. I'm shattered," she said.

"Well, maybe we won't get plastered, but have a bit of fun, just for a bit. Yeah? It's better than moping around here feeling miserable. Your granddad would have wanted you to be out having fun, wouldn't he?"

The corner of Kate's mouth perked up into a soft smile as, despite herself, she remembered how full of fun her granddad had been. She sighed. "Yeah, he would."

"Well what do you say then?"

They met Jenny and Flis, some nursing friends, at The White Horse just before ten; they had a couple of drinks and then headed off down the road to Helix.

By eleven, Kate was feeling wobbly. She had eaten only a sandwich and a packet of crisps before going out and had necked her first couple of drinks rather quickly.

"Feeling any better yet?" Sophie asked when they returned from the dance floor and plonked themselves down on a seat near the bar.

Kate nodded. "Much," she said. "Just give me a surgeon-ectomy and I'll be fine."

"Oh dear. Which one has been rattling your cage this time?" Sophie asked.

"Elliott," she said.

"What, old Jolly?"

"Who?" Kate asked her.

"Jolly. That's what we call him on our ward."

Kate was amused. "Appropriate." Then she thought she'd better clarify. "Young orthopaedic consultant, right? Quite new?"

"Yeah. Tall, dark and gloomy."

Kate chuckled. "That's the one."

"Why? What did he do to you?"

"He hauled me into Sister's office and tore strips off me, that's what," she said.

"What on earth for?" Sophie asked her.

"I was, and quite rightly, I have to say, objecting to his behaviour, and get this, *he* ended up threatening to report *me*!"

"He's going to report you? Why? What did you do?"

"Bastard was ripping into this poor lad on Aintree, acting the big 'I am' and I... kind of accused him of being a bully."

Sophie laughed, obviously surprised at Kate's nerve. "You go, girl!" she said.

"Oh, I wasn't as good as I would have liked to have been," Kate told her. "He was so... ugh... he was... infuriating. I tried to fight my corner, but I was rubbish and he was so icy and prickly. In the end he had me shaking in my boots."

Sophie put her arm around her friend. "I knew something must have happened when I found you scrubbing the house to death this evening. You don't normally go all manic if you're just a bit miserable. So how did you leave it?"

"With him threatening to report me."

"He's not going to, though, is he?" she asked.

"I don't know," Kate said. "I don't think so."

"And are you going to report him?"

"I should, shouldn't I? But what's the point? They're hardly going to take my word over his."

"Bloody surgeons."

"Yeah, bloody surgeons," Kate said.

"Speaking of the forbidden things... Do you ever hear from

Kate shook her head. "No, good riddance to the lot of them, I say."

"Here, here," Sophie said and clinked glasses. "Not that Guy was anything like Elliott."

"No." Kate laughed at the mere comparison. "At least Guy could be a charmer. Elliott on the other hand..."

"Oh, I don't know. I wouldn't chuck him out of bed," Sophie said.

"Ugh. No!" Kate was horrified.

"You're just mad at him. He can be a real love when he wants to be. He's meant to be very kind to his patients. They all seem to love him."

"Ha!" Kate found that very hard to believe.

"But Guy *was* gorgeous, you've got to admit."

"Yes," Kate conceded, "but unfortunately he had a little *too* much bedside manner. I doubt Elliott even knows what his is for. It probably dropped off years ago... with frostbite."

Sophie gave a wicked grin. "I dare you to find out."

"I'd rather snog Derek," Kate said.

"Not Dirty-Derek from Cardiology? The human octopus? Ugh!" Sophie shivered and they both burst out laughing.

Flis and Jenny joined them from the dance floor, slumping down in the seats close by.

"You look better," said Flis, brushing her blonde curls away from her face. "They're not a lot of fun, are they, funerals?"

"No. I'm not sure anyone has ever described funerals as 'fun', Flis," Sophie said. "But it's not that. The girl's got surgeon-itis again."

"Oh, lord. Which one now?" Jenny said, perking up.

"Elliott," Sophie said.

"Elliott?"

"Not like that," Kate added quickly. "We had a run in today."

"Which one's Elliott?" Flis asked.

"Orthopaedics. Took over from Mr Grant."

"Arrogant, self-righteous, pompous pillock," Kate muttered under her breath.

The other three looked at each other.

"How much has she had to drink?" Jenny asked.

"Not enough, obviously," said Sophie with a smile and she lifted Kate's hand with her glass in back up to her lips.

Kate swallowed back another gulp and shook herself. "Okay, I'm better now," she said. "Hey, have any of you seen the new anaesthetics registrar yet? The one everyone's raving about."

"I have," said Jenny, excitedly. "He's lush."

"Lush? How old are you?" Sophie asked.

"Well, if you don't want to hear about him."

"Ignore her," said Flis, straining to hear what was being said. "I do."

Jenny beamed. "He's gorgeous, isn't he? He's called Peter."

"Peter? Peter what?" Sophie asked.

"Florin," Flis put in.

"He came on to our ward today and he's… well… He must be over six foot tall, fair, well-built and such dreamy eyes."

Flis was daydreaming already. "I want to switch wards," she whined. "He's never going to come over to Age Care. The only time I ever see him is in the corridor at lunch times."

Jenny shook her head. "No, you wouldn't like him, Flis; he's far too good for you. He's a complete love with the patients: gentle and calming, but his eyes… What I wouldn't give to be stuck in a lift for an hour with those eyes."

"Are you sure it's his eyes you're thinking about there?" Kate asked her.

Flis flumped back into her seat, complaining that it wasn't fair, and Jenny grinned mischievously.

"Did you get to speak to him?" Sophie asked.

"Not much. I just showed him where his patient was. But you should see the way he looks at you… He really *looks* at you,

you know?" Jenny's eyes were wide as she fanned her face with her hand.

"Is he married?" Kate asked.

"I didn't see any ring," Jenny said.

Kate nodded over to Flis. "Keep bumping them off, Flis. He'll have to be on the crash team sooner or later," and the girls all roared with laughter at Kate's macabre yet practical approach to romance.

The following morning Kate was feeling a little more fragile than usual. She was woken at six-thirty by a punishing alarm that she'd forgotten to change from the previous day. She groaned, rolled over and went straight back to sleep. The next thing she knew it was a quarter past twelve, three quarters of an hour before her shift was due to begin.

She flew out of bed at Mach eight and just about managed to hurtle through the doors to A&E only a few minutes after the shift had started, still a little dazed and with the mother of all headaches. She slunk inside, downed a couple of Paracetamol and got straight to work.

Half an hour later she was volunteered, along with two more junior nurses, to join the junior doctors in an impromptu teaching session. Kate walked into the clinic room and sat down and then for the next twenty minutes was bombarded with a lecture on ethics and teamwork and when it was time to go, she walked back to her duties, exceedingly suspicious of the motivation that had sparked such an extraordinary talk.

Throughout the evening Kate made discreet enquiries to see if anyone could shed light on the reason for such a session and why she in particular had been chosen to attend it, but nothing was forthcoming.

On Saturday, everything was back to normal. Kate was on an early, Elliott was not on call, and so had no chance of being around, and she was left to get on with her work in peace.

~~~

17

"So who was the love of her life, then? Not Elliott, surely?" Lena asked. "Was it Peter?"

The woman smiled. "Would you like me to go on?"

Lena nodded, her curious gaze piercing her heavy fringe and the woman could feel the bond between them growing.

Chapter 2

That evening, Kate drove over to her mum and dad's house, to see how her mum was getting on since her granddad's funeral. Her Auntie Ann was there too, also a nurse, who worked at the local hospice. She was talking with her mum about what to do with their father's things.

Kate offered to help with the cleaning after the two of them had cleared his house and then she gave them a fruit cake that Sophie had made for them. "Oh, she's an angel. You must say thank you to her from us, won't you?" her mum said, carrying the cake out to the kitchen for slicing. "I don't know how you'd manage if she ever moved out."

"I'd starve," Kate said.

"You would an' all."

"But I wouldn't starve in squalor."

"No, that you would not," her mum replied and she smiled. "You both bring your strengths to the table, don't you?"

"Of course. Why do you think I chose her? She cooks, I clean. It's a perfect match. Shall I make some drinks?"

The three of them sat down around the dining table, with a piece of cake and a cup of tea. "How have you been, love?" her mother asked her.

"Okay, I suppose," Kate said. "I had a bit of a run-in with a consultant after the funeral the other day, but the girls took me out to Helix to cheer me up, so…"

"You had a run-in? Who with?"

"One of the consultants."

"What about?"

Kate paused, cautious of upsetting her mother any further. She shook her head. "Nothing much."

"Katherine?"

That was Kate in trouble. Her mother never called her by her full name otherwise. She scowled.

"Well, tell me then." Her mum gave her a 'you're going to tell me one way or the other, so you might as well get it over with' kind of look and Kate heaved a big sigh.

"I just caught him having a go at one of the patients on the ward."

"And?"

"And he was treating him like dirt."

Her mum looked at her for a moment. "And you thought of your granddad," she said.

Kate nodded and dropped her gaze to the table and her mum reached across and squeezed her hand.

"I should never have told you about that. It was probably nowhere near as bad as I made it out to be."

"Was Granddad upset?" Kate asked.

"Well, yes, he was, but-"

"And you were fuming?"

"Yes, at the time-"

"Then it was bad enough."

Kate's mum considered for a moment and then seemed to decide to let it slide. "So what did you do? Or, I guess more importantly, what did *he* do?"

Kate told them everything and then waited, a little anxiously, for their response.

"You'll be all right, Kate. You're a good nurse and you care

21

about your patients. He won't be able to make much more of it than that," her Auntie Ann said and she winked.

"Well I'm proud of you," her mum added. "If only more people stood up for those less fortunate than themselves it would be a better world to live in."

Auntie Ann smiled. "Which one was it?"

Kate looked across. "Elliott."

"Seriously?" She seemed bemused. "He's always seemed like such a lovely man when I've had anything to do with him."

"You know him?" Kate asked, surprised.

"Yes. At least, I assume it's the same one. His mother is in with us at the moment. You surprise me. I tell you, if I was twenty years younger…"

"Auntie Ann! I'll tell Uncle Malc," Kate said.

"I'm only kidding."

"You must be," Kate told her.

Her aunt looked at her watch and gasped. "Goodness, is that the time? I'd better get going or your uncle'll be round here banging the door down and demanding his tea."

They all stood up and cleared their plates to the kitchen and then Kate and her mum saw her auntie to the front door. Auntie Ann turned and called out a goodbye to Kate's dad and then hugged her sister. She turned back to Kate. "Don't let him get to you," she said and then agreeing to meet with her mum at their dad's house the following week, she hugged them both once again and said goodbye.

When the door clicked shut, Kate's mum put her arm around her and they walked back in to the living room. "Are you sure you're all right, love?" her mother asked.

"It did shake me up a bit," Kate admitted, "but Soph took me out to let off some steam."

"Good. I don't like the thought of some bully of a doctor having a go at my little girl."

They sat down in the living room, with its array of songbird figurines and were serenaded by the gentle ticking of the white china clock on the mantelpiece.

"Who's having a go at her?" Kate's dad asked, peering over his book.

"Just some grumpy old consultant at the hospital," her mum told him. "Don't you worry; she's got it all under control." She winked at Kate. "Haven't you, love?"

"Well, you let me know if you want me to go over there and beat him up for you, won't you, Kate?" her dad said and she giggled.

"Absolutely, Dad. You'll be the first to know."

Kate enjoyed what was left of the evening in the reassuring company of her parents and tried to forget about her clash with Mr Elliott. And as the evening turned to night, she remembered the reportedly gorgeous yet elusive Peter Florin and wondered when she was going to get to meet him, so that she might have the chance to judge for herself.

~

Around the same time that Kate was licking her wounds and scheming to try and catch a peep at the new registrar, Mr Elliott was walking into his lunchtime meeting with an irritation formed more from his encounter with the interfering nurse the week before, than his disinclination to hear about recent reviews in protocol. With his authority so rarely challenged, it was all the more startling when it was. He had had long enough to mull over the whole episode many times in his head since then and not once, in all that time, had his part in it gained any credence.

His conscience was troubling him. The hidden tears he had glimpsed briefly in her eyes, before she had averted her gaze and slipped out of the door, bothered him. He had not meant for it to go so far, but she had fought her corner with such passion that he had actually felt threatened and had barbed his words and fought all the harder. But the thought that he may have been so blinded by his prejudice that he attacked an innocent victim, weighed heavily upon him. He had now made certain the patient *had* been responsible for the accident, but he should never have lost control like that, with the lad, or the nurse. He had fought so hard to defend his honour, that in doing so, he now understood, he had lost it.

He admired her, if he was honest. For a nurse to stand up to a consultant, exposing his flaws, took a great deal of strength and conviction, he was sure. Had he really been that callous? He had witnessed the devastation wrought by irresponsible young lads countless times before, so often being the one left picking up the pieces. With Ali, he had even lived it. He felt the burden of his task keenly; duty-bound to tend them, when all he really wanted to do was rage at them for their thoughtless stupidity. But he had thought *her* magnificent and in recognising this fact came the understanding of his own reaction to her, and with that he was uneasy.

~~~

"He didn't want to like her?" Lena asked. "How miserable was he?"

"It seemed so. And he *was* miserable, you're right, but he did have good reason."

Lena held her gaze for a moment, searching the woman's expression before she carried on.

~~~

The following week the weather was dismal, the hospital seemed busier than ever and then a call came in.

There had been an accident on a farm and a man had been trapped inside machinery. He was badly injured and was due to arrive in A&E in five short minutes. The trauma team was called and Mr Elliott arrived at the same time as the anaesthetist on duty that day. They strode into A&E in the direction of Resus One.

Unaware of his arrival, Kate stepped out of a cubicle right into his path and their eyes locked for a second before someone called out his name and he was gone.

Kate retrieved the Tubigrip she had been searching for and walked back to her patient, suddenly on edge.

"Sounds like a lot of commotion going on out there," the gentleman said as she began to measure his arm.

"We're expecting a serious injury any minute," Kate told him. "They're just getting ready."

"Shouldn't you be out there with them?" he asked.

"I'll go in a minute. I've got to finish sorting you out first," she replied cheerfully.

"Oh, I'll be fine. You get over there."

"Mr Brimley, you're very kind, but I can't just abandon you like *this*. Now, who is going to look after you? You'll need a bit of help for a week or two until you can use your right arm properly again, won't you?"

"My daughter lives only a couple of doors away. She's on her way here right now. I'll be well looked after, don't worry about me. Now go on."

Kate finished up and looked at him. "Make sure you keep moving it gently so it doesn't stiffen up," she said. "Here's a leaflet about sprains. I'll wheel you out to the waiting room and we can see if she's arrived yet." Mr Brimley frowned as sirens began to approach. "It's no bother."

They reached the waiting room just as the gentleman's daughter was walking in. Kate handed the woman her father's coat and explained about his injury. "So there we are. Take good care of yourself now," she said. Mr Brimley shooed her away with his one good hand and Kate smiled and hurried down to Resus One to see if she was needed.

By the time she got there, the patient had arrived. Mr Cobham, the consultant, had assumed control and was barking out orders to the nurses and doctors around him. Mr Elliott was assessing the man's shattered arm, while the anaesthetist hovered around him, preparing to put the man to sleep, until the injuries to his chest and head could be stabilised.

There was a lot of noise in there at the time, so Kate found Stacey, the nurse in charge, and asked her if she needed any help. She looked across at Elliott, now talking to his registrar about what he had found and discussing the situation with Mr Cobham, his brow more furrowed than usual.

Stacey asked how the rest of A&E was doing and Kate told her it was in hand and not too many were waiting. So she asked her to run up to CT and find out how soon they would be ready.

Kate strode off as quickly as she could, happy to be out of danger, but she was soon back in Resus with the expectations of the team waiting on her. Mr Cobham and Mr Elliott were side by side and both turned round to look at her.

"Well?" Mr Cobham asked.

"They're ready for you now," Kate said. She felt the hard stare of Mr Elliott burning into the side of her face and so turned back to Stacey, deliberately avoiding his gaze. "Anything else I can do?" she asked.

"No. Thanks, Kate. If you could hold the fort round the other side while I take care of this end, that would be great."

Kate nodded and walked back round to attend to the walking wounded. A few minutes later she noticed the team pushing the trolley carrying the now anaesthetised patient in the direction of X-Ray and breathed a sigh of relief. Elliott was no longer a threat.

After break, a welcome interlude in an otherwise busy day, Kate assisted Dr Sarah with an old lady in Resus Two, who had slipped over in the street. She had several cuts to the fragile skin of her scalp and arms that required stitching. They took a side each.

When she was through, Kate looked around for the nearest yellow bin to put her sharps into and noticed something shiny tucked at the back behind a box of gloves, on the side in Resus One.

Checking with the doctor that she had everything she needed, Kate excused herself and wandered over to see what it was. As she neared the spot Kate realised it was a very elegant pen. She picked it up. There was nothing obvious to suggest who it belonged to. It could have been a patient's, Kate thought, but most probably it was Mr Cobham's, so she put it in her pocket for safe keeping.

Asking around the staff over the course of the evening, nobody came forward to claim it. Time passed quickly as the evening drew to a close and when the night shift arrived, Kate was more than ready to go home.

Monday morning was run of the mill: broken toes, sprained wrists and cut fingers. The sort of day where you could check your brain in at the door and cruise on through on autopilot. The gloom Kate had been feeling since her grandfather's funeral had lifted and apart from the barely audible calling of a lonely heart searching for a home, life was not too bad.

At break time, Kate headed to the canteen with a friend from general surgery. They were talking about the weekend when from behind them came a gruff-sounding voice.

"Nurse Heath."

Kate stopped in her tracks, instantly recognising the abrupt tone of Mr Elliott. Maisie looked round and Kate braced herself for what was to come, but refused to turn around to face him.

"Kate," came a warmer note from much closer to hand.

Kate turned around and there before her stood Mr Elliott. No ice in his eyes this time, but instead, a searching expression. "I understand you may have found my pen?" he asked.

For a moment Kate was bewildered and then the penny dropped. "Oh, yes," she said, reaching into her pocket and she pulled out the shiny silver pen she had discovered in A&E. She looked at it and then held it out and Mr Elliott took it. They touched, and as his hand moved over hers, caressing her sensitive fingers with his own, a charge of adrenaline shot up her arm, her stomach began to tremble and her chest struggled to breathe. Their eyes met and in that splinter of a moment, something brilliant shone out between them. Kate pulled back, disturbed by her reaction and saw the self-same look in his eyes.

He cleared his throat. "Thank you," he said. "This pen is very important to me." He hesitated for a moment as if about to elaborate further, but then he turned and walked away.

Kate took a deep breath, calming her heartbeat a little before turning back in the direction she had been heading, her feelings quite at odds with the sensations of his touch.

Maisie was instantly curious. "What were you doing with Mr Elliott's pen?" she asked, a broad grin on her face and her raised eyebrows suggesting all kinds of mischief.

"Nothing," Kate said quickly as she continued briskly on down the corridor, not looking to either side. "I found it last week. I didn't know whose it was. He must have left it in A&E when he came down for that mangled arm."

"You're blushing; you know that? I thought you hated him? That's what Jenny said," Maisie told her.

"What?"

"But then Kirst said you thought he was gay."

"I did no such thing," Kate heard herself exclaim. She deliberately hushed her voice in the hope that Maisie would follow suit and repeated the sentence quietly.

"But you did have a bust-up with him?"

"Yeah."

"And you still wouldn't shag him if he was the last man on earth?"

"I think that's a fairly safe bet, Maisie, yes, but you're missing the point. I didn't know it was *his* pen. I was just tidying up."

"Kirst's with you, you know?"

"What?"

"About Elliott's unshagability."

"Maisie!"

28

"But *she* thinks he just can't get it up. She says he never makes a pass at any women and he's not trendy enough to be gay, so he must just be a cold fish."

Kate was mortified. She didn't like the chap, not on any level, but it was quite breath-taking how quickly rumour could spread inside a hospital. "I never said he was gay," she hissed. "Look, can we talk about something else?"

The change in Elliott's tone had unsettled Kate profoundly. She found it hard to get the look he had given her, when their hands had touched, out of her mind. He had looked as surprised as she with the shock that rippled through them, confused even by the sensation. Kate would have assumed she had been the only one who'd felt it, but for that look. And then a thought drifted through her mind. He had known her first name. Perhaps he had found it out when he'd complained to her boss about her the previous week, or maybe it was in Resus the other day, but he had definitely called her by her name, 'Kate'.

In the canteen, Kate finished her piece of cake and she and Maisie were getting up to leave when a gorgeous doctor walked in. It was crowded in there and so Kate managed to catch his attention as he stood with his tray just beyond the till, searching the room for somewhere to sit. Heads were turning all around as whispers filtered through the air to Kate's ears. Kate pointed to her table as they picked up their things. The doctor walked over and smiled. Wow, she thought, so that was what all the fuss was about. This had to be the guy. He really did have a winning smile, and such amazing eyes, Kate was almost tempted to stay.

"We're just leaving," she said, not giving herself more time to reflect.

"Thank you. You're sure you won't join me?" he asked, his eyes not leaving hers for a second. Maisie started to sit down again, but Kate stopped her.

"No. We've got to get back. Thanks, though." She smiled at

the guy who really *was* very handsome.

"I guess I'll see you around then?" he asked, his eyes shining with expectation.

Kate nodded and smiled at him. Where was Flis when she needed her? "I expect so," she said and then dragged Maisie away.

That night, in bed, Kate thought about the new doctor. He seemed like a kind, decent guy who also happened to be seriously good looking, but try as she might, she couldn't get Elliott out of her head. She was still angry with him. He was an unfeeling, arrogant bully, but there was something about him…

The following day, Kate escorted a little girl up to the children's ward and was horrified to find out just how far the rumours had spread. As she was leaving the ward Kate heard a couple of auxiliary nurses chatting in the cloakroom about Mr Elliott. She heard her name and the expression: 'doesn't know what it's for' snuck out around the door and Kate paused, guilt climbing high in her chest, but she was at least a little relieved to hear that she had been quoted correctly that time. But if it had got round as far as the children's ward it must be everywhere by now. She was beginning to regret ever talking about the guy whilst drinking and just hoped the grapevine didn't spread so far that it would come back around to bite her.

Wednesday afternoon, Kate was down to assist the registrar in minor ops clinic, so with mask and gloves on, she set up theatre for the afternoon's list.

First there was a hand injury, brought in from A&E that morning, which needed the tendons exploring and suturing closed. Second on the list was a large sebaceous cyst from behind an old man's ear and the third was a lad who had been brought in from X-ray. He had been caught up in a pub fight a couple of nights before and had come in when his arm continued to be painful. There was glass to remove and the wound to explore and clean out and it was during this third operation, with her concentration entirely on the matter in hand, that Mr Elliott stuck his head around the door of Theatre, looking for Mr Cobham.

Kate was a little shaken by the sudden arrival of Mr Elliott in her calm, clean environment. Dr Penn, the Registrar, barely looked up from what he was doing. He didn't know, and after a brief glance in her direction, Mr Elliott withdrew. But Kate knew where Mr Cobham was and she wrestled with her conscience, lacking the will to speak up. He wouldn't recognise her with a mask on, surely?

"He's in Physio," Kate blurted out at the receding figure as he disappeared out of the door.

Mr Elliott stopped and peered back round at her. "Physio?"

She nodded.

"Thanks, Kate," he said and left.

The patient looked from the doorway, back up to Kate. "You've gone bright pink," he said. Dr Penn glanced up momentarily and then carried on with his work.

"Well it gets pretty hot in here, dressed in this lot in the middle of summer," Kate said and the patient smiled and they continued with their work.

On Thursday, Kate was on a day off and was with her mum at her granddad's house cleaning the rooms as they emptied. It wasn't easy walking around the house that had once been so important to her. It was a sad place now, soulless and hollow. All the things that held any memories had found new homes and the rest had been donated or sold.

Kate and her mum sat on the empty living room floor and ate their lunch, talking about the good times they'd had there. The new family would be moving in on Monday, so this was their last chance to see the old place before it was no longer anything to do with them.

Auntie Ann turned up a little after one and joined in with the last few bits of cleaning and then they said their goodbyes to the old place and drove away without turning back.

They decided to go to Farley's for a posh tea and cake to cheer themselves up. Kate chose a slice of carrot cake, her mum had a Chelsea bun and Auntie Ann had a big slice of chocolate fudge brownie.

"How's it going with Mr Elliott, Kate?" her auntie asked her.

"Yes, sorry, love. I've been so busy with all your granddad's stuff I forgot to ask," her mum added.

Kate didn't know quite what to tell them, so she decided to try to play it down.

"Not much to tell," she said. "I've bumped into him a couple of times."

"And was he just as obnoxious?" her mum asked.

"No." Kate's voice came out almost surprised, not the way she had planned it at all. "It seems he's managing to control himself."

"Good," her auntie said. "I told you he wasn't that bad really. Maybe he was just having a bad day?"

"Maybe? I can't seem to work him out."

"His poor old mother's been having a tough time, I'm afraid. We're trying everything we can, but..." She shrugged. "She's a lovely woman too. His father left them when he was just a lad, apparently. They're all each other has got now."

"What's wrong with her?" Kate asked, concern growing.

"Bowel cancer. Nasty one. And he's so patient with us, never gets grumpy, like some of the other relatives can do. Might not want everyone to know about it, though," she said and Kate nodded to show she understood.

For the rest of their time together Kate racked her brains trying to reconcile the differing accounts of Mr Elliott, but when she arrived home, she found Sophie sitting on the couch looking shaken and all thoughts of Elliott soon disappeared.

"What's happened?" she asked, pausing just inside the door. "You look awful. Are you all right?"

"My car," Sophie said. "It's been stolen."

Kate walked over and peered through the living room window

to the spot where Sophie's car was usually parked. "When did it happen?"

"A couple of hours ago. I didn't hear a thing."

Kate sat down and put an arm around her. "Are you okay?"

"Just in shock, I think."

Kate gave her a hug. "You're shaking," she said and she got up. "I'll make you a cup of tea.

A few minutes later she reappeared carrying a hot cup of tea and a packet of chocolate biscuits. "Go on, get that down you. Have you rung the police yet?"

Sophie sipped her tea. "Yeah. Straight away. They've already been and gone."

"You've given them the details?"

"Yes."

"Well, I guess there's not a lot more you can do. Have you rung your insurance company?"

"No. I thought I'd walk into town and tell them in a bit. When I'm more in control of my bodily functions." The mug shuddered to a stop as she placed it back down in the tray on the table.

"I'll come with you," Kate said.

"No. I'll be okay. I'd rather have a bit of time on my own to get my head together," she said. "Is that all right?"

"Of course," Kate said. "Whatever you want."

While Sophie was out, Kate spent an hour or two tidying the house, doing the laundry and pondering on the conversations of the day. Her heart reached out to Mr Elliott and she thought about her granddad. His death had been horrendous at the time, but in retrospect, it was only a matter of a few days for him, not weeks and months of suffering. And Mr Elliott had no family around to support him? The poor guy.

Sophie got home far later than expected. In fact, Kate was starting to worry, thinking she should never have let her go off on her own as shaken up as she was. But when she finally returned, Sophie was grinning from ear to ear.

"You're looking better," Kate said. "Everything sorted out?"

Sophie beamed.

"What is it? You look like you've just won the lottery, not lost your beloved car."

Sophie said nothing.

"Sit down there and tell me what's happened."

Sophie sat down and started from the beginning. "I wandered about for a while, just trying to get my head around it all and then, when I was on a bit more of an even keel, I walked into the insurance place and this guy stood up from behind a desk and asked me to sit down and Kate, he was *gorgeous*. I mean, my mind was a little fuzzy before I saw him, but after… He had to virtually walk me through the whole thing; I was so out of it. And then he had a word with his colleague and took me out for a drink to settle my nerves. And he's just - arghhh! He's funny and sexy and easy going and we just sort of… clicked."

Kate rolled her eyes. "Sophie Turner, only *you* could manage to make such a crap day turn out so well." She shook her head, amazed. "So I take it you're over the disappointment of losing your car then?"

Sophie beamed.

"Good, because I'm starving."

"Oh. Rich is picking me up in an hour to take me out to dinner. Sorry."

"Wow. He doesn't hang around, does he? Rich, eh? Okay, just me for tea then, is it?"

"Would you like me to show you where the kitchen is?" Sophie teased.

"You're all right," Kate said. "I clean the thing often enough. I think I can find it."

The following afternoon Kate started a long haul of shifts. She had swapped a couple to help a friend get to a wedding, so it was a bigger set than it should have been and she was very aware of the amount of work she had to get through before her next day off.

For days the department ran like clockwork. Patients came and went, each leaving their mark on her life to a greater or lesser extent, but the following week a call came in for the A&E department to expect casualties from a big car wreck just outside of town. Kate was on duty in Resus One. It was almost nine o'clock at night and her shift was nearly over, but the night staff were not yet in.

Gloria put out the call for the trauma team to come to A&E and informed the rest of the staff to prepare and so Kate rang coronary care to see if they could take her patient as quickly as possible and the two of them began to ready the bays.

Chapter 3

It wasn't long before the casualties began to arrive. The first ambulance brought in a woman with cuts and bruises and a child with what seemed little more than a broken arm, but the mother was hysterical. Kate took control, whisking them through to a cubicle within A&E and found a free nurse to get them checked in and taken care of before hurrying back to Resus. As it turned out they were also expecting the other daughter of this woman, the girl who had been worst hit by the car, so she quickly ran back around and promised to let them know the moment the girl came in, but insisted they get seen to while they waited.

Doctors came hurrying down the corridor and entered Resus just as the second ambulance was arriving. They pulled on gloves and hovered about, trying to glean what information they could about the casualty expected.

Mr Cobham appeared and began to take control. An elderly man strapped to a back board arrived. He was handed over and assessed by the team. They got to work and soon X-ray were there too. It was Kate's job to fly around making sure everything was being done and chasing up anything that seemed to be taking too long.

Another ambulance arrived and all but the few staff needed to deal with the gentleman in bed one moved over to bed two along with the paediatrician, who had been waiting in the background for the girl to arrive.

Mr Elliott left his registrar to handle the man and came over to see the girl. The child was in the process of coming round and appeared to be very distressed. They had been told that she was nine years old and called Sasha. She had been hit by the car when the elderly man appeared to have collapsed at the wheel. Kate moved around to the head of the bed and started talking to the girl very calmly while Fiona, the paediatrician, got a needle in the back of her hand and then Mr Elliott stepped up to take a look.

Kate tried her best to comfort the girl as Mr Elliott began assessing her limbs and asking her questions, but the child was too scared and began to cry again. Her legs were hurting and Kate leant in closer still to talk softly into her ear. The girl grabbed her, her pleading gaze searching Kate's, and then her face just crumpled.

"Sasha," she soothed. "I'm Kate and I'm going to stay with you until you're safely on the ward. Your mum and your little sister are already here waiting to see you, but they have injuries of their own and they need to get those seen to before we can get you all back together. Now these nice men and women here are just trying to find out what's hurt and what's not and then we'll get you comfortable and we can bring them in, okay?" Sasha sniffled and looked up at her. "I promise I'll stay with you."

Kate looked across and caught Elliott's eye. He held her gaze for a moment and then nodded. "See that handsome doctor down the end there?" she said. Mr Elliott smiled uncomfortably. "Well *he* needs to ask you a few more questions and when he's done, this nice lady here is going to get you something else for the pain."

Mr Elliott called down instructions, asking Sasha to wriggle her toes and if she could feel him touching her legs and Kate did her best to keep the girl calm. After he was satisfied with her legs, he moved up to her arms and went through the whole process again, with Kate trying hard to comfort the girl as they went.

Fiona drew up the pain relief and injected it through the line in the back of the girl's hand and Kate checked that she was more comfortable as the doctors and nurses began to disperse to their various tasks.

With her hand firmly by Sasha's side, Kate called across to one of the other nurses. "Pam, you wouldn't fetch Sasha's mother and sister for me, would you? I think they're in Cubicle Six. They'll probably have just about enough time to see her before X-ray are ready."

Mr Elliott nodded his thanks and wandered over to the side to write in the notes. Suddenly the little girl started fitting and Kate called across to Fiona, who was back by her side in an instant.

The final ambulance arrived with the wife of the old man. She had been trapped in the car and had just been released. Reluctantly Kate had to leave Fiona and a junior nurse to deal with the little girl and hurried to the main door to receive the last casualty.

The lady was lifted onto the third bed where Mr Cobham appeared at Kate's side. His registrar, who had been dealing with the gentleman in the same bay, finished writing and moved over to help. Orders were called out and staff began to materialise around the trolley.

Kate picked up the scissors and started to cut away the clothes so that the doctors could better examine the lady and a shout went out from behind the curtain next door: Cardiac arrest.

Looking over, Kate realised they were running short of staff, so she shouted for the medical student to carry on cutting and dashed over to pitch in.

Staff flew everywhere chasing equipment and drugs needed for all the casualties, like ants in a burrow, each one a part of something greater.

Sasha's mother appeared around the corner with the smaller child at her side and Kate shouted at the nearest nurse, "Get them out of here!"

Kate was still busy with Mr Cobham, doing chest compressions on the man in Resus One, when the anaesthetist peered round the curtain to see if he was needed. Fiona was managing Sasha and Mr Elliott was working on the old lady.

They lost the old man.

Kate pulled the curtains around the trolley and checked round the other casualties. They were all in hand.

The Anaesthetist stayed to help out with the elderly lady, whose injuries seemed to be mainly to do with her right leg. Mr Elliott checked around the other casualties too, deciding which ones were a priority for Theatre, and then he returned to Mr Cobham, who was arranging a plan for each one.

Mr Cobham turned round and put his hand on Kate's shoulder. He looked at his watch. "Kate, it's nearly ten. Go home. The cavalry's here and they're stuck in. We'll be fine. Thanks for staying on."

"I'll just check in on Sasha," she said.

"She's intubated now and Fiona's with her," Mr Elliott said, coming to stand beside them. "She won't know."

"What about her mother? Has anyone gone to talk to her?"

"I think Sue's with them right now," Mr Cobham assured her. "Go home, Kate."

"Thank you," Mr Elliott said. "With the girl."

Kate looked at his furrowed brow, aware that he had a long night's work ahead of him. "No problem," she said and as she made her way out to her car and drove home, she wondered, had she really described Mr Elliott as 'handsome'?

Letting herself back into the house, Kate called out a hello to Sophie and was reassured by a reply. He had thanked her for her help, spontaneously. That in itself was a surprise. Maybe the man was feeling guilty? Maybe he wasn't so bad after all? Whatever the workings of his mind, Kate knew she would be back again tomorrow and Mr Elliott would still be there, but for the rest of that night she had a date with a glass of wine and a pillow, and nothing and no-one was going to get in the way of that.

A few days later Mr Elliott stopped by in A&E and asked to

speak to her. Kate was in a cubicle when she heard his voice. Her body froze as she wondered what he could want with her this time and she excused herself from her patient for a moment to step outside and speak to him.

"Kate, I thought you might want to know that the girl from the other night is going to be all right."

"What, Sasha? Oh good," she said. "Is she still here? I wondered if she'd end up on a neurosurgical unit."

"No. Her CT didn't show any bleeding, just a bit of swelling which we can handle here. She's off ITU and recovering up on the children's ward if you'd like to go and see her. She's been asking after you. She thought you were an angel."

Kate laughed. "Not quite. But thanks for letting me know. I'll pop up in my break."

"Good. Well…"

Kate looked down at the floor, uncomfortable at being the focus of his attention once again, even though it was in a good way this time.

"You worked like a Trojan the other night. You must have been exhausted by the time you got home," he said.

"A little. But you had to carry on after I left. And your bit was far more important than mine."

"Not in the eyes of that little girl," he said.

Kate shifted her feet uncomfortably and blushed. "Well, let's not disillusion her too quickly, eh?" She smiled, and for a moment she could swear she saw a trace of a smile on his lips too. A cough came through the curtains from her patient within and Kate excused herself politely and returned to her work.

Seeing Sasha so much better at lunch time put a spring in Kate's step, despite the mountains of bandaging and tubes surrounding her. She was comfortable now and her mother was with her.

"Thank you so much for what you did the other day," her mum had said, after Kate had been introduced to Sasha again.

"Not at all. I was just doing my job. I'm just sorry I ended

41

up having to yell at you," she said. "I felt awful doing that, but it had just gone a bit mad at the time."

"It doesn't matter. I quite understand. Sasha's in one piece, that's what's important."

The father walked in just then.

"Mark, this is Kate, the nurse from casualty Sasha was telling us about," the mother said.

The gentleman shook Kate's hand firmly. "Thank you for everything you did," he said.

"But I was just saying, I didn't really do much," she told him. "It was Fiona Phillips, the paediatrician, who saved the day. She's great, isn't she?"

"Yes, she's lovely, but the surgeon who saw her in A&E came up this morning too and he was very complimentary about you. He told us you were amazing, getting Sasha to stay calm and quiet so that they could deal with her as quickly as possible. And you stayed with her, reassuring her when all the other doctors and nurses were scaring her to death with their questions. She thought you were an angel."

From the bed, Sasha groaned with embarrassment and Kate smiled at her and winked. "Not quite, but I'm very flattered." Then she whispered a loud aside to the girl, "Blame the strong pain killers, I would," and Sasha giggled. "Anyway, I'd better be getting back to work. I'm glad you're on the mend, though."

It was always nice to get good news and for the rest of the day, Kate breezed along with a contented smile on her lips.

On the last day before her long awaited days off, Kate came across Mr Elliott in the corridor. He was talking with another consultant. She caught his eye as he walked past.

"Kate," he called out. He put a hand out to stop her and excused himself from the other consultant. "You went to see Sasha then?" he asked.

"Yes. She's looking much happier. Thank you."

"You know she's determined to be a nurse like you when she's older now."

Kate smiled. "I'll have to have a long talk with her, then, won't I?" she said. She wrestled with the idea of apologising for her behaviour the other week, or should she just leave it to blow over? Their gazes held, as words, waiting to be spoken, lost their moment and went unsaid and then he nodded slightly, turned away and continued to talk to the other consultant.

Kate walked back down to A&E. "What are you looking so happy about?" Gloria asked her. Gloria always seemed to know when something was bothering them. It was like having your own mother around. Kate smiled to herself but quickly straightened her face. A few minutes later Gloria walked past again, carrying a suture pack and dressings.

"Well?" she asked.

"Nothing," Kate replied, her cheeks flushing with the fib.

"Hmmm, looks like it," and she walked on, calling back over her shoulder. "I'll get it out of you, Katy Heath, don't you worry."

Kate rolled her eyes and picked up the next card in the box, calling out the name to a sea of expectant faces sitting in the waiting room.

Returning home that night, Kate collapsed into the armchair. Sophie was on a day off and was already in the party mood. "You're home. Come on, Mr Crickland from orthopaedics is having a house warming and we're all invited," she said.

"But I've just worked twelve days straight," Kate said. "I'm exhausted. Besides, I barely know him."

"But I do and I'm allowed to bring a friend and I've been waiting for you to get home to go."

"Oh, Soph. Don't make me go, please. I'm done in."

Sophie gave her a stern look and then sighed in resignation. "Go on then. I've put some lasagne in the fridge. You can bung it in the microwave when you're ready. Don't wait up."

Kate looked around the room. Two whole days off. She really wanted to get out of her uniform, but she just didn't have the

43

energy to move.

Sophie sauntered down the stairs around ten o'clock the following morning and found Kate sitting in the front room, cuddled up under a blanket, watching some of the TV she'd missed out on across the previous two weeks. Sophie yawned and Kate looked round. "Morning, you dirty stop out. Sleep well?"

"Eventually," Sophie croaked.

Kate studied the smug expression on Sophie's face. "Go on, give us the dirt, then," she said. "You know you want to."

Sophie grinned. "It was good. You would have liked it. Great house. It was one of those refurbished barns outside town. The carpets are going down today, so they decided to have the party last night in case anybody spilled their drink. And they did. Jenny tipped a whole glass of wine down some poor guy. He was very good about it. Probably one of her stupid stunts to get attention."

"Did it work?" Kate asked.

"I guess so, yes."

Kate shook her head. "That girl's incorrigible. Who was it, do you know?"

"No. It might be one of your lot, though. Medium height, brown hair, got a mole by his right eye."

"Oh, Carl. Dr Penn. Really? Well, it takes all sorts, I suppose."

"Was Jolly there?" she asked.

"Jolly? At a party? Are you mad? No he was probably at home devising new tortures for A&E nurses. Or maybe he was at a gay bar?"

"I never said he was gay!" Kate snapped. "That was Kirsty."

Sophie looked at her. "Okay."

There was a pause in the conversation as Kate wondered why she had reacted so sharply. "I was just angry at him that day," she said.

"Really?"

Kate shot her friend a look. "I wish I'd never told you all," she said sagging. "I was just as bad as him, wasn't I?"

44

"Ooh. I bet that hurt to say, didn't it?" Sophie said. "You mean you may actually have been in a bit of a bad mood that day, having just buried your granddad and all, and it's possible you might have shot your mouth off at him because he caught you slagging him off behind his back?"

Kate winced. "You didn't have to put it quite like that. You're meant to be on my side."

Sophie raised her eyebrows. "Don't worry. Consultants never listen to gossip and what he doesn't know won't hurt him... or *you* for that matter. Have you managed to swap a few hours next Saturday night so we can go to the ball?"

"Yes. Gloria said she'd cover for me. She reckons she's too old to be out partying till all hours anyway."

~~~

"She is," Lena added and a small smile crept into the corner of her mouth and settled there.

~~~

"Good," Sophie said. "Then you can make it up to him there with an apologetic snog."

"Is he going?" Kate asked.

"What is this I detect? Is the ice maiden beginning to crack?"

"Like he'd ever look at me that way? No."

"I wasn't thinking about *him* being after *you*."

"Oh, shut up! Is Peter going to be there?" Kate asked.

"The delectable Dr Florin? I honestly don't know." Sophie got up and walked out to the kitchen singing, "Adam and Katy sitting in a tree, K-I-S-S-I-N-G."

Kate threw a cushion at her, but smiled. 'Adam?' she thought. 'Adam Elliott'.

On Saturday night, Kate rushed in around six and jumped into the shower. Sophie was walking round in her dressing gown and slippers, busy ironing her dress and straightening her hair.

"I wish Rich could come with us," Sophie said as she arrived in Kate's bedroom doorway, pulling a long-handled black comb through her hair.

"He could have. If you'd wanted," Kate said.

"Would you? If you weren't medical?" Sophie asked.

"No. Probably not. But he's still going to give us a lift, isn't he?" Sophie smiled. "Yes, of course."

"You've got him wrapped around your little finger, haven't you?"

"Absolutely, and quite right too," she said.

At a quarter to eight Rich rang the bell and Sophie hurried down to the front door to let him in. She kissed him and stood back to show him her dress. "How do I look?" she asked, twirling from side to side and bobbing a little curtsey.

"Stunning," he said, pulling her into his arms.

Sophie beamed. "I'll do then?" and Rich kissed her emphatically.

"More than 'do'," he growled. "I'm beginning to regret not coming with you now. You're going to need someone to fight off all those young doctors."

Kate appeared on the stairs wearing a long flowing dress in deep turquoise-blue, embroidered with pale gold. It had tiny thin straps and stopped just above her ankles. Her strawberry blonde hair hung loosely down her back with only a single clip to stop it falling across her face. She smiled. "You do realise half those doctors are actually women? Hello, Rich. Doesn't she look amazing?"

Rich turned back to look at Sophie. "Beautiful," he said. "You both do. But we'd better get a move on if Cinderella here doesn't want to be late for the ball."

Rich helped them both into the back of his car shutting the door behind them and then he produced a cap from the passenger seat and put it on. "Where to, milady?"

The girls collapsed with laughter in the back seat of the car.

"The Ambassador, please, Tibbs," Sophie said, through a splutter of giggles.

Rich winked at her in the rear view mirror. "Right away, milady."

They arrived at the hotel and Rich opened the car door. He bowed as they stepped out and Sophie beamed at him. "Thank you," she said.

"Just you mind you don't go swanning off with any of your dashing young doctors. Male or female," he added. "You're mine now and don't you forget it."

Sophie saluted obediently and Rich turned to Kate. "I'm relying on you to keep her on the straight and narrow, Kate."

"No problem," she said dragging Sophie away from him to get inside before they missed the start of the meal.

Inside, the hotel was filled with light. Huge arrangements of flowers adorned magnificent pillars and chandeliers sent sparks dancing around the marble walls.

The doorman directed the girls to where they could deposit their coats and from there the cloakroom attendant pointed them in the direction of the drawing room. On their arrival, they accepted a glass of wine from a waiter and then wandered into the room.

Kate looked round and spotted a seating plan on an easel. They looked for their names and found them on table ten. Searching further they found Mr Elliott on table thirteen, Carl, on table ten with them, but there was no sign of Peter Florin for Flis. Kate sipped at her wine and watched the waiters, busy setting the tables in the dining room.

From where they were standing, Kate found she was in the perfect position to keep an eye out for new arrivals. Thus far there had been no sign of Mr Elliott, but by the time they took their places to eat, there he was. There were a couple of tables between them, but with his table being diagonally across from her own, Kate could see him quite clearly.

"You've gone very pale all of a sudden," Sophie whispered as she placed her napkin in her lap. "What is it?"

"He's here," Kate whispered back. "I'm looking straight at him."

"Who? Peter?"

"No, Elliott."

Sophie stifled a smirk. "Isn't that a good thing?"

Kate looked sideways, horrified that Sophie seemed to have such insight into her predicament. It was becoming horribly plain to Kate that she was attracted to the man, despite her reluctance to accept it. Sophie smiled an all knowing smile, which Kate found fell hopelessly short of reassuring. "Why? Do you think there's any point?" Where had that come from? What on earth was she thinking?

"Of course," Sophie said.

"But…"

"Look, he's a good-looking, successful, single guy and you're a gorgeous, caring – despite recent events which may make him think to the contrary – intelligent woman. What could be wrong about that?"

Kate fiddled nervously with her hair as she racked her brain trying to work out what it was she really wanted.

"You look lovely. Don't fuss," Sophie said. "And I don't want to find you hiding in a corner, polishing the silver if he tries to ask you to dance later on. It's fine."

Kate took a deep breath and let it out slowly. "I wouldn't need to polish this silver anyway," she said. "Have you seen it? It's positively gleaming."

As the starter was being served Kate glanced over and saw Mr Elliott talking with his colleagues. One of the senior nurses from Ascot Ward was sitting on the far side of him and Kate found herself for the moment feeling glad that he wasn't talking to her.

The conversation began to liven up on Kate's table as the group settled in and started to eat. It was a welcome distraction for Kate, enjoying the conversation until the waiters began to clear the plates and she felt something pulling her eyes to look across again, and this time she caught Elliott's gaze. Immediately she looked down and then, after a second or two, back up. He was busy with his table, his own plate being cleared. But he looked back over and caught her still looking at him and they were fixed there, a moment captured in time, as her pulse raced and her breath held. The heat rose in her cheeks making her dip her face and turn back to her friend for refuge. She swallowed and took another sip of water. She had to find something to focus on.

Kate reached for the dinner menu and looked in the direction of the words, but nothing was going in. She tried again. Was she *so* nervous? Not a word of encouragement had passed his lips. In fact he had probably said more words to her in anger than anything else, but still she found she was captivated. She knew she had a history of failed relationships, but then again, who didn't?

"What are we having next?" someone asked from across the table.

Kate was confused. "Oh… Er… Chicken in tarragon with white wine sauce and seasonal vegetables," she managed to croak out, realising she was still holding the menu. She took a deep breath and placed it back on the table.

"Brain shorting out a little?" Sophie whispered and Kate rolled her eyes and heaved a sigh of exasperation. Sophie smiled and tucked into the food in front of her, but Kate found she could barely stomach a thing.

"No wonder you stay so lovely and slim, Kate," one of the women on the table called across to her. "You eat like a sparrow. I wish I ate less, but I just love my food."

"Oh, don't you believe it," Sophie told them. "She eats like a horse when we're at home."

"Don't you like the food?" Carl Penn asked.

"No, it's fine. I'm just not very hungry," Kate said. "I might pop to the bar and get another drink, though. Anyone else want one?"

Kate had to take the chance to catch her breath. She walked back to the bar in the drawing room, breathing deeply. The stuffiness in the dining hall had become quite suffocating. She ordered some drinks and returned to the table carrying a tray only to find Jenny now sitting in her seat.

She handed out the drinks and stood beside the table. Sophie looked up. "We thought Jenny could sit in your seat while we're having pudding and you could go and natter to Flis. You've ordered the same thing. You don't mind do you, Kate?"

Kate thought it a little odd, until she remembered Jenny's penchant for Dr Penn and then she agreed happily. "Where's Flis, then?" she asked looking around.

Jenny stood up and pointed to the near side of table six, where a place was now sitting empty. Kate could see the back of Flis sitting next to it but suddenly realised sitting there would put her directly behind Mr Elliott. Only inches away in fact. She looked back at her friend in panic. But Sophie just turned to her with that all knowing smile of hers and nodded. "Go on, then," she said. "See you after."

"But…"

Sophie turned back to talk to Jenny and Kate was left to walk through the dining hall to her new position, right behind Mr Elliott.

She took a deep breath and tidied her hair and then picking up her drink, she walked over and sat down at table six.

Sitting so close to Adam Elliott, Kate found it difficult enough to breathe, let alone hold down a decent conversation. His presence flowed around her, enveloping her in a haze of sexual tension. Flis was gushing on about the beautiful decorations and gorgeous dresses and Kate had to just sit there and let it all wash over her. Breathe in; breathe out, she thought, her pulse surging faster and faster. Kate's ears strained for any words at the next table Adam Elliott might utter, but he was distinctly quiet throughout and she could do little else but play with the edges of her dessert.

When all the crockery was cleared away and the coffee was served, the guest speaker, an American lawyer, stood up and began a very amusing tale about medico-legal claims in the USA. Everyone turned their chairs to face the front, leaving Kate almost side by side with Mr Elliott. She was convinced she could feel the heat from his body warming her own. Her palms were sweating as her eyes found their focus on his right knee. It was a firm-looking knee, not too bony and not too big. His dinner jacket was black and his shoes were smart. God, how she wanted to touch that knee.

The noise of laughter around her became distant and muffled, allowing only the pressing thud of her heart in her ears.

At last the speech came to an end and the audience clapped and cheered enthusiastically, except in the small space between table six and table thirteen, where only the sound of a poor heart beating wildly could be heard.

Music struck up on the dance floor and people started to talk again, sipping their coffee and laughing at each other's jokes.

Kate excused herself and walked away through the cool corridors to the sanctuary of the ladies' room. Only one girl was in there when she arrived and *she* left soon after. Kate looked in the mirror and spoke to herself. "You're a mess. He's just a man and he has no interest in you anyway. Hell, you don't even like him; it's just a stupid obsession. For heaven's sake, get a grip."

A group of nurses walked in and she quickly clawed back control and checked her make-up in the mirror. It was fine. She dabbed her cheeks with a little cold water and then walked back outside to find Sophie. Sophie would know how to handle her stupidity. She would understand how to put Kate at ease. Her mother hen abilities were the stuff of legend.

Walking back down the corridor, Kate suddenly saw Mr Elliott walking towards her. One of his hands lay casually in his pocket and the other swung loosely by his side. His cummerbund and bow tie were both midnight blue and his shirt was crisp and white. Dark, blue-grey eyes pierced her as he moved slowly closer. Kate couldn't think. Where should she look? What should she do? Mr Cobham walked out of the drawing room as Mr Elliott passed by. They exchanged a look and Mr Cobham disappeared again and

Mr Elliott's eyes moved back to her.

Kate felt sure her face must have been scarlet under such scrutiny, or else deathly white from fear. She tried to smile as he approached, though it took all her courage to do so. And then he stopped.

"Kate. You look... stunning. I'm only used to seeing you in your uniform. Your hair, it's so long. It's beautiful."

Kate suddenly lost the power of speech, her higher functions having long since left her. She stuttered. "Y-You're looking very handsome too, sir."

"Adam. Please, Kate; call me Adam. We're not in work now."

"Adam." A world of expectation hung between them, raising the tension to breaking point, and then Kate snapped. "Look I'm really sorry about that day on Aintree. I was completely out of order. I'd just had a very bad day and I-"

He stepped closer and placed a warm finger on her lips. "No need," he said. "You were right. I had lost my composure. It got out of hand. I'm sorry. It won't happen again." His finger moved slowly away from her lips and brushed a stray lock of hair from the side of her face. He stepped a fraction closer. Their gazes mingling. Kate's breath quivered, as she realised the moment she had been subconsciously hoping for was rapidly approaching.

"Kate, there you are," Jenny called out from the doorway of the drawing room. "I've been looking for you."

Jolted, Kate turned abruptly, like a child caught stealing from the cookie jar, and when she turned back, Mr Elliott was walking away, back down the corridor and into the hall.

"That was close," Jenny said. "I'm not going to let him have a go at you tonight. We're here to *party*. Come on. We were all starting to wonder where you'd got to."

With her pulse still pounding through her body, Kate followed Jenny back into the drawing room and soon found her friends again.

"You found her, then. Where were you?" Flis asked.

"I just went to the toilet," Kate said.

"I caught her in the nick of time," Jenny announced. "Elliott was about to get his claws into her again. Close one that, wasn't it, Kate?"

Kate pulled a strained face, making a non-committal grunt that in no way fooled Sophie, who looked at her, seeming to assess the situation. A few of the A&E nurses pushed past her, grabbing her arm. "Come on, Kate. It's time to dance."

Kate looked at her friends as she was dragged up onto the dance floor, none of whom seemed keen to follow her. "You dance," said Sophie. "We'll see you in a bit."

Kate moved through the crowd onto the dance floor and started to dance, but it wasn't long before she spotted Adam Elliott with some of the surgeons just to the right of the room. He was looking at her, making her feel… naked. She looked back a moment or two later and he was still there, looking at her intensely. Bravely she managed a small smile and felt sure his eyes gleamed a little brighter than before. What could she do? She could hardly walk up to him and ask him to dance. Well, she could, but she wasn't nearly brave enough or drunk enough to do that yet. That was the answer, she thought, she needed more to drink.

Kate excused herself and headed to the bar in the drawing room and bought herself a long drink. She was just about to leave again when Kirsty came in. "I heard you nearly had another run in with Elliott tonight," she said.

Kate's mouth dropped open in disbelief. "What?"

"Elliott. It's a shame he wasn't on call tonight instead of Barker. I don't care if he is straight, he's about as interesting as a dry stone. 'Cold-hearted, pompous prick who wouldn't know what it was for' I heard you said? Yeah, well, I pity the poor girl who ends up with him. We'd have to hold a wake for her. Ooh, there's Bianca. See ya."

Kate was mortified. Kirsty had always been a bit of a tornado, but she hadn't even given Kate chance to reply. She looked back across to the dining room and her world began to cave in, as there, standing just inside the doorway, looking at her, was Mr Elliott. His eyes dulled as his gaze fell away and he turned around and left.

Kate panicked. Had he heard the words Kirsty had said? It wasn't true, any of it. Well not exactly. Not anymore. She promised herself there and then that she was never going to do something so stupid ever again but that did nothing to help her current situation. What could she do? Should she chase after him and throw herself on his mercy? Should she pray that he hadn't heard anything and was just waiting to catch her on her own? But he had left *after* Kirsty had left her on her own. She felt sick. She hurried out into the hall to look for Sophie.

She found her chatting to a couple of junior doctors. Sophie took one look and excused herself. She took Kate by the hand and walked her round the hotel until they found a quiet corner where they could talk. "Okay, talk to me. What's happened?"

Kate didn't know where to start.

"Take a deep breath," Sophie said, "let it out slowly and then tell me what's gone wrong. It's obvious he's attracted to you."

Kate shook her head, unwilling to face up to her fears.

"Really? Because it definitely looked that way to me."

"I thought he was," Kate said. "I even thought he was going to kiss me at one point. That was when Jenny butted in."

"I knew something like that must have happened," Sophie said. "But that's good, isn't it? At least now we know he does like you."

"But I went to the bar a few minutes ago and on my way out I was collared by Kirsty and she went on and on about what I thought of Elliott, at least what she *thought* I thought, that night at Helix, and… he was there."

"Where?"

"Behind her, in the doorway."

"He overheard?"

"I think so."

Sophie pondered this for a few seconds while Kate stood there, fidgeting anxiously, her heart aching and her spirit in turmoil.

"What are you going to do?" Sophie asked at last.

"I don't know," Kate told her. "I was hoping *you'd* know what to do. You're always so much better than me at this sort of thing."

"You need to talk to him," Sophie said. "See how he is and then judge for yourself if he's upset by what he may or may not have heard. Do you care enough to fight for this one?"

Kate knew she was right, but could she be that brave? She nodded.

"Do you want to get back in there? Get it over and done with? Or do you want to have another drink first?"

"Now, I think," Kate said.

"Come on then. Let's strike while the consultant is hot."

Chapter 4

Wandering back through the corridors towards the dining room, Kate's heart rate was rising with each step that she took. She scoured the rooms, but there was no sign of him. Sophie looked over and Kate gestured that she had no idea where he could be. She walked out into the drawing room and looked for him there. Still nothing. She searched the corridors and back into the dining room with increasing unease and still he was nowhere to be found. Bravely, she decided to ask at Reception. "Excuse me," she said. "Have you seen a dark-haired gentleman with a dark blue bow tie and cummerbund passing through here recently?"

The lady behind the desk smiled as best she could, considering the whole place was full of similarly dressed men. "A gentleman fitting that description *did* take a cab from the front steps just a few minutes ago, miss," she said. "Would you like me to order a taxi for you too?"

Kate walked back into the dining room and downed the rest of her drink. He had heard. Her chance had passed her by and it would never be coming again.

Sophie found her a short while later, sitting in a dark corner, drowning her sorrows. "No luck?" she asked.

"He's gone," Kate told her.

"Really?"

She nodded.

Sophie sat down next to her. "I'm sorry, Hun. I don't know what to say."

Kate shook her head. "What the hell was I thinking of, losing it over *him* anyway? If only Peter was here to ogle at."

Sophie opened her mouth to say something, but the look on Kate's face seemed to halt her in her tracks and so she just put her arm around her friend and rested her head on Kate's shoulder. "Do you want to get out of here?" she asked.

Kate nodded.

"Come on then."

~

Out on the road, Mr Elliott loosened off his bow tie and let out a big sigh. That had been too close, he thought to himself. He did find Kate very attractive, but she was a difficult one to fathom. Some days he would swear there was a kind of spark between them and some days not. The girl was complicated, or maybe he was out of practice. He didn't pay any mind to what he had heard. It was what it was, gossip.

He hated gossip of any kind and hospital gossip was the worst: people meddling and prying into your life, never leaving you alone. He'd had enough of that for one lifetime. All he wanted now was to be left alone.

He stared out of the window as the bright city lights came back into view and thought of Ali. He remembered the way she had looked at him when he had done something wrong. He leant his head back against the seat and tortured himself some more. Soon he would be back in his bachelor pad, his sanctuary, his home, with no one else to trouble him and no-one now to care. Whatever he felt for Kate, he wasn't prepared to take things any further. It had been the wake-up call he had needed and he determined to put some distance between the two of them, to give him time to forget about her, while the yearning ebbed away.

~

Monday morning Kate was back in work and still sore from the events the night of the ball. She couldn't face seeing Adam Elliott again so soon. She had no idea what to say to him, so she kept a low profile in the hope that she would not be seen. And as a plan, it worked. Nothing big came in to A&E and the morning passed without drama. Tuesday, however, she wasn't nearly so lucky.

A patient in A&E needed to be escorted up to the trauma ward and try as she might, Kate could not find anyone else free to take him. It was mid-afternoon; chances were that Elliott would not be roaming the hospital at that time of day, so reluctantly she headed off to Ascot Ward, more subdued than usual.

She buzzed at the ward entrance to be let in. Walking slowly down to the nurses' station, Kate found herself suddenly face to face with Adam Elliott. He looked at her, without a hint of acknowledgement and then walked straight on.

Kate was crushed. It was obvious he had overheard Kirsty the other night and against that, Kate felt she would be hard pushed to defend herself. Her frame sagged as he strode out of the ward, leaving her heart pounding so fiercely in her chest it made her body physically ache. He hated her.

She didn't see him again for the rest of the week and several people asked her if anything was wrong, but she could tell them nothing.

Saturday evening, Sophie persuaded Kate to go to Vin-Deux, a new wine bar that had opened up on the other side of town. They had heard it was a dressy establishment, so had made an effort. Kate was wearing a deep green cocktail dress and heels and Sophie was in a little black top, some smart trousers and sparkly earrings. It was just the two of them. Rich was out with his mates that night and had arranged to meet them at the monument around half past ten. Until then, their nights were their own.

The atmosphere was buzzing in Vin-Deux. The music was good, not too loud so they could still hear each other speaking, yet still upbeat enough to keep the place lively.

After a few drinks, the girls moved upstairs to the dance floor and headed in and a short while later, Sophie spotted the much swooned after Dr Florin. Poor old lovelorn Flis still hadn't managed to meet him properly, so Kate pulled out her mobile, moved away from the blare of the music and gave her a ring, but there was no answer.

"She must be working," she said.

"Poor Flis, always in the wrong place at the wrong time. She'll be gutted when she hears we went out without her and bumped into him."

Kate caught his eye across the room and he spoke to one of his friends briefly before making his way towards them.

"Don't look now, but he's on his way over," Sophie hissed.

"Ladies, you're both looking very lovely tonight. I'm Pete. Can I get either of you a drink?"

Kate shook her head, having a full glass already in her hand.

"I'll have a white wine, if you're offering," Sophie said and handed him her glass. He paused for a second, looking from Sophie to Kate and back again and then walked over to the bar.

The girls huddled closer. "I don't think he recognises us," Sophie said.

"I know." They watched him at the bar.

The gorgeous Peter Florin returned, passed Sophie her drink and turned back towards Kate. "You know, you look very familiar," he said. "You haven't by any chance been in hospital recently, have you?" Now this was too much fun to pass up. Kate had the upper hand here and was going to use it. She nodded.

"I thought you had. An operation, perhaps?" Kate held a straight face. "Or maybe an injury? Have you been into accident and emergency?"

Kate had to struggle hard to hold a straight face. "That's amazing. How on earth did you know that?"

"Ah, well, I'm a doctor as it happens." He was obviously used to impressing the girls with this.

"Really? Goodness, how wonderful. You must be very good with your hands." She winked at Sophie, who almost lost control of her bodily functions until Kate dug her in the ribs and patted her back.

"Sorry, went down the wrong way." Sophie coughed a little and turned her face away.

"Well it's a good job we've got a doctor in the house," Kate told her with a big smile. "You'll have to excuse me; I've just spotted someone I need to talk to." Grinning from ear to ear, Kate walked around the dance floor to say hello to an old acquaintance.

Pete turned back to Sophie, obviously more than a little taken aback that a woman had wandered off on him when he was in full charm offensive.

"She's a nurse, you fool," Sophie told him. "Her name's Kate. She works in A&E. She was just messing with you."

"And you're a-"

"Nurse, too. Yes. Sophie." She held out a hand. "Ascot Ward."

Not long after, Kate drifted back across the room, a little surprised that Pete was still standing there. She smiled and he raised an eyebrow in return.

"I'm afraid your cover's blown, Kate," Sophie confessed.

Kate looked at him. "Sorry," she said. "I couldn't resist it."

Pete tried his best to smile. "You can't blame a guy for trying. With such a beauty in the room, I had to give it a go."

Sophie's eyebrows rose and, making an excuse about needing to go to the ladies', she quickly left Kate and Peter alone.

Kate flushed, flattered, but a little unsettled by Sophie's disappearance.

"You've gone bright red," he said, suddenly amused at her expense. "What is it? Aren't you used to a man telling you how beautiful you are?"

If possible Kate flushed even harder. "No, absolutely not."

"Now I don't believe that. You must be. You're just playing with me again, aren't you?"

"I am not," she said. "In fact I think it's *you* who is toying with *me*. Trying to get your own back, I expect. Please don't take me for a girl who is deluded about her own appearance. I know I'm pretty average and I'm okay with that."

"I wouldn't dare toy with you, Kate. I know when I've met my match. But you're wrong, you know. You're the most beautiful girl in here, easily. Would you like to dance?"

The very thought of showing off how ungainly she was in front of a gorgeous guy was hideous. "I don't dance very well," she said.

"Neither do I. We could always be bad together?"

What was he suggesting? Kate shook her head. "No thanks."

"Are you sure I can't get you a drink?"

"Well, perhaps a drink. Could I have a bitter lemon, please?"

Pete pulled a face. "Really? That nasty stuff?"

"I like it," said Kate.

"Are you sure I can't get you something more exciting?"

"No, thanks," she told him firmly. "I've put a cap on my exciting drinks lately, after I did something completely stupid under the influence of several of the things."

"I'm intrigued." He smiled. "Does this something have a name I would recognise?"

Kate laid her most reproachful gaze on him. "Bitter lemon, please."

"Coming right up."

Sophie returned and looked around. "How's it going?" she asked quietly. "You know, I think he's into you."

Kate really hoped not. "Maybe, maybe not. He's probably used the same lines on half a dozen girls already this evening. But whatever you do, don't let Flis hear you saying that, or she'll never speak to me again and I'm really not that interested."

Sophie sighed. She looked at her watch. "It's almost time to meet up with Rich. Are you ready?"

"Oh, I'm ready."

"Ready for what?" Pete asked, returning with Kate's drink.

"I was just telling Kate that it was nearly time for us to go."

He passed Kate her drink. "Really? Not already, surely?"

"Afraid so," Kate said. She swigged back her drink. "Got to work tomorrow and I have to get my beauty sleep."

"No you don't." His face was a picture of charm.

Kate cast him a cynical smile and knocked back the rest of her drink. "Thanks anyway," she said. "Come on, Soph, we'd better be off. It was nice to meet you, Pete. Thanks for the drink."

"Wait. Won't you give me your number?"

Kate looked across at Sophie. If Flis hadn't been so besotted with him she might have considered it. Might. He could have been just what she needed to help her forget about Adam. But no. "I'll see you around," she said and they made their way out to the door.

Sophie had been right, of course, the night out had done Kate the power of good and the fun of meeting Peter Florin had lifted her spirits immensely.

Kate wandered into work on Monday morning no less uneasy about the way things had been left with Adam, but knowing now that he was just one man. It was a good place to be in for her. Things were unlikely to be able to get any worse and there was a chance they may actually get better, so she decided to ride out the storm of Adam's disapproval and try not to let it bother her any more than it should.

She began to see light on the horizon when she managed to organise three full days of therapy. Anna had been Kate's friend since school days and she was about to get her PhD and Kate was definitely going to be up there to help her celebrate. She managed to swap a couple of shifts, which meant she was working almost ten days straight, but it was going to be worth it. She had been longing to see Anna ever since the situation with Adam had blown up in her face.

On Wednesday afternoon she bumped into Pete in the corridor at work and he asked to take her out the following night. Kate gave him marks out of ten for persistence, but told him she was busy, finally promising to think about it, to get him off her back.

The next morning she was off on the train to meet up with Anna. The taxi pulled up outside the last house on the right and she rang the bell. A minute later the yellow door flew open and Anna came rushing out, throwing her arms around her.

"Katy. You're here. Come in; come in."

Kate walked inside and was introduced to Anna's housemates, two of whom she'd met before. They chatted for ages, catching up on what everyone had been up to and in the evening they went out to one of Anna's friend's parties where Kate was finally introduced to John, Anna's boyfriend. She had heard a lot about the guy in their phone calls, but hadn't yet been able to meet him.

"So what did you think about John?" Anna asked at the end of the night. They were sitting in their pyjamas on top of Anna's bed, each with a blanket around their shoulders and a hot cup of tea in their hands.

"He's lovely, Anna."

"He is, isn't he?"

"And he's obviously very into you."

"And why wouldn't he be?"

"Absolutely. So what's going to happen to you both now?" Kate asked.

"What do you mean?"

"Well, you're leaving, aren't you?" she said.

Anna hung her head. "Ah, yes."

"So…?"

Anna looked back up, her eyes alight with excitement. "Can you keep a secret?"

"Of course."

Anna hushed her voice. "He's asked me to marry him." Her face split with happiness.

Kate was stunned. "Well, that's… wonderful."

"He's just the best thing that's ever happened to me. He's gorgeous and kind and thoughtful and I just know I can trust him. I love him."

Kate looked at her and couldn't help but smile. "Wow." Then she threw her arms around her friend and hugged her, careful not to spill their tea. "I'm so happy for you. I'm jealous, obviously, but…"

"You can't tell anyone. Not yet," she said. "He's going to talk to my parents after the ceremony tomorrow."

"Of course." Kate was quiet for a minute. "This doesn't mean I'm going to lose you, does it?" she asked, suddenly worried that John was bound to take up her place in Anna's life.

"As if. I'm going to need a bridesmaid for starters and then I'm going to need my best mate to keep me sane when I come to my senses and realise I've turned into a nagging wife and need to get out of there for a bit."

Kate laughed. "Glad to see you've got realistic expectations, anyway," she said.

"And, of course, I'm going to be closer to you when I move to Brisely."

"You got the job?" Kate chirped.

"Yes."

She squealed with delight. "And John?"

"He's got an interview for a job in the area too."

"You've got it all planned out, haven't you?"

"And what about you?" Anna asked her. "You've got a good job you enjoy."

"I suppose so."

"Any new men on the horizon?"

Kate paused, just for a second, but it was long enough. "No."

"Katy Heath, there was hesitation there. Tell me everything."

"There's nothing to tell," Kate said, realising her mistake. "So when's the wedding going to be?"

"Don't you 'wedding' me. Who is he?"

"Nobody. There's no-one."

"I don't believe you."

"It's nothing, honestly."

Anna tilted her head and gave Kate a look that eventually made her crack.

"You'll end up marrying him, I bet," Anna said when Kate had finally brought her up to date.

Kate spluttered into her tea. "Yeah, right. Did you not get the bit when I messed everything up by running my mouth off? I probably just need to find a nice uncomplicated guy."

"Is there such a thing?"

"Then I'll be able to get Adam Elliott out of my head. It's probably just an infatuation. Maybe I'm deficient in something?"

"Yes: a good man," Anna told her.

"Thank you. It's okay, I'll probably clash heads with him again next week and remember exactly why I hated him so much in the first place."

"Or he could be the perfect guy for you, but you're too chicken to try?"

"What?" Kate was struck dumb.

"Face it, Kate. You throw yourself into these relationships, until they're just starting to go really well and then you panic. You find something miniscule that you don't like about them and blow it up out of all proportion and then finish with them. It's the way it always happens."

Kate was astounded. Where had all this come from? "I thought you were supposed to be my friend?" Kate joked back, but there was an edge of hurt in her voice that she couldn't seem to hide.

"Don't look at me like that. I'm only saying this because I want you to find someone who makes you as happy as John makes me.

You're my best friend, Kate. It's just that you seem to really like this guy. Is there no way that you could save it? Be brave for once and give it a go."

Kate laughed sadly. "Don't hold your breath," she said. "Anyway, you'll be far too busy drooling over your new fiancé to worry about little old me. Oh, Anna, I'm so pleased for you. And I can't wait until you're living closer to me."

Anna gave her a serious look and then like a light switching on, she beamed. "I know. It's going to be great, isn't it?"

On the train on the way home, Kate looked through her pictures of the party and the ceremony on her shiny little camera. She smiled at the shots of Anna in her silly hat and gown, the pair of them together, and then a lovely one of Anna and John.

Kate thought back to her conversation with her friend. Her relationships had all been complete disasters to date. Was she just being too picky? Did she panic, as Anna had suggested? She paused, unable to process her inner fears. One man out there had to be right for her, surely? And then maybe she would no longer have to fight.

Kate walked back into the house and found Sophie and Rich looking serious. She stood in the doorway and smiled, but neither of them smiled back. "What is it? What's up?"

"It's your mum, Kate. She's in hospital," Sophie said. "Your dad rang about an hour ago. We've been trying to contact you, but your phone was turned off."

Kate immediately grabbed her mobile and found the battery was dead. "What... What's happened?"

"She's all right." Sophie quickly came over to stand beside her. "She tripped up at the top of the staircase and fell all the way down."

"Oh God!" Kate's hands flew to her mouth and her knees became weak.

Sophie put an arm around her shoulders and sat her down in the nearest chair, crouching before her. "It's okay. They're with her now. And Rich'll give you a lift in as soon as you're ready."

"I can drive," Kate said.

"No, you can't. Not in this state."

Kate looked over at Rich. "Can we go now?" she asked.

Rich nodded. "Of course."

Sophie gave her a big hug and helped her to her feet. "Go on then," she said. "Send her my love, won't you?"

It was a Sunday night and the streets were clear and in no time at all Kate was running through A&E in search of direction.

Sheila, the night sister, was on. She stopped Kate as she went hurtling through. "Kate. What's the matter?" she said.

"It's my mum," Kate replied. "She was in here about an hour ago. She fell down the stairs."

"Of course, I should have realised. She'll be in Theatre by now. But don't panic, she wasn't too badly injured. It could have been a lot worse." She turned to another nurse passing by and held a leaflet out to her. "Amy. Take this to Mr Conner in Cubicle Three, please, and then send him on his way. I'm just going to take Kate up to find her dad. I won't be long."

The two of them marched through the hospital up to Kempton Ward, talking about her mother's injuries on the way. In the day room they found Kate's dad looking small and lost. Kate rushed up to him and hugged him fiercely, tears springing to her eyes.

"Kate, you came. I didn't know what to do." He clasped his daughter so close to him that Kate was rocked by a vulnerability she had never known.

Sheila made sure they were okay and then left them to it and Kate sat down next to her dad. "What happened?" she asked him, holding on to his big warm hand.

It turned out that Kate's mum had suffered a broken ankle, the bone in her wrist had been sticking out through her skin and at first they had feared for a broken neck but the scan had cleared her of that. Kate drew in a big sigh of relief. "You poor old thing," she said. "And poor Mum."

"But you're here now," he said. "Everything will be all right now, I know it will." And he patted Kate on the back of her hand as they sat there, waiting for news.

About an hour and a half later, a surgical registrar walked in and told them that the operation had been a success and that her mother would be up on the ward very soon. Kate asked which consultant her mother was going to be under and the doctor told her, "Mr Elliott."

After the doctor left, her dad turned to her. "Is he good?" he asked.

Kate's head was reeling. "Em… yes, Dad," she said. "He's very good."

The next day Kate was on duty and eager to see how her mum was getting along, so she grabbed the earliest break possible and took the stairs two at a time up to Kempton Ward and buzzed to be let in.

When she arrived, her mum was sat up in bed, wearing a soft collar. Her left ankle was in plaster and her right wrist was strapped up high in a sling. She smiled when she saw Kate and Kate walked in and kissed her.

"Mum. Are you okay? Are you in any pain?" Kate asked.

"No. I'm quite comfortable, thanks, dear. They've all been very nice to me in here."

"What about your wrist? How's it feeling?"

"A little sore."

"Can you wiggle your fingers?"

Her mum concentrated on moving the little she could. "See. I told you I was all right. How are you, love? You look shattered."

"Really? Because my mother only went and threw herself down the staircase last night, completely ruining my evening off. Some people are so inconsiderate, you know?"

Kate's mum chuckled but then she winced.

"What's the matter?" Kate asked.

"I don't know. I've probably bruised my ribs, or something. I think I bashed every part of me on the way down those stairs."

"You poor thing," Kate soothed.

"Oh look, there's my doctor. Over there. See? The one in the dark grey suit. Oh good, I think he's coming over."

Kate's body froze. Mr Elliott walked past the end of the bay, he stopped and looked across at her mother and Kate reached for her charts and pretended to be looking at them.

"Mrs Heath. How are you feeling this morning?"

"Much better, thank you, Doctor. Sorry to be such a nuisance."

"You are nothing of the sort," he said. "I'm glad you're feeling more comfortable now. Are the nurses treating you well?"

"You are all being wonderful. Far better than I deserve, silly old woman that I am."

"Nonsense, there is nothing silly or old about you."

Kate's mum beamed and then unwittingly scythed down her daughter in one fell swoop. "I believe you know my daughter, Kate?"

Mortified, Kate turned around, preparing to witness the disapproval in Adam's eyes.

"Of course. Kate, I hope we are treating your mother to your satisfaction?"

Kate couldn't help but feel the barb in his words, even if his tone was painfully pleasant. "She seems very comfortable, thank you," she said, and she was sincere in that, even if her voice betrayed the tension that he caused. Her eyes lowered, unable to meet his gaze and she longed for a hole to open up in the floor so that she could fall right through and disappear.

"Good. I'll pop by again tomorrow, but if you need anything, I'm sure the nurses will be able to see to you." He nodded a goodbye and withdrew.

"Such a lovely man. I don't know why you had such a hard time with him? He's been sweetness and light to me."

Kate was dying. Her mother had done that on purpose, she

70

was convinced. In fact it was no wonder Kate found difficulty maintaining a moderate level of tact when her mother seemed devoid of even the basics. At a time when she wanted nothing more than to forget the entire sorry incident, the world seemed to be conspiring against her, and her mother obviously wanted in on the act.

At dinner the following evening, Sophie brought up the subject of Mr Elliott and Kate gave her a pointed look.

"I'm sorry, but I told Rich all about it," she said, sheepishly.

"Soph!" Kate was horrified.

"Don't worry, he won't tell anyone, will you?"

"Scout's honour," he said, holding two fingers up beside his head.

"I just thought it would be good to get a man's point of view on things."

Kate humphed in reluctant acceptance.

"Men don't work like women, Kate," he said.

"Tell me something I don't know."

"They're far less complicated."

Kate looked at him as if he was mad.

"No, honestly. If we like a girl, we'll go for it. If not, we won't."

"Like: good, don't like: bad. I'm with you so far."

Rich shook his head. "We don't do subtle changes in the tone of our voice, or a look in a different direction. If we're pissed off at you, you'll know about it. If we're angry, you'll hear it. Same goes for horny."

Sophie joined in. "If they're ignoring you, they'll smile and nod."

"Exactly. You're getting it." He grinned at his girlfriend. "Don't try and read more into the guy than is actually there."

"Okay, so what *should* I do?" Kate asked, open to hearing any pearls of wisdom that Rich was willing to offer.

"Nothing."

"Nothing?"

"Nothing. Don't always be trying to *do* something, Kate. If he likes you, he'll get around to it. If he doesn't, he won't."

71

"As simple as that?"

Rich nodded. "Yep. Pretty much."

Kate let out a large sigh and started clearing the dishes. What did he know? He'd never met the guy. Adam Elliott was far more complicated than most other men she knew. She was swimming through fog to get to him and why? It was still a mystery to Kate why he had such a hold over her.

She spent the next few days dashing between work, her mother and helping out her dad. She saw nothing of Adam and had little time to be either sorry or thankful for it.

A week or so later, Kate was out in town doing some shopping when she stopped off in a coffee shop for a drink. She set her tray on the table and placed her bags at her feet and then settled herself down. A moment later Pete walked in. He spotted Kate and smiled. Kate smiled back and then pulled out a magazine and started to read.

A few minutes later a chair pulled up on the other side of the table and Pete peered over the top.

"So I've finally got you out for a drink," he said. "This can be our first date."

Kate set down her magazine and looked at him. "*This* is not a date."

"But it could be. Come on, Kate. Give me a try. What have you got to lose?"

"My rarity."

"Oooh. Touché!"

"I've heard about you, Peter Florin: serial philanderer and heart-breaker extraordinaire! Can't say I'm eager to join the club."

"I'm cut to the quick. I had no idea you had such a low opinion of me," he said feigning injury.

"I think you're a great guy, all that aside. I just have no interest getting my heart broken. Although I know of at least one nurse who might be willing to give it a try." She smiled.

"Really? We'll get back to that in a minute. So why can't I

tempt *you*, Kate? Heart already taken? Already broken?"

Kate was suddenly less amused.

"It is, isn't it?" he said, curiosity most definitely engaged. "But which one? And by whom?"

Kate looked into her coffee. "Why so interested? Is it just that you can't have me, so you feel the call of a challenge?"

"No. I like you, Kate. You tell it like it is. I can respect that. I wouldn't want to break your heart, whoever has got there before me. Talk to me, Kate. Come on. Who is it?"

"Only if you tell me why you go through women like a bullet through butter."

"Ah. Well, that's the million dollar question." Pete took a swig of his drink and then looked back at her, thoughtfully. "I lost someone a few years ago. Someone who was dear to me. After that I guess I felt it was time to really live."

Kate looked at him. "I'm sorry," she said. "I wasn't expecting you to be as honest as that. That must have been very hard."

"It was. It still is some days. Especially now I'm here."

"Why here?"

"Because I find myself haunted by a reminder. Adam Elliott."

"Adam?" Kate's mouth went dry. She tried for a normal voice. "You and he don't get on?"

"It's a long story." Pete looked at her. "Are you all right?"

"Yeah. Sure."

"Only you seem a bit... disturbed? I haven't said something to upset you, have I?"

"No. No. We're just obviously haunted by the same person."

"What, you and Adam?"

"Not really. I don't know. You won't tell anyone will you? I would die if anyone found out." She heaved a big sigh.

Pete shook his head and reached over to cover her hand. "Your secret's safe with me, Kate. I may be many things – desirable, intelligent, debonair..." He grinned. "But I'm a good friend."

Kate gave him a sad smile.

"He's a good man, Adam. You could do a lot worse."

"Yeah, well. If I ever manage to dig myself out of the mess I've made with him, I might find out."

Pete's phone went off. He looked at her. "Saved by the bell," he said and answered the phone.

Kate sat there sipping her drink while Pete made plans to meet up with his latest woman. She smiled to herself as he put on the charm. Perhaps she had had a rare glimpse of another side of Peter Florin and he seemed to be a pretty decent guy underneath.

Weeks went by without seeing more than a fleeting glimpse of Adam. Kate began to hope for even his passing displeasure. A cross word from him would be better than nothing at all. Willing a big trauma into existence wasn't something she was proud of, but at least then she might get to spend some time with him. But with her luck, it would be someone else's turn on duty if a call actually did come in.

Rich was spending more and more time round at the house. Sophie and he were becoming inseparable. Many a night Kate would wander off up to bed leaving the two lovebirds downstairs, kooched-up together on the settee. And although she was happy for the two of them, it only seemed to accentuate how thoroughly alone Kate actually felt. No, not *alone* exactly, but with a growing awareness that she wanted to be with just one person: Adam.

Finally a call came in. A young man had been badly injured in a fall and a call went out for the trauma team. Kate felt a shiver of excitement race through her and she immediately went to find out who was on duty that day, but it wasn't Adam and her heart deflated.

Still, she got ready to receive the patient and when he arrived he was bleeding out fast. The lad had fallen from the height of a roof, or that's what they had been told, and they were prepared for that, but what control had forgotten to mention was that he had fallen through glass. He was cut to ribbons. Paramedics had tried to stem the flow and had given all the fluids they could, but what he desperately needed now was blood.

Kate was put to the task of getting on to blood bank, but the line was engaged. She waited a few seconds, tapping her pen on the mountain of paperwork lying across the desk and then she tried again. Still no luck. She looked for the list of consultants' numbers, usually pinned above the desk, but it wasn't there. She rifled through the paperwork littering the area and still she couldn't find it. She tried the department again. The tone beeped out a busy rhythm and after a third try, with Mr Cobham shouting at her to report, Kate jumped up and ran.

She ran down the corridor, out of A&E and shot through into the main corridor of the hospital. She ran as fast as her legs would carry her, weaving in and out of staff and visitors, eventually arriving in the labs. She rushed up to the desk and gasped out the problem. The technician looked confused, until he noticed the phone lying just off the hook. He apologised profusely, shouted abruptly and the team jumped into action.

They assured her they would get more blood down to A&E as fast as possible and the head of department rang through to apologise to Mr Cobham. Kate took a moment to catch her breath and thanked them before walking back down to A&E at a far steadier pace.

Turning a corner, she almost crashed straight into Mr Elliott. She was flushed and her skin moist from running the length of the hospital at pace. She realised she must have looked a state. Adam met her gaze momentarily and then walked on, nothing further passing between them.

Kate felt the full force of his disapproval in that one brief look and her pace slowed perceptibly. By the time she got back to A&E, the vascular surgeon had arrived and was preparing to take the lad to Theatre and Mr Cobham thanked Kate for her presence of mind and her speed.

"Are you all right, love?" Gloria asked later that day. "You don't seem yourself."

"I'm fine," Kate said. "I've just got a lot on my mind at the moment, that's all."

Gloria tilted her head.

"You know, my mum," Kate fibbed.

"Oh, yes. How is she doing? I should have asked."

"Not bad," Kate told her, glad of the diversion. "Frustrated because she can't do much, but I'm going round later, so I'll be able to help out a bit."

When Kate arrived at her parents' house later that afternoon, she found her mother being waited on hand, foot and finger, by her weary father. The house was very different. The dining room had been made over into a temporary bedroom while her mother was tied to a wheelchair. Unable to use crutches because of her broken wrist and not yet allowed to walk on her broken ankle, for everyday chores she was pretty much useless. Getting to the toilet was a mammoth task in itself and her parents had discovered a few shortcuts in the time since she'd been out of hospital, which her mum talked her through as and when they were needed.

Kate tried to give her dad a bit of a rest and took over the fetching and carrying for a while, releasing him to go and spend some time with his friend, and Kate decided a take-away was in order.

Auntie Ann called by and enquired after her sister's treatment.

"Such a lovely man," her mother repeated. "Spoke very highly of you as well," she said, turning to Kate.

Kate was immediately alert, although she tried hard not to look it. "Really? Why? What did he say?"

"He said you were very capable and that you cared a lot about your patients. 'Very intuitive', I think were the words he used."

Kate was confused. She had been convinced the man hated her. Perhaps it was all just part of his bedside manner. He might not actually think these things.

"I told you he was a nice man," her auntie said. "So sad his mother's not going to pull through."

Lost in regret, Kate's heart wept. The man who was all on his own and looking after a dying mother, was the man she was - surely it was time to admit it? - falling for. He, who was patient, kind and dedicated, had been inadvertently slandered by her own lips, even questioning his sense of compassion. She had guarded against all his attempts at conversation and yet was unable to get him out of her mind. What had she done? At last she had found a decent guy, a man of compassion and integrity, and she had driven him away.

"Are you all right, Kate?" her auntie asked. "You've gone quite pale."

"No, I'm fine, really. I've just remembered something I was meant to do, that's all. It's no big deal. I'll get off home in a minute and sort it out." She wasn't about to confess to anything yet. There was far too much still to feel and to fathom for words.

~

Adam felt shattered at the end of a busy day but he knew his mother was fading and she needed him.

He pulled up outside the hospice and walked the lonely walk into hell. Alone with his fear, he moved quietly through the corridors to his mother's room. She was sleeping. Adam crept inside and sat down by her bed. After a minute or two she was disturbed by the pain and he took hold of her hand and soothed her.

"Adam, you're here." Her face tried to smile.

"How are you, Mum?" he asked softly.

"Can't complain."

Of course, she never did, even when she had reason to. She was a brave woman and had struggled too much for one lifetime. He *had* hoped that by becoming a doctor he could have kept her in a manner that would have eased things for her, but fate had stripped him of that and now his hands were tied and he was helpless but to hold her as she fell.

"You look weary," she said. "You need to take better care of yourself."

"I'm all right, Mum. It's just been a busy day, that's all."

His mother looked at him. "I wish you'd find yourself someone new," she said. "Someone who could take care of you and make you happy. I worry about you, after I'm gone."

"Don't, Mum. Don't... I'm all right, really. Can I get you anything?"

She shook her head. "Ali's gone, my darling boy. It's time to move on. She would understand, you know? She would."

Adam blinked back the tears and looked out of the window. "I'm not sure I can, Mum. I've tried, but..."

"No one said it would be easy." She squeezed his hand. "The best things rarely are," and she winced again as the pain gripped her.

"Is it getting worse, Mum?" he asked.

"Perhaps just a little."

Adam wandered into his apartment and sifted through the mail, letting it flop down onto the sideboard to be dealt with another day. He rubbed his face with his hands and then, letting out a deep sigh, he sank down onto the settee. The remote was to hand and soon mellow music was mingling with the sandalwood scent of his living room and he allowed it to soothe him for a while.

He tried to think about something else. Kate. He smiled to himself remembering the way she had looked as she ran into him in the corridor earlier that day, so wild and free. But then his smile slipped away and he rose to his feet. He walked purposefully into his bedroom and picked up the photograph from beside his bed. The gold band shone up from the bedside table as he brushed the fine features of the woman in the frame. He smiled sadly. "Help me out here, Ali," he said. "I don't know what to do." Then he studied the picture for a minute longer, searching for the answers he needed, before putting it back down in its spot and walking out to the kitchen.

This job at St Stevens was not forever. It was the sleepy backwater he'd needed to disappear in for a while and take care of his mum. But something had been brewing inside him. Ali had always wanted to go to Italy and his heart had been set on a job in Milan. He picked up his laptop and went back to the living room. He would find that job and he would make it happen, for her.

~

Kate's conscience was far from easy over the days that followed. She decided to speak to Adam and own up to her mistakes. She was doubtful that she would find the forgiveness she craved, but she had to try. She wanted him. Kate was determined to find an opportunity to get herself not only alone with Adam but also with time to talk. Even then, it was by no means a given that he would understand. But the alternative of living with the daily fear of seeing him despise her very existence was far, far worse.

~~~

"So what did she do?" Lena asked.

The woman seemed pleased that Lena was following the story. She had been so quiet and still, there had been little evidence that she was even listening. "What *could* she do?" she said. "She could hardly tell him how she felt without owning up to everything he'd heard."

Lena chewed at a ragged nail. "And Ali?"

"Kate had no idea."

~~~

Kate decided she would probably have to settle in for the long haul, but in fact it was only three days later that she got her chance.

Chapter 5

Kate opened the clinic room door to start setting up for Mr
Cobham's clinic and walked right in on Adam. He was perched
on the radiator with his back to the window, one arm laid across
his chest, talking into a Dictaphone. He paused mid-sentence
and looked up. Kate saw the notes of a patient lying open on
the desk and realised he was still finishing off his own clinic from
the morning.

At first Kate thought she would excuse herself and hurry back
out. But indecision made her pause and she hovered for a moment,
uncertain.

"I'm sorry. Am I in your way?" he asked. "I won't be long."

Kate tried to speak, but her mouth was suddenly useless and
nothing would come out.

He continued dictating his notes, still looking at Kate off and
on and then, when he had finished, he put his hand down and
looked at her. "Kate-"

"Mr Elliott. I'm so sorry about what you overheard at the
ball. All the rumours flying around. I never meant any of it to
happen," she blabbered, unable to meet his gaze as he took in the
sight of her.

Adam's eyebrows rose.

"It's just... I was so angry. I'd had a really bad day and... I never said you were gay. I mean…"

His eyebrows rose further.

"You know what it's like when you're angry and you've had a few too many to drink… well maybe you don't." She took a deep breath. "I might have implied that you… Well that… That you never… God, I'm just really sorry." Kate turned to leave, wanting to be anywhere but there. What had she been thinking? It had to have been the stupidest plan ever.

"What don't I ever do, Kate?" he asked, halting her retreat.

This was torture. Was he actually going to make her stand there and say the words? If he'd have had half a heart he would have just accepted her apology and been done with it. She turned back, still clutching the notes to her chest, her eyes searching around the room for distraction.

"What don't I do?" he asked again, standing up from his perch on the other side of the room.

She was dying here. Adam started to walk toward her, his expression dark and unreadable. Kate was flustered. Her thoughts were scrambling inside her brain and she was desperate to be out of there, to be *anywhere* else but there.

"Look, it was the day you had a go at me."

"*I* had a go at *you*? From what I remember it was the other way around." He was still walking towards her, slowly, very slowly.

"Well it didn't feel that way to me and I… My housemate took me out that night, to let off steam and… well I might have implied that you…"

"Yes?"

Beginning to shake, she took a deep breath again. Blood was rising rapidly in her cheeks. She hugged the notes against her as if by doing so they might afford her some protection. "Wouldn't be at all… very… passionate."

His brow quirked. For a moment he seemed to think about this. "And what lead you to that particular conclusion?" he asked.

Oh, why was nobody walking in? Any other day and half a

dozen people would have come and gone in the time she had been standing there. Kate desperately needed it to end.

"Should I have been flirting with all the nursing staff?" He picked up his last set of notes from the desk. "Would I have scored more points with you if I'd slept with half the women in the hospital and flirted shamelessly with the rest?" His tone was cutting now. Angry even. She was a foolish child being reprimanded by the headmaster.

"No!" Kate exclaimed.

"Really?"

"Of course not."

Adam approached her. He leaned down and put his head right next to hers. His lips were millimetres away from her ear. She could feel the warmth of his breath on the side of her neck. Her heart was hammering inside her chest.

"Good," he said. He pulled back, looked her in the eyes for a second, letting her know he had the upper hand and walked out, and Kate was left shaken and reeling and falling apart.

There was no way now, no way in hell that this man would ever look at her the way he had done before, just for the briefest of moments, at the ball. She had ruined herself in his eyes and he had never been more magnificent in hers.

Unfortunately, Kate still had the better part of her shift to go and the rest of her time staggered slowly on.

She was desperate to be out of there that day and lived in dread of anything happening that might cause her to have to collide with Adam again.

At last it was time to go home and she was gone. She was first out of the car park and she didn't look back.

Sophie was buzzing when Kate walked in that evening. Rich appeared at the kitchen door.

"Hello, Kate. Can I get you a drink?" he said.

Kate slumped down into a chair and let out a large sigh. "No thanks, Rich. I'm not really in the mood."

"Something wrong?" Sophie asked, her face suddenly serious again.

"I owned up to Elliott today."

"You did what?!" Rich walked in, rolled his eyes and sat down next to Sophie, passing her a glass of wine.

"What on earth made you do something like that?" Sophie asked. "Had he heard?"

"He must have," Kate told her.

"Did he say so," Rich asked.

"Not in so many words, but-"

Rich held his head in his hands and then looked up again. "What did I tell you about making assumptions?" he said. "I thought we agreed you were going to stop trying to *do* things all the time?"

"I know, but-"

"But you thought you'd do it anyway."

"And how did it go?" Sophie asked.

"Excruciating," Kate told her.

They sat there for a minute as Kate told them about her day and finally Rich said to her, "Next time, save us all the agony and just kiss the bloody man, will you?"

Kate laughed a hopeless kind of laugh and grabbed a cushion to her chest, squeezing it tightly. "Yeah, right," she sighed. "Like I'd be brave enough to do something like that."

The pair of them looked over at her as she sat there, feeling sorry for herself and then it began to percolate through Kate's crowded mind that Sophie was looking sickeningly happy. She studied the pair of them. They were grinning inanely. "What is it?" she asked.

Rich and Sophie looked at each other and Rich put a hand on Sophie's knee. A smile split Sophie's face and she held out her left hand. A ring shone from her finger and all at once Kate forgot her troubles and leapt across the room. "No! You're engaged? Oh my God! Let me take a look at that ring. Wow, it's beautiful." She glanced up at her friend. "That's really wonderful, both of you, but isn't it a bit quick?"

Sophie squeezed Rich's hand and looked into his eyes. "Is it? I didn't know there was a time frame for these things."

"I've had longer bouts of indigestion!" Kate told them.

Rich smiled at Sophie. "It's never too soon to start the rest of your life."

"Ah, that's brilliant, you guys. Look at you. You're so happy. I think I'm going to cry. So when's the big day?"

"Hopefully sometime next June," Sophie said. "I definitely want to be married before I turn twenty-five."

"Absolutely," Kate agreed. "Because that would be just ancient!"

Sophie gave her a guilty smile and Kate laughed.

"It's all right; I know I'm left on the shelf, at least that's what my mum keeps telling me anyway. I'm probably going to be one of those nurses who dedicates their life to their patients and then retires to a nursing home for old nurses and grumbles on about how much better the care was in their day."

Kate lay on her bed that night going over the events of the day in her head. Sophie was getting married. And although she really was the most sensible of Kate's friends, Sophie was two whole years younger than she was and Kate had never been anywhere near a serious enough relationship to think about marriage. But they were good together, she couldn't deny that. All she could do was pine for a love she had no chance of holding. And the more she came to understand the man, the more that reality hurt.

Adam intrigued her. And as for passion? If the way he made her insides shake whenever she was near him was any indication of how things would be between them, he would definitely have no problem there. When he had leaned down right next to her ear, she had barely been able to breathe.

Kate groaned and rolled over and tried her best to get to sleep. Maybe he would come round. Perhaps. Given time. She had tried an apology. All she could do now was wait and see how it was when they saw each other again. Only then would she have some idea of the damage she had done.

Naturally, because she now wanted to more than ever, Kate didn't see Adam for days after that. Two weeks passed without so much as a glimpse of him. The weather changed for the worse and although A&E was busy, nothing major was coming in.

She began to check every morning, to see if his name was on the trauma list, just in case anything came up. She desperately wanted something to happen, anything really. It didn't have to be fatal. In fact it definitely shouldn't be, because then they wouldn't need to call the team. Just something reported as big that when it arrived was much less serious. How awful was that? She knew she should be ashamed of herself, but so much of her longed to see him that her conscience was forced to abide.

Days dragged by as shift after shift passed without incident, and then at last they got a call. A car crash on a country road outside town had caused three to be seriously injured and a fourth dead at the scene. Kate leapt into action. Something was coming in and Adam Elliott was actually on duty. She informed Mr Cobham and the rest of the staff and then put the call out for the trauma team.

Excited, but nervous, she started getting ready for the arrivals, clearing bays and freeing up as many nurses as possible. The doctors started arriving, congregating in Resus One, but there was no sign of Adam.

Kate put out a fast bleep for him and Mr Crickland, the surgeon standing right beside the desk, was alerted. He looked around and Kate stared at him in confusion. "I was trying to get hold of Mr Elliott," she said.

"Oh, no. Mr Barker's covering for him today. And *his* calls are being diverted to me at the moment because he's in a meeting. But I've let him know. He won't be long. Did you want anything in particular?"

Kate's heart sank. "Er, no." Then she started to worry. "Is he ill?" she asked.

Mr Crickland turned back again. "Who, Mr Elliott? No, family issues, I think. He's got a few days compassionate leave. He should be back on Friday."

Sirens blazed and everyone fell into place. The casualties came in, were processed and shipped out to various wards or straight into theatre as needed. And when all the smoke had settled and the back-log whittled down, Kate found a moment to reflect on Adam's disappearance. His mother, she thought, it had to be his mother. Losing a much-loved grandparent had been bad enough, but an only parent? Kate couldn't possibly imagine what the poor man had to be going through.

On Friday Kate was watchful. She scanned the cases in casualty for broken bones. She walked slowly off to break and wandered back a tortuous route, hoping the more time she spent and the more ground she covered would increase her chances of seeing him. But it wasn't easy falling for a shadow. Every time the sun stopped shining, he seemed to disappear.

A few days later Kate had the task of escorting an elderly man with a broken hip up to Ascot Ward. As she walked on to the ward she could hear voices ahead of her raised in battle. She wheeled the gentleman down to the nurses' station and passed a side-ward where a middle-aged couple, obviously unhappy with the treatment of their relative, were making their feelings known. She glanced sideways and saw the harrowed face of Adam Elliott and suddenly her heart wrenched. His brow was stoical, but in the brief moment that she saw him, Kate could see a world of pain hiding behind those lonely blue-grey eyes and she longed to reach out and comfort him.

She handed over the patient, all the while trying to hear what was going on further up the ward.

"Kate?" the nurse prompted.

"Sorry. Um, Mr Green. Yes, er... fractured neck of femur, right side, analgesics given in A&E."

"Don't you walk out on me when I'm talking to you!" a shrill

Kate looked over and saw Adam rapidly making his way out of the ward, in the other direction. "It's all there," she said, a sense of urgency rising in her voice. "Okay, Mr Green?" Desperate to get away, Kate handed over the notes and raced off in the direction Adam had taken. She reached the door seconds behind him. Which way had he gone? Then she spotted him, striding down the corridor to the right, his fists clenched at his sides and his shoulders square and rigid like a soldier.

Kate walked as fast as she could, but failed to keep up with his forceful pace. She stepped up to a jog and only then began to gain on him. Down the staircase and along the other corridor she followed him. But he took a door to the right and Kate arrived outside and paused, wondering what she was about to crash in on. It was a tutorial room with no window. She had to take the chance, so she took a deep breath and walked in.

Adam was alone. She found him leant over a table, with his arms outstretched and his hands spread wide. He turned, startled by the intrusion in his private retreat and in that first moment, before the shutters went down, Kate could see the anger and desolation burning inside him. She closed the door behind her and walked towards him. Adam held a hand up to stop her. "What do you want, Kate," he growled. "This really is neither the time nor the place."

"I just thought you might need… someone," Kate said, her voice soft and tremulous as she fought to stay her fears as she knew she must.

Adam turned back toward the table, saying nothing and Kate approached cautiously, like a child with a wounded bird.

"Don't pay any attention to those people," she said softly. "They're just upset. They'll probably calm down in a bit and want to apologise. Don't let them get to you." She was close now. She could almost reach out and touch him, his broad, tense shoulders and strong, skilful arms. She stretched out her hand and slowly ran it down the firm ridge of his shoulder blade.

Adam's body stiffened at her touch, but he did not pull away. Kate swallowed hard and stepped round to the side of him, letting her palm smooth down his side, feeling his warm firm body beneath her fingertips. The sensation thrilled her and made her brave. Adam stood up straight, but could not meet her gaze. Turmoil raged through his features as she stroked his warm cheek with her cool hand. His eyes met hers and Kate's gaze fell to his lips. Her heart began to pump hard, harder than it had ever done before, unable to believe she was being so bold. And she felt again the electricity surging through her as she reached up on tip toes and touched her lips to his.

Adam received the kiss without objection, but nothing more. Kate began to step back and he looked into her eyes and must have seen the longing there for he scooped her up into his arms and pulled every inch of her body against him. His lips, now hot and needy, were pressed on Kate's and she was lost in wonder. His body was strong and hard against her own. His mouth ravaging hers with urgent desire. This gorgeous, sad man was hers, even if it was only ever going to be in that moment, and she wanted him.

The acid tones of the couple from Ascot Ward passed by outside their door and Adam's frame froze, breaking the spell. His body tensed and he pulled away.

Kate looked up into his face and then took his hand in hers, squeezing it gently, but Adam looked down and slowly pulled his hand away. Kate gazed at him in earnest, but he seemed once again unable to meet her eyes. "What's the matter?" she managed to utter, although even then she knew her heart was breaking. "What is it?"

"Nothing," he said shortly. He turned to Kate and looked at her, the wall firmly back in front of his eyes. "Nothing." He moved his hand to reach out and touch her face, but could not even manage that. He let his hand fall back away, defeated. "I've got to go," he said, and he left Kate standing there in an empty tutorial room, her lips tender, wondering what in the world had just happened.

After a couple of minutes Kate realised he wasn't coming back. She looked at her watch. She had been away too long and she hurried back to work.

Returning to A&E, Kate was hoping to just carry on undetected, but Gloria noticed her walking in. Of course she did.

"You took your time," she said.

"Yeah. Sorry. It was the lifts," Kate fibbed. "They were playing up. They're all right now. I managed to get one of the engineers to come and sort them out. Anyway, I'm here now. Did I miss anything?"

Gloria studied Kate's face. "You look flushed," she said.

"Yes, well, I had to run all the way back, because it took so long to get out, didn't I?"

Kate made it through what was left of her shift and went home. Sophie was on a late shift that day, so there were several hours to spend at home on her own before Kate had someone to talk to. At half past five she rang Anna, but Anna wasn't home. She went over the day in her head a hundred times and still she had no idea what was going on between them. After a kiss like that, Kate had expected some declaration of… well… something. But he had acted as if he'd been coerced into it and seemed desperate to get away.

By the time Sophie got in, Kate was in a state. She sat down quickly and listened to what had happened.

"Don't worry too much," she said kindly. "He might just be the shy type. You know, one of those guys who takes a little time to warm up, but just wait until he gets going. At least he didn't push you away, or tell you to go to hell. He could have."

Kate sniffed, her eyes still a bit watery from the hours of self-torture. "I guess so," she said.

"Maybe he was taken aback? You might find that when you get in there tomorrow, he'll throw you over his shoulder and carry you off into the sunset."

At last Kate managed to splutter out some laughter.

"That's better. I hate to see you looking so miserable," Sophie said. "It puts me right off my supper."

Kate thumped her playfully.

"Come on. Enough of your moping. Let's get something to eat before I crash out. And you'd better get some beauty sleep, if you're going to go around snogging poor consultants willy nilly – I still can't believe you did that, by the way – You'd better be looking your best for whatever is going to come next."

Kate rolled her puffy eyes. "I can't believe I did it either. I don't know where I got the courage to do something like that from." She grinned anxiously.

"But it was good, though?" Sophie asked.

Painful as it was to remember, Kate spent a second reliving the storm that had raged through her body at the touch of his kiss. "Fantastic," she said.

"I've got a good feeling about this one. He's got hidden depths, I'd say," Sophie encouraged. "Strong silent types normally do. Just you wait and see."

"Well, I think *I've* done enough, don't you?" said Kate. "I've made my feelings pretty clear."

"Rich will be proud of you."

"He will, won't he? But will it actually do any good?"

"Of course it will. He's probably sitting alone at home right now wishing he had played it better himself. I bet you anything you like there will be a bunch of flowers waiting for you in A&E in the morning. Now cheer up, you miserable cow! You got to kiss the man, didn't you? Come on; let's see what we can rustle up. I'm starving."

The next morning Kate went into work with a tiny spark of hope in her soul. She tried to convince herself that Sophie was right. Surely Adam would have thought over his reaction to the kiss and realised how distracted he had been? She greeted people happily and kept up her good mood throughout the rest of her shift, but there was to be no word from Adam.

A little dejected, Kate left the department at the end of her shift. She needed distraction, so she rang Anna and drove over to Brisely, arriving there just after three. The woman next door let her in with Anna's spare key and she was left alone to nose around the apartment. It was Spartan in there, Anna having only recently moved in. There was a comfy settee and a small table and a unit that held the TV, but apart from that, there was little else to fill it. Kate settled down in front of a chick flick and waited for Anna to get home, which she did around a quarter past five.

Anna was over the moon to see Kate again. "So what do you think of the place?" she asked. "I see you've made yourself at home."

"It's great. I like the... space," Kate said, searching hard for something to compliment.

Anna burst out laughing. "Well, at least that's something. It'll be lovely one day. Besides, I've got to leave room for John's stuff, haven't I?"

"How's that going?" Kate asked. "Has he got a job yet?"

Anna's face fell. "No, not yet. But he's got another interview tomorrow, so... fingers crossed."

Together they found something for dinner and sat down to eat.

"So, what brings my hard-working, under-appreciated, poorly-paid nurse out here to see her old friend in the middle of the week?" Anna asked, looking at Kate seriously and her chewing paused for a moment while she waited for an answer.

"Oh, nothing really," Kate said. "I just felt like a trip out."

Anna raised an eyebrow. "I'm not daft, Kate. It's got to be quite important to bring you out here."

"Do I need an excuse to come round and visit my oldest friend?" Kate asked her.

Anna laid down her knife and fork and looked at Kate. "Is it him?"

"Who?" Kate asked, innocently.

"You know very well who. The guy you were falling for the

last time we mentioned your love life."

A small smile rippled the corners of Kate's mouth. "It's him. But I wasn't falling for him back then."

"Oh, really?"

Anna listened to the latest of Kate's escapades and picked up her fork to continue eating.

"So? Aren't you going to tell me I've been a complete idiot? Surely you've got something?"

Anna thought for a moment before starting to speak. "I've been thinking a lot about you and your love life since we last met and I've got a theory. Feel free to tell me it's a pile of cack, but… Do you think you're afraid of getting in deep with someone? Of letting go and really giving your all to them. A man, I mean?"

Kate frowned. This was not something she had wanted to hear. What she really wanted was for Anna to tell her everything was going to be okay.

"Are you maybe a bit scared?"

Kate thought. "I don't know. Not consciously."

"Well, perhaps I'm wrong. It was just an idea. I thought perhaps… after your brother… But you can't do any more with this one. If he doesn't want you after all that, I'm afraid you're just going to have to lump it. Sorry, Hun, I know he means a lot to you. Are you sure he's not married?"

Kate thought for a moment. "I don't think so. No-one has mentioned a wife lurking in the background and he was on his own at the ball, I'm sure of it. I knew everyone else at his table."

"And there's no ring?"

"No. But that doesn't mean a lot. Most of the surgeons don't wear one. All that scrubbing up; it gets in the way."

"Well, maybe he just thinks you're an ugly old troll?" Anna teased and the light relief was welcome.

Kate thumped her. "It's certainly a possibility. Or maybe he's just got something against ginger."

"You're not ginger, you're strawberry blonde," Anna defended.

"Okay, light ginger," she sighed. "Oh, I don't know."

"Listen to me, Kate. He's an idiot if he doesn't snap you up and nobody wants an idiot."

"Quite right too," Kate said, but she didn't mean it. She did want him, more than ever now, and after that kiss, the pain went even deeper. Kate had never known how rejection could physically hurt. She desperately wanted him to want her back. She couldn't give up on him, not yet.

It was ten o'clock by the time she arrived home. Sophie was in. She had just put the kettle on. "Dirty stop out!" she called out from the kitchen. "Where have you been?"

"I went over to Anna's," Kate said.

"Birmingham?" Sophie enquired.

"No. She's in Brisely now. It's only thirty minutes away."

"How's she settling in?"

"Good."

Sophie walked in to the living room with a cup of tea in each hand. "Have you eaten?"

"Yes, thank you."

"So… tell me. How did it go today?"

Kate sighed. "Nothing."

Sophie looked downcast. "I'm sorry. And I feel really guilty being so happy now."

"Don't you dare," Kate scolded. "You and Rich deserve your happily-ever-after. The two of you are perfect together and lovely people, although I think we've now established that Rich's advice on love life completely stinks and I hope you're going to tell him that from me. I may even sue." A small laugh escaped Kate's lips. She sighed. "What are the rules on becoming a nun these days?"

Friday morning Kate was at work. Nothing much was coming in and it gave the staff a few minutes peace to get the department in order and catch up. But the time dragged. As the shifts were changing a call came in that a car had collided with a lorry and overturned outside town and the passengers were on their way in, one of whom had a serious limb injury. Mr Cobham asked Kate to contact the trauma team before she went off.

Within minutes Mr Barker was with them. Kate spotted him arriving through the windows of the A&E doors. Adam was standing by him, just outside the department.

As Mr Barker entered, Adam saw Kate. He blinked, his body unmoving. No warmth could be seen in those blue-grey eyes as he hovered in the doorway looking back at her. He turned and walked away and all Kate's hopes disappeared with him. She collected her things and walked out into the car park to find her car, tears welling up behind her eyes as the biting wind met her skin.

"Kate."

A voice called out her name from close by. Kate's breath caught, she blinked and turned around. Adam stood there, immaculate and composed. His face changed as he saw the tears in her eyes and she hurriedly wiped them away.

"It's the wind," she explained.

He paused for a moment seemingly searching for something to say. His lips moved a little, but nothing came out.

Kate dropped her gaze to the floor and made to go.

"I'm sorry, Kate," he said. "I don't know what to say. I never meant anything like that to happen."

And that was the worst part. Kate lifted her chin, forcing back the tears that threatened to flow once more. "No. It was my fault," she said. "I'm sorry. You just looked so unhappy. I heard about your poor mum and I-"

"I don't need your pity, Kate." His tone had changed.

"It wasn't pity." Kate suddenly found herself having to defend her actions. He had taken it all the wrong way. What she had wanted to say was that she adored him, him and his moody ways and his high walls. She wanted him any way she could get him, but what she needed more than anything was for him to want her too. "I just couldn't bear you looking so sad," she said, her forehead crinkling as she fought to keep her equanimity. "And when that awful family started having a go at you…"

"You thought you could just kiss me and make it all better? I'm not a child, Kate. I'm a grown man. Life is a bit more complicated than that."

"I'm sorry. I didn't mean to… I never thought-"

"I'm married, Kate."

Kate forced her gaze to meet his stormy eyes as pain and confusion suddenly took their toll and a weight the size of a cannon ball dropped inside her heart. All the pieces of the puzzle finally slotted together. She had been a fool. Of course he was married. Why wouldn't he be? He was gorgeous. Humiliation and regret battled for place inside her as hope disappeared. She turned and got into her car, backed out as quickly as she could and pulled away.

~

Left alone, Adam leant on the bonnet of his car. He had panicked and he knew it. Whatever he did he seemed to make a mess of it. All he had wanted to do was apologise for the way he had treated her the other day and he'd only ended up making matters worse, his anger flaring at the thought of the gossips talking about him again.

He sighed. He knew he had been losing it on the ward the other day too. Why couldn't he just keep control of his temper? He believed Kate really cared about him and what had he done? He couldn't bear to think of how kissing her had awakened in him something he never thought could breathe life again. He had imagined it, of course, every time he saw her. He knew Kate hadn't really kissed him out of pity. He knew that. He could see in her eyes that she wanted him; though for the life of him he couldn't think why. But he couldn't do anything about it; not yet. It wasn't right. Until he learned to let go of Ali, there wasn't room enough in his heart for two.

Why was life so hard? Why couldn't he just love again? He

wanted to. He needed to. He just couldn't. It felt like he was being unfaithful to Ali and that was something he could never do. It was the guilt of wanting to move on, that was the struggle he was battling with.

He stood up. What should he do? A letter? Flowers, perhaps? Or was it better that she hated him? He thought about that. His chest ached and his head was pounding. He rubbed his face with his hands and looked up at the sky as his heart spoke out to the woman he had loved. Then his gaze dropped down to the place where Kate had been and he shut his eyes tightly, turned back and walked in.

~

Kate pulled up outside her house and hurried inside, her heart breaking. How had she messed up quite so badly? He must actually hate her now. All she had wanted to do was go to him and comfort him, tell him everything would be all right and all the time she had been kissing a married man.

She dumped her coat and keys inside the door and headed upstairs for a shower, where she stayed, until she had collected herself again and then she went back downstairs to cuddle up in front of the TV and lick her wounds. She rang her mum and her dad answered, worrying her a little. "Hello, Dad. What are you doing home?"

"I had a meeting arranged for this afternoon and they had to cut it short, so I came home to see your mum. Don't worry. I can hear that nurses' brain of yours kicking in. So before you ask, she's fine, so you can stop your fretting now. Is everything all right with you?"

"Yes, fine thanks, Dad," she fibbed and spent a few minutes talking with him before he passed her over to her mother. Kate grilled her mum about her symptoms and whether she was doing her exercises and she found a kind of safety and reassurance in hiding behind the mask. Her mum still had an appointment left with Mr Elliott.

"He's such a lovely man."

"Yes, you may have mentioned that, once or twice, Mum," Kate said.

"Well, he is. No ring either. You could do a lot worse for yourself than him. You're not getting any younger, you know."

"Mum!"

"I'm only saying."

"Well, don't."

"Your father and I would love some grandchildren before we die."

"You're fifty-two, mother!"

"Exactly. And I was twenty-five when I had you. You'll soon be twenty-seven and you're not even married yet."

That was it; Kate was not in the mood for a lesson on her failings. She needed no reminder of either her loneliness, or the overwhelming distance between her and Adam. Both these things had been painfully etched into her life already that day, so she pulled out her trump card, the tried and tested diversion technique that never seemed to fail. "How's Marcus doing?" she asked. Marcus was her adventurous older brother, always travelling the world and fighting injustice wherever it might be. He had had several close shaves over the previous few years, a couple with the law and once even with his life. He was always good fodder for a conversation with her parents. And thankfully it worked.

Kate spotted Adam several times over the following week and she tried hard to relax and pretend to have moved on, even though she had to fight the urge to throw herself at his feet and beg him to forgive her, which wouldn't have been good for anyone involved. She smiled when she could, and when she couldn't, she just gazed levelly back at him and defied him to disapprove of her. Had he not also kissed her? And how was she supposed to have known?

As the cold weather set in, broken bones appeared in A&E with increasing regularity. People in the streets slipped on ice and skidded on the roads. Old women broke wrists, old men broke hips and children broke any bone they fell on.

Kate found herself escorting patients up to the wards on a regular basis but never a word passed between them.

One particular day Kate overheard a relative complaining about Mr Elliott, about his gruff bedside manner. The gentleman in question was in quite a temper and the nurse at the desk was taking it in the neck about his father's treatment, hearing about how unfeeling Mr Elliott was being. The nurse was looking harassed and more than a little uneasy.

Now Kate had had first-hand experience of Mr Elliott in full sail and understood where the gentleman was coming from, but she also knew now what a wonderful man and gifted surgeon he was, so despite his reluctance to settle a peace with her, Kate hoped she might be able to help and so she stepped in. "Excuse me, sir; I wonder if I could be of some assistance. Trisha, would you like me to take over?"

The nurse seemed confused by the suggestion, but after the last five minutes of being shouted at she was more than willing to let someone else have a go.

"It's all right. I was about to go on my lunch break anyway," Kate said. "Would you like to go somewhere more private and tell me what the problem seems to be, Mr...?"

"Johnson," Trisha offered.

"Mr Johnson, please; follow me."

Kate walked down the ward looking for a private space and found an examination room lying empty. She invited Mr Johnson and his wife to sit down, closed the door and slid the shutter across and then she perched on the examination couch beside them. "You'd better talk me through it," Kate said. "Why don't you start at the beginning?"

Chapter 6

A few days later, when Mr Elliott walked onto Ascot Ward to do a round before his weekend off, Kate's dealings with Mr Johnson were already the stuff of legend. The round continued as usual, until they were about to leave, at which point Sister Pritchard asked for a word in private.

Adam obliged willingly, assuming there must be some very good reason for her obvious unease and he arranged for his team to go ahead of him, to meet him on Kempton Ward as soon as he was through.

Sister Pritchard closed the door to the office and took a second to consider her words. "I thought it best that you became aware there has been some tension with one of your patients," she told him. "Well, their relatives anyway."

"Which one?" Adam asked.

"Mr Johnson. His son."

"Mr Johnson's son?" Adam's eyebrows flickered. "I'm surprised; he was all politeness and gratitude when I passed him in the corridor the other day."

"Well, perhaps that was after Staff Nurse Heath had worked her magic on him," she said.

"Nurse Heath?" Adam's very blood reacted.

"She's from A&E. Don't ask me how she came to be involved in this, but apparently she swooped in out of nowhere and diffused the whole situation."

Mr Elliott settled back on a short filing cabinet. "I think you had better tell me exactly what happened, don't you?" he said.

Sister pulled up a chair and sat down. "It was Tuesday, late morning I think. Trisha was at the nurses' station catching up on some paperwork when Mr Johnson's son started kicking off. It was something to do with what you had or hadn't done with his father's treatment and what he seemed to think you should be doing."

"Yes, he had been a bit prickly that day, come to think of it," Adam said. "I seem to remember him wanting a second opinion, or something."

"And what did you say to that?"

"I told him he was perfectly entitled to do just that if he wanted to, but that it wouldn't do any good."

The nurse seemed to weigh this up. "Well, whatever it was, he didn't appear to take it very well and he started stamping around the ward, shouting abuse and threatening to sue you. He wanted Trish to give him the name of the person to contact to set up a complaint and then he began ranting about the standard of care and anything else he could think of, from what the staff told me. And then, like an angel, Kate drifted through the ward, calming the whole situation. She took him and his wife into a side room and when they came out... he was a kitten. Don't ask me *what* she said. I don't really care, but he's been as quiet as a mouse ever since. She did us *all* a favour."

~~~

"What did she do?" Lena asked, but the woman just smiled and gently shook her head.

"Patience."

Adam took a deep breath and let it out. He nodded. "Thank you, Sue. Leave it with me. I'll take it from here."

Sister Pritchard nodded and let herself out and Adam stayed where he was for a few minutes and then strode off to re-join his team.

The day was busy and afternoon clinic ended late. At six o'clock he was finally ready to leave. He walked outside and sat in his car. His fingers hovering for a minute over the mobile phone in his jacket pocket. He picked it out and rang the hospital switchboard and asked to be put through to A&E. "Hello," he croaked. "I was wondering if Nurse Heath was on duty today."

The person on the other end of the line rustled through some papers. "I'm afraid not, sir. She won't be back on until tomorrow afternoon. Can I take a message?"

"No, thank you," he said. "I'll talk to her tomorrow." Kate wasn't there.

Adam's apartment was in a new, modern building. He had paid a top notch price for a designer lifestyle that somehow left him hollow. He let himself in and slumped down in his leather settee. He looked up at the picture Alison had loved and frowned. "You'd like her," he said, his voice laden with melancholy and he turned on the TV to slip away, but it was no good, he couldn't concentrate. What had Kate said in there? What confidences had she broken? And how, without undermining him completely, could she have placated the situation so thoroughly? He rested his head back and closed his eyes. The image of Kate talking softly to the little girl sprung vividly to his mind. She may be passionate about her patients, making her jump in too eagerly sometimes, he thought, but she wasn't cruel or unkind. Kate was Sasha's angel and his too now it seemed. She had taken care of Sasha, whispering words of tenderness in her ear when she needed comfort and now she was doing the same for him, despite his turning her away.

He had tried hard not to want her. He had done his best to avoid her whenever he could, but fate wasn't making it easy for him. Could he go to her? Just talk to her? Would she still want to listen to him after all he had put her through? Adam wasn't sure. But he knew then that he had to try.

But was he ready to talk? He was still afraid to look in a mirror in case he saw the reproach in his own eyes. His demons were always with him, reminding him of what he'd lost. He couldn't bear any more pity. He had been glad to leave his last job behind, to get away from all the sad looks and tilted gazes. He wasn't about to risk seeing that in Kate's eyes. Kate had to see him for himself, a solitary figure who still wanted her, even though he battled every day with himself to avoid it.

He loved Ali, he really did, but Ali was gone and Kate was here. She was flesh and blood and he wanted her. He wanted the companionship, the intimacy of loving. He couldn't bear to keep hurting her and if he couldn't manage to live without her, he was going to have to try.

~

Kate started work on Saturday afternoon with her head pounding. She had slept a little too heavily the night before and her neck ached. She eased her head from side to side and felt the pull.

The night seemed to have started early, with drunken teenagers and hordes of cuts and breaks queuing up to be tended to, so they were dealing with a hefty backlog by the time the night shift came on. Fortunately, Sheila, a very experienced night nurse, had just had a basin full of her eighteen-year-old son and was in just the right mood to take on the drunks. Kate stayed ten minutes longer to finish up with her gentleman with heart failure who was waiting to go to coronary care, and then finally, with great relief, she was out of there.

Outside, she took a deep breath of fresh air. The cold crept in and she wrapped her coat around her. Looking up at the clear night sky, Kate let out a deep sigh and walked over to her car. A man stepped out of another car close by and looked at her. Kate stopped and looked a little harder in the dim light, anxious to recognise him as a friend. He started to walk toward her and Kate hurried to open the car door, but as the light from the street lamp fell across his features, Kate suddenly recognised the dimly lit face of Adam. She hesitated and then continued to unlock her car.

"Kate."

Kate turned back round, shivering. She hugged her coat tighter about her. Adam approached and his face was difficult to read. Was he going to be pleasant, or not?

"It seems I am indebted to you for your efforts with Mr Johnson the other day," he said.

Kate struggled for a second to think of what he could be referring to, but then she remembered. "It was no bother."

"I think it was," he said. "Sister Pritchard told me everything that happened."

Kate shook her head trying to play down her part. "I just listened to him really," she said. "All he needed was someone to vent at. He was just worried."

"I very much doubt that was all there was to it, but thank you anyway." There was a more comfortable silence between them now, as his sincerity showed. "Are you hungry?" he asked. "I was just wondering because I would really like to take you out to dinner to apologise."

Kate was speechless. What did this actually mean? She was just beginning to sort herself out. She still yearned for the man but she was back in control of her life again and his attentions, however desirable they might be, were only going to cause her more pain. "Er, that's really not necessary," she said. "I was just glad to be able to help." She looked into his gorgeous eyes and smiled warmly. "But it's very kind of you to offer, thank you." She turned to go.

"There's nothing kind about it, Kate. I want to," he said, stopping her with a touch on her arm.

Those words she had *longed* to hear. Why was he saying them now? "You're married, Mr Elliott."

"I'm not."

What was he saying? "But you said-"

"I know. I'm not, Kate. I was, but I'm not anymore."

Kate was confused.

"I'm sorry. I shouldn't have said that. I panicked." He shrugged. "Forgive me?"

Could this be real? Could she trust him? This was too much. But she hadn't wanted him to come to her out of duty or some kind of misguided gratitude. She hadn't done it for that. She would have been happier if he had never found out about the whole thing. Her only thoughts had been to protect him, if she could. She had wanted to make his life easier. She wanted his patients to understand what a wonderful surgeon they were dealing with and having achieved that much, she had been happy enough, until now.

"Well?" he asked.

Kate looked at him. "So you're really not married?"

He took a step closer and smiled the sort of smile that warms your heart and melts your soul. "I promise," he said softly. "I can explain… if you'll let me."

Kate took a deep breath. "Okay, then," and she shivered in the bitter evening air.

"Come on. We'll take my car."

"What, now?"

"Do you have somewhere else you need to be?" he asked.

"No."

"Well then."

"But what about my car?" Kate said.

"Don't worry," he told her. "I'll drive you back here later to pick it up. Or drop you home. Whichever you like. You're not on in the morning, are you?"

"No. Monday," Kate said.

"Good. Come on then. Let's get out of here."

Kate locked her car again and with trembling limbs, she walked with Adam across the car park to his black Audi R8, parked further up the row.

He blipped the car and told her to hop in and Kate climbed into the passenger seat. The interior was spotless. A flash of dirty uniform screamed out from across her knee. "I'm in my uniform," Kate said as he climbed in next to her. "I can't go anywhere dressed like this."

Adam paused. "Would you like to go home and change first?" he asked.

Kate looked at her watch. "It's too late for that," she said. "By the time I could get ready no-one would be left serving."

"So we'll get a take away and take it back to my place," he said.

Kate thought for a moment. Her heart was racing as everything she had hoped for seemed to be finally falling into place all at once. "All right."

"That's settled then. What would you like? Chinese? Indian? Pizza?"

"Mediterranean," Kate said.

"Mediterranean?"

"Yes. There's a great place on-"

"Church Street."

"You know it?"

Adam nodded. "It's practically my second home." He started up the engine and pulled out of the car park.

"You know Niko then?" Kate asked. Niko was the owner of the restaurant, a lovely man and Kate had a real soft spot for him. "Yes."

"He's a sweetie, isn't he? He always puts something extra in my order."

Adam raised an eyebrow. "I'm not convinced his motives are

entirely altruistic there."

"Don't be silly, he's about fifty," she said.

Adam shrugged. "Your point being?"

"Well, he wouldn't think of me like that."

Adam shook his head and smiled. "You've got a lot to learn about men, Kate."

Kate looked at him for a second and then moved her gaze back to the window.

They turned into Church Street and Adam parked the car. Kate hopped out and huddled up in her long winter coat. But it wasn't long before the icy wind had her shivering again. Her teeth started to chatter and Adam looked round.

"Is that you making that noise?" he asked. Kate stuttered out a 'yes' and he put his arm around her and tucked her against him. "Come here," he said and held her close until the chattering ceased. He soothed her back and let his breath seep through the layers of wool around Kate's neck until her mind was spinning and she was losing her grip. Traces of aftershave and washing powder tangled with her senses, hurtling sideways in a whirl of panic and excitement.

"Come on. We'd better get you inside and then back to my place to warm up."

Niko was pleased to see the pair of them together. "Belissima. My two favourite customers here together. You two are…?" His face lit up expectantly. But Kate shuffled awkwardly as Adam cleared his throat. "No matter; no matter. I will rustle you up something extra special."

They waited in the warm shop front while their food was being prepared. Their gazes shifting from each other to the ornaments on the wall, neither of them knowing what to say or what to do and then Niko appeared once more, smiling from ear to ear. He held the bag open and then popped another dish on top. "You will like this, I think. You let me know, okay? It's a new dish I'm trying out." He handed it over and took the money from Adam.

"Remember to tell me what you think. Okay?"

Adam agreed and they said goodbye. "Come on," he said. "Are you up for a bit of a jog?"

The pair of them sprinted back down to the car and climbed inside. Kate put the bag of food on her lap. "Smells great," she said. "How far away do you live?"

"Not far," Adam told her. "Why? Can't you wait?"

In a little more than five minutes they were pulling up outside a magnificent apartment building.

Adam got out and opened Kate's door and she passed up the food and climbed out. She looked up at the building, all steel, glass and elegance.

"Wow," she said.

"Come on. Let's get you inside before you start shivering again."

Kate took one more look at the stunning building she was about to enter and then looked back at Adam. He blipped the car and they walked inside.

At the door to his apartment Kate realised Sophie might be worrying about her. "I'd better ring home," she said. "To say I haven't been abducted by aliens or anything."

Adam looked sideways, concern showing in his features. "Is someone at home waiting for you?" he asked.

Kate saw his expression and smiled. "Only Sophie, don't worry. She works on Ascot Ward?"

"Oh. I thought perhaps…"

Kate shook her head.

Adam opened the door and they walked in.

Kate looked around the tastefully decorated hallway as she took off her coat and Adam slipped out of his. He was wearing an off-white cotton shirt rolled up at the sleeves and dark green combats. It was a surprise to see him out of a suit. It was a far more casual look than Kate was used to and it helped to put her a little more at ease. She tried to remind herself that this was just a friendly matter, that he was showing his gratitude for her help the other day, but it wasn't working. She had once been a little girl and this was her frog turning into a prince.

"You give Sophie a ring and I'll just whip around and make sure the place is presentable," he said, disappearing into the living room as Kate picked out her phone.

"Hi, it's me."

"Where are you? Are you okay?"

"I'm fine. I just bumped into someone and I thought I'd better let you know that I'm going to be late."

"How late?" Sophie asked.

"I don't know. I've got to go. See you."

Adam appeared at the door. "Everything okay?"

"Fine," Kate said.

"Great. Then let's eat."

She was shown into a living room that could have graced the inside of the best glossy lifestyle magazine. There wasn't a speck of dust or untidiness anywhere. Kate was impressed. It was a smart bachelor pad, simple and functional, with little in the way of ornaments, or soft furnishings. Adam placed some logs in the fireplace on the wall and lit them and now Kate was doubly impressed.

"I've never seen a fire as posh as that before," she said, walking over to take a closer look.

"It's only a log burner," he said. "They've just set it inside a wall, that's all."

The flames started to build and Kate moved closer until she could feel the warmth coming off them, and she shivered as the heat settled in. Adam noticed and came to stand behind her, rubbing his hands up and down the sides of her arms to warm them and then he fetched a small blanket from another room and wrapped it around her shoulders. His hands rested for a moment around her and then he went back to the table to dish up.

When it was all set out, he walked over and handed Kate a glass of wine. "Ready?"

Kate nodded, wondering just how much she was actually going to be able to eat. But before long they were chatting easily and Kate quite forgot about being nervous. "So, I know you don't eat your salad and that you like Mediterranean food. You live in a very smart flat and you seem to have every opera CD ever made..."

Adam looked at her quizzically.

"I saw them on your sideboard," she said.

"Wow, you don't miss a trick, do you?"

"Oh, and you always have shiny shoes."

Adam laughed. It was the first time Kate had ever seen him laugh and it was fascinating. He was striking when he was serious but when he laughed, he was... breath-taking. His eyes twinkled in the light of the fire and his whole body was glowing in the soft light of the stylish wall lamps.

"So what else should I know about you, *Mr Elliott*?"

"Adam."

Kate sat back in her seat. "Adam." She tilted her head and nodded. "It suits you."

"What, better than 'that obnoxious, pompous prick, Elliott'?" Adam seemed amused, but Kate cringed remembering her hideous display. She thought for a moment to correct the errors Kirsty had made that night, but on reflection decided it would make it little better, and closed her eyes in dismay.

"I'll take that as a yes." He smiled. "I'm glad you think so. Deed Poll can be so tedious these days."

"I'm-" Kate began to apologise, but Adam just waved it away. "Would you like some more to eat?"

"No, thanks. I'm full," she said.

"More wine?"

"I'd better not. I've got to drive home later. So have *you* for that matter," she said. "You promised to drive me back to my car, remember?"

"You don't have to go," Adam offered.

Kate's eyes almost popped out of her head as her smile fell

away. What was he saying?

"I mean, I've got a spare room you could borrow," he said quickly. "I could drive you back to your car in the morning. If you like?"

Kate was confused, unable to process all the implications of that last suggestion in her present state.

"It would be such a shame to waste such a good bottle of wine," he added.

"But I haven't got anything with me," Kate said.

"What do you need?"

Kate racked her brain. "A toothbrush," she said.

"I have a spare."

"Hairbrush."

"I can manage a comb?"

"Spare underwear?"

Adam winced. "Ah. You've got me there." He thought for a moment and then came up with an idea. "I've got it. You can have the spare toothbrush and I'll lend you a T-shirt to sleep in and we'll put the clothes you're in now through the wash overnight." He sat back then, looking thoroughly pleased with himself.

Kate smiled as she looked at him. "So that's how you've ended up as a consultant."

"By washing women's clothing overnight?" Adam asked.

Kate laughed. "No, by solving tricky problems."

He laughed and then his face turned more serious again. "So it's sorted then? You'll stay?"

Kate's heart stilled and from somewhere inside her a voice said, "Okay," and it was settled.

Adam stood and started to clear away the plates and Kate decided to follow him into the kitchen, a pristine, gleaming, culinary heaven. "I'll wash if you dry?" she said.

Adam thought for a second and nudged shut the dishwasher in front of him. "Excellent."

Soapy fingers touched a few times while plates were being passed from one to the other and Kate was rapidly dissolving into a bag of nerves wondering where all this was leading. Adam was going to see her wearing just one of his T-shirts. Thank God she had shaved her legs that morning.

"So what's the big deal with opera?" she asked him, trying to turn the spotlight on to him for a change.

"Would you like to hear some?" he asked. "Then you can judge for yourself."

"Okay," Kate said.

They wiped their hands on a dry cloth and then walked back into the living room.

"Is there some opera you'd like in particular?" he asked as he picked out a disc to place into the music system.

"I can't say I've tried any; you'd better choose. I'm more of an R&B girl myself."

"Really?" Adam sounded surprised. "Well, we'll have to do something about that. See if you like it. If you don't, we can turn it off, or find something else. There's plenty of other stuff to choose from."

And then the most stirring music Kate had ever heard drifted out of the walls and carried her away. Adam watched as she listened to the music right the way through an entire track without a word being said. Kate was enthralled. As the track came to an end, Adam topped up her wine glass. "Is your Kate short for Katherine?" he asked.

"Yes," she told him.

"I like that. Katherine."

Kate had always hated her parents calling her by her full name, but now, from Adam's lips, it sounded beautiful.

The next track started up and Kate listened again. Flames flickered on the far side of the room and the good food and red wine had warmed her through, or was that being alone with Adam?

Kate looked up into seductive blue-grey eyes and smiled and Adam put down their wine. He held her gaze, unswerving. His body moved purposefully toward her as she waited, pulse racing for him to make his move. Strong, gentle hands reached to cup her face and he leaned slowly down and kissed her.

Being in such close proximity to Adam Elliott was intoxicating. It was a drug Kate did not feel inclined to give up and she sank into the kiss without reservation. His arms wrapped around her and pulled her against him as she slid her fingers up his back, so hot and firm beneath his cotton shirt, and pulled him closer. Adam's kiss became deeper and more intense and Kate was overwhelmed by the desire igniting inside her. Sparks shot through every corner of her body. Her limbs were turning to cooked spaghetti and she was rapidly losing her grip. Adam's frame supported her with the strength of one hand and his other caressed the delicate skin at the side of her neck.

Her taste of heaven lasted until the end of the track and as the music faded away, Adam ended the kiss and looked at Kate through those deep dark eyes of his. "You are so beautiful, Katherine," he said. "I have wanted to do that ever since the first day you hauled me out on Ascot Ward. You were such a force to be reckoned with. I was quite in awe of you."

"But I was… hideous. I was so angry with you."

"I know. You were magnificent."

"I was a trembling wreck," she told him.

"You were beautiful," he said and he kissed her again making her blush even deeper than before.

Kate shook her head. "I'd just come back from my granddad's funeral that day. We were very close. Only granddaughter." She looked up. "I really thought you hated me."

"Not at all. I… I've just had a lot of things on my mind recently. I'm sorry I took so long. And now I feel really bad. You had just lost your granddad and I laid into you. What a bastard I must have seemed." Adam looked around the room. "Come on, sit down, you've been on your feet all day. You must be tired out."

Kate sat down on the dark brown leather settee and Adam

115

settled a short distance away. He reached out his hand and touched Kate's hair. "Even when you've done a full day at work your hair still looks perfect. How on earth do you manage it?" he asked.

"Hundreds of pins," Kate said. "I pin it up so tight it wouldn't dare come loose."

"Ah, a control freak. I see what I'm up against now."

"Afraid so. But then I doubt you're too happy when things don't go the way you want them to either?"

Adam chuckled. "No. Maybe not. So we're as bad as each other, is that what you're trying to say?"

"It would appear so."

Adam ran a finger down the edge of her cheek searing the skin where it touched, opera played softly in the background, and Kate finally felt like she had come home.

"Why did you tell me you were married the other day?" Kate asked after a couple of minutes summoning up the courage.

Adam let his hand drop away from her face. He took a deep breath and looked down at his fingers. "I *was* married once, but not anymore. I just sometimes have difficulty coming to terms with that fact. Not that she's gone, you understand, I know that, but that I'm no longer married. It's not easy learning to move on from a love that was so new and untainted by life."

"What happened?" Kate asked him. "If you don't mind talking about it."

Adam looked at her for a long moment. "Her name was Alison. We met in our house year when we were first qualified. She was wonderful: beautiful, clever, caring. You'd have liked her. We got married a year later and we were just thinking about starting a family… and then she died."

"Oh God," Kate whispered.

"She was in a car crash. It was late at night and I was on call." He stopped to compose his thoughts. "She hadn't wanted to go out that night, but I made her. I thought she would like it once she got there. She did so loved to dance, Ali, and she had found

116

a friend to drive her. She never made it home."

Kate reached out a hand and touched his knee. Nothing she could say would make it any better.

"I tried to get there. But she was at another hospital and by the time I got someone to cover for me, she was already gone." Adam's gaze dropped to the settee beneath him. "I sat beside her on ITU, watching the machines keeping her alive, but in the end…"

Kate squeezed his hand and he looked up. What could she say?

"I'm sorry, but you deserved to know." He took another deep breath and let it out.

"How long ago did she die?" Kate asked him.

"A couple of years ago."

"Shit. I'm so sorry."

"Yeah. Still, life goes on, as they say." He got up to fetch another bottle of wine and changed the music and when he returned, he had lost his shadow. "So tell me about *your* love life then, Kate, and please try and make it more entertaining."

"Oh, Lord. Mine's far less moving and sadly not even entertaining," she said. "Unless you count the time I went out with a policeman I met in A&E, only to find out later he was really a male stripper. No, I've not been half so lucky in finding love." And she squeezed his hand and smiled fondly.

When she could suppress her yawns no longer, Kate looked up at the display on the music centre and realised it was past two in the morning. "I'm really sorry," she said arching her back as she yawned. "I'm afraid I'm going to have to get some sleep soon. I'm done in."

Adam checked his watch and apologised for keeping her talking so late. He got up from where he was sitting and held out his hand. "Come on sleepy head," he said.

Kate followed him into the little corridor off the living room. "Your room," he said as he pushed open the door on the right. It was an immaculately decorated guest room in shades of terracotta and soft cream. "It should have everything you need in there and your bathroom is just through that door," he said, pointing to a door on the far side of the room. "My room is down there," and he nodded to the end of the corridor. "If there's anything you need, just give me a shout."

Kate stepped inside.

"Is it all right?" he asked.

"Yes, it's gorgeous. I'm just a little afraid of getting lost in here." She held up a finger to point to her hair. "You might never find me again with this hair."

"Oh, I would always find you, Kate," he said and Kate's heart raced. "Besides, I love your hair. I won't hear a word said against it. I'll just get you something to sleep in." A minute later he was back at her door with a large blue T-shirt. "There you go. Now I will definitely be able to find you in the morning. I'll wait out here. You go and try it on. See if it will do."

Kate shut the door and looked around. She had a double bed made up in the centre of the back wall with a bedside table on either side. To the right was a dressing table below the window and on the left sat an easy chair and the door to the bathroom. She quickly undressed and pulled on the T-shirt. It was vast on her, stretching half way down to her knees and to her elbows on either side. Kate was relieved. She slipped off her tights and knickers and bundled them up inside her uniform and then taking a deep breath, she walked back outside into the corridor.

Rather self-conscious of how little she had on, she bobbed a small curtsy.

"Perfect," he said. "Shall I take those for you?"

"No," she snapped, flushing slightly. "I can do it." As if she was going to let him touch any of her dirty washing on a first date! Was this a date? She still wasn't sure. "Just point me in the right direction."

Adam took her to a door behind the kitchen that looked like a cupboard. Inside was a tiny laundry. She put her bundle in the drum and threw in a capsule and then Adam set it to run.

"Right, all sorted." He looked at his watch. "It's twenty past two and you're shattered. You'd better get yourself to bed. I'll see you in the morning." Closing the door on the steady hum of the machine, they walked back to their rooms.

At her door, Kate stepped inside and Adam hovered in the hallway. "Goodnight," she said.

"Goodnight, Katherine."

Kate closed the door, drifted into the en-suite to brush her teeth and then collapsed into the fresh clean bedding, buzzing with adrenaline. She really thought she might stay awake for hours with all that had happened between them that night, but as the adrenaline suddenly dropped away, it took her down with it and before long she was fast asleep.

It was just before ten when Kate awoke. She looked around, disorientated and confused at first, until she remembered where she was. She was at Adam's. Kate sat up and stretched and listened intently. There was not a sound from the apartment outside.

Rediscovering the bathroom with morning eyes, she was not surprised to see it was spotless too. There was a fresh white suite, with beige walls and a brown floor. A stack of fluffy white towels were standing to attention in the corner of the bathroom, beside an immaculately clean power shower. Kate tidied up the mess of packaging she had unravelled the night before and wondered at the amount of thought that had gone into creating such a glamorous spare room.

~

In the kitchen, Adam heard the shower turning on. He smiled. He had been up for an hour already and was eager to see Kate again. He had folded her clothes neatly and they were sitting on the arm of the settee, with the underwear tucked discreetly inside, waiting for her.

119

Kate emerged, her hair hanging loose and still damp. She was wrapped in the largest towel imaginable but still seemed very uncomfortable with how much flesh she was exposing. "Do you have a hair dryer?" she asked, fidgeting on the spot.

Adam stood in the doorway to the kitchen, as fresh as a daisy after a peaceful night's sleep. "Sorry," he said. "Not much need for one."

Kate hovered for a minute, obviously wanting to say something more. "My clothes?" she asked.

Adam smiled. "Over there on the couch."

Kate grabbed the pile and scuttled back into her bedroom.

Once again his mind trailed over the kiss they had shared the night before. He could do this, he told himself. It was nothing he couldn't handle. He wouldn't let it go too far too soon. One step at a time. But a few minutes later his control was sorely tested when she emerged from the bedroom in her clean uniform and bare legs. Her hair was loose and her eyes were bright. Her hand rested above the draw where he had stowed Ali's picture the night before and his gaze lingered a moment as guilt threatened to engulf him, but he forced it back down and distracted himself with breakfast. Nothing serious had happened. Not yet.

~

Kate realised her hair would have to dry naturally, a true test of any man's mettle in her opinion. Could he handle all that unkempt ginger hair? Having no mascara was a bit of a problem too, but she had remembered this of old and had been very careful not to wash too vigorously around her eyes the night before and it seemed enough was left from the previous day not to look too hideous.

"Good morning," she said, sheepishly.

"Coffee?" he asked. "Tea?"

"Tea, please," she told him.

"Can I get you something to eat?"

"No, thank you. I'm not very good at breakfast."

Adam poured a mug of tea and passed it over. "Your hair," he said pointing to the wayward strands around her face.

"I'm sorry." She winced.

"Sorry? Why? It's wonderful. You should wear it down more often."

"In A&E?" Kate said. "It'd be caked in vomit in no time."

"Good point," he conceded.

They sat down at the dining table so that Adam could eat his toast and Kate sipped at her cup of tea. "Did you sleep well?" he asked.

"Like a log, thank you," she told him. "I was out for the count as soon as my head hit the pillow. I hope I didn't snore."

"I didn't hear a thing."

Kate wondered if he was just being polite. It was strange, but now they had had a chance to cool off from the night before, Kate wasn't completely sure she knew where she stood. It *felt* very much like they had slipped into friends mode and she was unsure about how to go on. Kate had no car to make her way home, so she was reliant on Adam to take her back at least as far as the hospital. She didn't really want to leave, although a change of clothes and a hair brush would have been nice, so she said nothing and waited for him to set the tone.

"Do you have any plans for today?" Adam asked her.

Kate shook her head. "Not really. I was planning on doing a bit of cleaning, but that can always wait."

"I'm afraid I'm hopeless at cleaning. I don't have the patience for it," he told her.

"You're kidding me. This place is immaculate. And I'm obsessional about that sort of thing, so I should know."

"I have a cleaner," he confessed and a sheepish smile touched the corners of his lips.

"A cleaner? You cheat! All this time I've been so impressed and it wasn't even you."

Adam chuckled and got up to clear away his things. Without thinking he loaded them into the dishwasher.

Kate leaned back in her chair and peered into the kitchen after him. "And you've got a dishwasher? Why on earth did we do the washing up by hand last night, if you had one of those things?"

Adam walked back over and rested a hand upon her shoulder. "Because I wanted to do something with you," he said.

Shivers rippled down Kate's body. "I can think of nicer things to do," she said and then instantly realised what she was saying and flushed bright pink.

Adam stooped down and leaned close to her ear, the same way he had done that time in the clinic. "So can I," he said.

Okay, she thought, obviously *not* in *friends* mode any more. Phew!

Kate realised she should try and relax. Hadn't her being there come from learning to step back and let him take control? She put her mug in the dishwasher and walked back to where Adam was perching, on the arm of the settee. He pulled her by the hands until she was standing between his thighs. "I'd really like to spend some time with you, Kate. I'd like to take you out somewhere today. Would that be all right?"

Kate's pulse rate quickened but then she looked down at her clothes. "Dressed like this?" she asked.

"No, maybe not. I could drop you off at your car and follow you home and then we could go on from there. What do you think?"

"All right," she said. "Where are you taking me?"

"It's a surprise."

"But how will I know what to wear?" she asked.

"Wear something warm," was all he would say.

Kate looked into his eyes and wondered how she had ever been unable to see what a gorgeous man he really was. His silky dark hair and his blue-grey eyes were so beguiling and as for his firm - only yet tentatively explored – body, hidden beneath the thin burgundy sweater; they were all just a frame for the kind, passionate man he was within.

Kate's eyes dropped to his supple mouth, moving just a little as he searched for the right words to say. Then she noticed a tiny scar on the right of his top lip. It was so small she had never even noticed it before. She reached out and rested a fingertip on it and Adam's breathing hitched. "What happened?" she asked.

Adam looked at her so intensely, studying every curve of her face, searching for what, she couldn't be sure. "I fell off my bike when I was six," he said.

She looked back into seductive eyes and leaned forward to kiss the tiny mark and Adam let out a soft guttural groan, took her in his arms and claimed her mouth with his. No dim lights or crackling fire could be blamed for setting the mood this time. No music was playing and no wine was being drunk. It was just one body reaching out to another and two hearts yearning to belong.

Chapter 7

In its honesty, their kiss was devastating. Kate's body gave in to every flicker of Adam's will. It moulded seamlessly to his as their breath mingled effortlessly in the crush. But from somewhere just behind her right shoulder, Kate suddenly felt the burden of living up to such a perfect wife rushing in on her and the weight of it drew the air from her lungs. Adam had spoken of Ali the night before in such whispered tones of worship that Kate felt all at once ill at ease and she froze at his touch.

"What's wrong?" Adam asked, concern drawing lines on his face.

"Nothing. A sore back, that's all. It must have been lifting that drunk we had in last night," she assured him, for what could she say? She could hardly tell him the truth.

Adam turned her around and started rubbing her back, melting her muscles with his touch. A small appreciative groan escaped her lips, betraying her, and he turned her back round and held her face in his hands. Dark passionate eyes met hers and more might have happened had Adam's mobile not chosen that very moment to go off.

Kate pulled away, allowing her time to gather her senses and Adam cursed under his breath and reached into his back pocket to answer it.

"Hello?"

This was the voice Kate was used to. The stony, authoritative tone of the consultant. It had to be the hospital. Surely he wasn't on call? Kate straightened her dress and tidied her unruly hair behind her ears, whilst bracing herself for disappointment. As she studied Adam, concentrating on his call, she noticed that he still had hold of one of her hands and did not seem inclined to let go of it, his fingers intertwining with hers, even as he spoke serious words to the caller.

"Okay," he said at last. "I'll be there as soon as I can."

Adam put down the phone and looked at Kate. "That was work," he sighed. "I'm sorry, but I'm going to have to pop over there. John has asked for my help on a patient just in."

Kate couldn't help but feel somehow that it had been far too good to last anyway and maybe a little of that showed in her face, because a moment later he lifted her chin with a finger so that her gaze was level with his.

"Don't worry. I shouldn't be long," he said. "Can I come and find you when I'm finished?"

Kate nodded and he squeezed her hand for reassurance.

"You'd better write down your address and phone number in case I get lost."

She smiled, happier now and he kissed her tenderly. "Come on, I'm afraid we're going to have to get a move on. Grab your things."

Kate arrived home just after eleven and wandered in trying to act her most nonchalant. Sophie was with Rich and leapt up as she arrived, rushing over to meet her.

"Where have you been till this time, you dirty stop out?" she asked. "We were beginning to think we should send out a search party. You were so evasive on the phone last night. Come on, sit down here and tell me everything."

Kate couldn't help it; try as she might her face was betraying her with the most decadent smile. "It was just a friend, I told you. But it was late by the time we finished talking, so we decided I should stay over. And now I really must get out of these clothes."

She walked quickly upstairs, leaving Sophie and Rich to specu-
late on what had really gone on. In her bedroom Kate crashed
down face first onto her bed and quietly screamed into the pillow.
She was happy, if a little insecure. It was astonishing how things
had changed in the past twenty-four hours. She wondered where
he was taking her and whether they would even still have enough
time to go after he was through at the hospital.

Looking through her wardrobe, Kate picked out some jeans,
thick socks, a warm blouse and jumper. Not knowing how much
time she had, she pulled them on and then dried and brushed
out her hair. She thought about Adam and how he had liked her
hair loose and so she left out the pins for a change and just tied
it back in a long plait.

She looked in the mirror. A little work was needed and
removing what was left of yesterday's make-up, she reapplied
afresh. She looked again. Better, she thought.

Emerging back downstairs, she saw Sophie looking up at her
with suspicious eyes, her arms folded across her chest. "What's
going on, Katy Heath?" she asked.

Kate tried to give her an innocent look but she was fooling
no-one.

"Come on, spill."

A car pulled up outside and Rich got up and peered out of the
window. "Well, there's a very smart Audi just pulled up outside,"
he said.

Sophie looked at Kate and the doorbell rang. Kate rushed over
to reach the door before the other two did and Rich and Sophie
leaned around the living room door expectantly.

Kate took a deep breath and opened the door and there was
Adam, looking magnificent. He smiled and then noticed the two
onlookers standing behind her and waved.

Reluctantly Kate asked him in, giving Sophie a very hard stare.

"Mr Elliott," Sophie stated in surprise.

"Hello, Sophie."

"And this is Richard, her fiancé," Kate added when Sophie seemed incapable of further intelligent conversation. "Rich, this is Adam."

Adam walked inside and shook Richard's hand and congratulated them both on their engagement. Then an awkward silence settled among them and Kate tried hard to avoid their enquiring gazes.

"Are you ready to go?" Adam asked, ending the drought.

"Yes," Kate said a little too quickly. "Let's go."

Kate sat in the passenger seat as they sped off into the countryside. It was almost half an hour of fields, trees and small talk, with the radio playing quietly in the background before they finally pulled up in a small parking spot a short way off the main road. "Here we are," he announced.

Kate stepped out of the car and a chill wind whipped across her face. She reached into the back seat and pulled out her coat and knitted hat. Her breath was misting in front of her face.

"Are you warm enough?" Adam asked, shrugging into his big padded jacket and gloves.

Kate looked down at what she was wearing. "I think so."

"You haven't got any gloves," he said.

Kate pulled one out of each pocket and held them up.

"Okay. Come on then. This way."

He held out his hand and Kate took it gladly. They walked for a while up a gentle slope and then the going started to get a little harder. Adam helped her along the steepening path as Kate began to wonder what on earth could be worth driving all the way out there for. They were in the middle of nowhere, with only a handful of sheep for company. It was dull and barren and cold and she was struggling to discern the appeal.

As they reached the top, all obstacles suddenly fell away and the view opened out before them.

"Well? What do you think?" Adam asked.

Kate stood and looked around, taking in the scene. "It's wonderful," she said.

Adam led her over the brow of the hill to a little ledge on the far side, where he laid out a plastic mac and they sat down and looked across at the panorama before them.

"I come out here when I need to get away from everything," he said.

Kate looked at him.

"That doesn't include you."

She raised an eyebrow.

"Okay, maybe a little."

Kate nudged him playfully and looked back at the view. "It's beautiful, isn't it? You can see for miles."

"You can today," he said.

He took her hand in his and held on to it. "I would like to keep seeing you, Kate," he said. "But I wonder if we can keep it just between us for the time being?"

Kate looked at him, not unduly concerned, but curious as to why he would feel that way.

"You know what hospitals are like," he said. "The grapevine would have a field day."

Kate was reminded of her comments in Helix back in the summer and how far they'd spread in such a short time *and* how they'd altered along the way. She nodded solemnly. "You might be right."

"Just until we're... well... until we get used to each other. The last thing we need is everyone else's opinions and advice coming between us."

"I can handle that," she told him.

"Good." Adam kissed Kate's gloved hand and then turned back to the view. "Do you see that plume of smoke down there, just to the right of the river?"

"Yes," she said.

"That's a place called The Hooded Monk. It's a little pub that serves great food and has an open log fire, or so I've been told. Are you feeling hungry yet?"

"Starving," Kate said.

"Great. Come on then, I'll race you down."

Of course he beat her back to the bottom despite Kate's almost dangerous levels of cheating and once they got back to level ground, they walked hand in hand as far as the car and then drove off in search of food.

Inside the inn, they found a table next to the fireplace. Kate took off her gloves and coat and pulled off her hat.

"Oh, shame," Adam teased. "I thought you looked adorable in that hat."

Kate gave him a stern look.

"Honestly!"

But she was not convinced. Adam's eyes were still twinkling.

They ordered the steak and ale pie and the hunters chicken and Adam was obviously impressed when Kate finished first.

"Wow, you can eat fast," he said.

"I grew up with three brothers," she told him. "It was eat or be eaten in our house."

He nodded. "I guess so. And there was me thinking you were going to be one of those women who pick at their food, barely eating enough to feed a sparrow."

"Me? Why?"

"Because I saw you at the ball. You hardly ate a thing that day."

Kate looked at him then, a little surprised.

"Yes, I noticed."

"I was nervous," she admitted a little shyly.

Adam smiled. "Why?"

Kate was squirming in her seat. "It doesn't matter." She looked up and saw in Adam's eyes that he knew very well why and she smiled at him.

"Can I get you another drink?" he asked.

"I'd love an apple juice, please," she said.

"I'll be right back."

Adam walked up to the bar and the old man serving there acknowledged him and walked over. "Yes, sir? What can I get you?"

Adam ordered the drinks and the man picked out a couple of glasses and began to pour. "Cold out there today," he said.

"Yes. Nice and warm in here though," Adam replied.

The man nodded. "Visiting the abbey, are we?"

Adam raised an eyebrow. "Which one's that, then?"

"Durbent Abbey. Just down the road a way."

"I didn't even know there was one there," Adam said.

"Well, it's more of a ruin than an abbey these days, but there's an interesting story surrounding it. That's what gave this place its name."

A few minutes later, Adam returned to their table and retook his seat. "Cheers," he said and they clinked glasses and took a large swig. "I thought we could take a look at the abbey after we've finished, if you like?" he said. "There's an old ruins not far from here. It might be worth a look?"

"Okay," said Kate.

After pudding, Adam settled the bill and they walked back outside to the car.

"Right, I need you to spot for me," he said. "Apparently we need to go left out of here and then the next right and follow the road for about a mile until we reach a fork. It should be up on the right. It's hidden from the road by the trees in summer, but it shouldn't be too hard to spot this time of year, apparently."

The pair of them drove down the winding country roads until they reached the fork and then Adam slowed down to give them a chance to look around.

"Over there," Kate said, pointing. "Behind the trees. See?"

Adam pulled over and got out of the car. He took hold of Kate's hand and they walked together up to the abbey.

Moss clung around the crumbling walls and noisy crows hovered in the sky overhead, like vultures waiting to descend.

Kate stepped through a doorway and into a large roofless room. Looking up she saw the clouds gathering around them. The light was already fading, adding to its eerie charm. They walked on into another room, still mostly hidden from the sky and wings flapped. From the rafters above them, pigeons swooped out, startling Kate and making her jump.

Adam chuckled. "Seen enough of that room?" he asked. He squeezed her hand and led her on out of the gloom and back into the open air. Brambles snared the stones of the north wall, like a clawed hand grasping at its prey and Kate stepped carefully into a clearing, where all but the superficial rubble had been lost over the years. It was lighter there, but offering fewer walls for protection, the cold wind churned about them and Kate hugged her coat tighter.

Darkness was approaching from the west and although it was still early for the light to be fading, no romantic sunset was going to be visible that night. Adam grabbed Kate making her jump and he rolled up laughing.

Kate thumped him. "You scared me half to death," she gasped. But he was soon forgiven as he pulled her into his arms and wrapped his coat around her, making her feel safe and warm.

Kate laid her cheek against his chest, in no hurry to pull away. From inside his coat she could feel his warm body surrounding and protecting her. The mixture of scent, touch and heat was incredibly seductive and had she not been out in the middle of nowhere on a cold winter's afternoon, Kate was convinced she would have been putty in his hands.

"Apparently this abbey saw a couple of grisly murders in its day," Adam said, releasing her from his safety, as he began to wander on through the ruins. He held out his hand to help her over the fallen masonry. "They say a long time ago a local farmer's daughter was caught in the woods in the arms of a monk."

Kate looked up.

"So the farmer marched them up to the abbey and insisted on a marriage between the two. But the abbot refused and the villagers turned against the monks and bad feeling rose up between them."

He stepped a little closer.

"Not long after that, the abbot was found dead in his chamber; his throat had been cut and his cloak was gone, but *no traces of his killer were ever found*."

Kate rolled her eyes as Adam tried hard to make it spooky.

He paused. "But a new abbot arrived and then the girl from the village had a baby. The new abbot got to hear about the baby and he kept the monk confined, going to meet her in his place and soon *she* was dead too. They say the girl's cries could be heard across the valley and the abbot… had *vanished*.

Kate took a deep breath and let it out. "So who was the murderer then?" she asked.

Adam turned his head to the sky and then looked back towards her. "The abbot."

Kate thought for a minute. "But I thought he got his throat cut?"

Adam looked at her. "Well it must have been the second abbot then. The one they sent to replace the first."

"But, how could he have killed the *first* one if he didn't arrive until after the first one was dead?"

Adam looked thoughtful. "No. Actually I remember it now. It was neither of them. It was the carpenter.

"What carpenter?"

"The one that loved the girl."

"You never mentioned a carpenter. So why did the carpenter kill the girl if he loved her?"

Adam shrugged. "I don't know. Because she had her wicked way with a monk, I suppose."

"But why kill the abbot then?"

Adam grabbed her and bundled her against him. "Oh God, I don't know. Just look impressed, will you. The chap in the inn only told me the story a few minutes ago. I can't remember."

Kate rolled up laughing. "I'm sorry. It was a great story… if a little flawed," and he tickled her until she begged him to stop.

A white shape swooped silently by them in the darkening sky and Kate yelped, grabbing on to Adam, who wrapped her up in his arms and followed its arc. He leant down to kiss the top of her head. "It was only a barn owl," he said softly. "It's gone now."

Kate's heart was beating fast as she slowly pulled away and looked up into the sky. "I think I've had enough of abbeys for one day," she said. "Can we get out of here?"

"You are a funny thing," he said as they wandered back across the field to the car. "So full of fire one minute and as soft as a kitten the next."

Kate considered that. "That must be what makes me so loveable," she said and Adam nodded. His eyes dipped down to meet hers and he pulled her against him and kissed her with a simmering passion that promised so much.

"You are far too tempting," he growled through dark hazy eyes and Kate took a breath and let it out, hugging herself against the wind.

Large drops of water began to splash down on them and Adam held out a hand and looked up at the sky. "I think it's about to chuck it down," he said and they ran the rest of the way back to the car, hopping inside just in time to watch the heavens open and the sky empty out all around them.

Back at Kate's house, Adam walked her to the door. "Would you like to come in?" she asked him.

"Not this time, sadly" he said. "I've got a hundred and one things I need to do before the morning. But another time?"

Kate nodded.

"So when can I see you again?"

"Thursday I'm on an early, with a late the following day," she said.

"Great. I'll pick you up around seven?"

"Okay."

"Good." He kissed her again more tenderly than before and

groaned as he pulled away. "Katherine Heath, you are killing me." His lips met hers again very briefly and then he said goodbye and walked back to his car.

Kate stood and waved him off and then went inside and closed the front door.

Sophie was standing just inside the living room with a huge grin on her face. "Well?"

Kate's face creased into an enormous smile as the pair of them squealed with delight. She collapsed down into the armchair and Sophie sat close by.

"So? Come on. You're not going to do this to me again. I'm fit to burst here. How did you end up staying the night with our handsome Mr Elliott? That *is* what happened, isn't it? Tell me that much at least."

Kate filled her in from the beginning of the evening. "And then we went to bed," she said.

Sophie's eyebrows could get no higher. "You harlot!"

"Not together."

"What?"

"I slept in the spare room. Oh Sophie, it was beautiful," she said.

"I thought you said you slept in the spare room?"

"I did," Kate assured her. "I was talking about the spare room. It was immaculate, tastefully decorated and *so* clean. Just gorgeous."

Sophie sat back. "You are seriously deranged, woman. You finally get to spend the night at Mr Elliott's house after mooning around after him for... well... *ages* and the thing you get most excited about is the house?"

"No, of course not. It *was* a very nice apartment, but *he* was fabulous."

"And absolutely no funny business?"

Kate shook her head. "He's picking me up again on Thursday."

Sophie slumped back into her seat and sighed.

"But you can't tell anyone," Kate added.

Sophie sat up again. "What? The hottest news of the year and

I can't tell anyone?"

Kate shook her head. "Not a word. Please. Just for a bit, Soph."

"Why not?"

"Hospital gossip. You know what it's like. We just want to have a bit of time to ourselves before the guys at work get hold of it. You won't tell anyone, will you?"

Sophie zipped her mouth shut. "Not a word. But tell me, is he the one?"

Kate looked into her friend's excited, happy face. "I hope so, Soph," she said. "I really hope so."

Sophie squealed again and stamped her feet on the floor in excitement. "I knew it. I told you you would know it when you felt it. Oh, I'm so pleased for you, Kate. Just think, if you get a crack on, we could even make it a double wedding."

At this, Kate virtually choked with laughter. "Give us a chance, Soph. We've only been out once."

"Okay. Okay. I'll ask you again in a month."

That night Kate was back in her own bed, thinking about the night before and how much had changed in such a short time. All failings now forgiven, they had fallen for each other in a big way. Kate knew that if he asked her, she would give him her heart without so much as a moment's hesitation. She felt secure with him. He seemed to adore her and *she* him, and soon they would be able to tell the world and watch the faces of the rest of the staff as they looked at Kate in surprise, wondering what she could possibly see in grumpy old Jolly. But Kate knew what they did not, that Adam was a gorgeous, kind, funny and passionate man. And if they had made the effort to get to know him better, then maybe they would have been able to see that too. Just as long as none of the prettier nurses began to appreciate him, Kate hoped she would be safe. For a moment there her heart quivered. Maybe the secrecy was a good thing, she thought.

Back in work, life carried on as usual. Kate moved through her day hiding her wonderful secret and Adam was... nowhere to be seen. It was as if nothing had even happened. And yet so much had changed in Kate's life. She was now... Adam's girlfriend, she supposed. *She* was going out with Mr Elliott, the stony-faced orthopaedic surgeon who everybody recognised, but nobody knew, and she wasn't even allowed to talk about it.

Tuesday saw another early shift and Kate was finding it harder and harder to believe that what she thought had happened over the weekend really *had* taken place.

Wednesday she was on an early again and still no sign of Adam. By now she was desperate to see him, if only to reassure herself that it had been real. He hadn't called even and Kate started to doubt everything. Did he really like her? Was there something special between them? What if it had just been a bit of an awkward mistake, by a man too polite to dump and run? Her days should have been filled with excitement and happiness, a woman blossoming in the first flush of love, but instead his words were twisting in her mind and she was beginning to feel more and more rejected. She had to talk to him.

That night Kate sat by her phone, wishing she had taken his phone number too. Butterflies beat their wings at the lining of her gut as she waited for Adam to call her. And then he rang.

"Hello?"

"Kate. It's so good hear your voice. I've been thinking about you for days. I wanted to see you last night, but I didn't want to just bowl up when you weren't expecting me. You may have been busy or with someone else."

"I would have *loved* to have seen you. At work it's all just been same-old-same-old and it just feels so odd, like the weekend never really happened."

"Oh, it happened, believe me. And I don't want you swanning off with some other guy while I'm stuck in clinic staring at mangled hands, okay?"

And as easily as that Kate relaxed. Her smile remembered how much she had to be thankful for and they talked a little longer before, joyfully, Kate realised she now had Adam's number and they agreed to meet earlier than previously arranged the following evening.

The next day Kate was back on form. She bounced into work and raced through her day with a sunny smile and methodical diligence.

On the way to break she spotted Adam. He was walking down the main corridor in the opposite direction. He didn't seem to have noticed her. Kate approached, closer and closer, and still he gave no hint that he had seen her. He was almost in front of her when finally he looked her way. Kate's breath held. His dark grey pinstriped suit was tailored perfectly to show off his lean masculine physique and his blue-grey eyes shone out from his handsome face as time slowed down, and just as he was almost out of sight, Adam winked and their fingers touched ever so briefly and then he was gone. Accelerating back up to speed, it was over in an instant and he was half way down the corridor behind her, but he had looked, and winked, and touched. Kate let out a big sigh and walked on up to the canteen with a contented smile playing merrily around her mouth.

She arrived home just before two and was struck by the thought: What if it happens tonight? She began to beautify as if her life depended on it. Something she definitely planned on doing was taking some spare underwear, tucked away discreetly in a pocket. What should she wear? Most of her wardrobe was pulled out and discarded in the race to find something suitable. In the end, she decided to go with the first thing she'd tried on, a long floaty skirt and matching top in forget-me-not blue with a white collar and cuffs; maybe a little dressy for an evening at the pub, but unlikely to look out of place at Adam's.

~

Adam sat in his car in the hospital car park. He had finished work early for a change and was as nervous as a teenager on a first date. This was a real date, he thought. He couldn't deny it any longer. The other night had just developed of its own free will. He had spent time with Kate the next day too, but still nothing serious had happened. *This* was different. *This* meant far more.

Part of him was desperate to see her; the spark between them was undeniable. Kate challenged him and impressed him with her strength and compassion, he found her compelling but he had given his heart before and he had promised it would be forever. Ali's image drifted through his mind, searing his senses and tearing at his scars. What did it say about him, loving again so soon? About his endurance, his fortitude? Could he really bear to go down that road again? Yes. He had to.

He arrived at half past five, half an hour before Kate was expecting him. He knew he had to move fast or he would lose his nerve and so, game face on, he knocked.

~

Kate answered the door, her heart rate leaping with excitement, and there he was.

"I'm early. I hope that's okay?" Adam said. "Are you on your own this time?" He was looking round her.

"Sophie's on a late," she told him.

"Good." Adam stepped inside closing the door behind him and kissed her more passionately than ever before. Kate blushed, breathlessly steadying herself. "I've been thinking about that all day," he said. "So, do I get the guided tour?"

What was there to see? "Oh, of course. Come in." Kate showed him round their living room and kitchen. Pointed out the toilet, the tiny garden and then arrived back at the front, job done, she thought.

"Don't I get to see upstairs?" he asked.

Kate shook her head, remembering the state she had left her bedroom in. "Absolutely not. It's a complete mess."

"I don't care, come on." He pulled on her hand, but Kate stubbornly refused to move. "You haven't got a dartboard up there with my face on it or something, have you?" he asked.

"No."

"Perhaps you've got another man tied up, waiting for you?"

"Certainly not!" she exclaimed.

"Well, come on then. How bad can it be?"

Adam pulled on Kate's hand again and led the way upstairs. At the top he asked which way to her bedroom and Kate reluctantly pointed to her door and then quickly rushed in front of him barring his way. Slowly Adam approached.

"I don't remember you showing me *your* bedroom," she said to him trying anything to put him off, but Adam was having none of that.

"I'll show you mine if you show me yours," he said, his eyes gleaming with the challenge. And then he leaned down and breathing hotly into her ear, he whispered how much he wanted her, kissed her neck and pulled her against him, devouring her. But distraction had been the heart of *his* plan all along and one delicious moment later he flipped her round and was staring at the mother of all messes on the inside of her room.

The walls inside were blue and the bed too, under the pile of clothes that was. He looked back at her, amused. Kate marched inside and gathered up all the clothes into her arms. "I didn't know what to wear," she huffed.

Adam turned to face her and took the bundle of clothes out of her arms, dropping them back down onto the bed. Then he took Kate's chin delicately in his fingertips and looked into her eyes. "You look stunning."

Pulling her against his side, he looked around her room. It really was very blue, she realised. Mid blue walls gave way to watery-blue bedding with darker blue on the carpet. On one wall, opposite her bed, was a picture of the ocean with a small sandy island, green trees, and a pair of flip-flops at the waterline.

"I take it you like the colour blue?" he said.

"It's the sea," Kate told him. "And the sky. I like the idea of floating on calm blue waters, with just the stars above me and, apart from the gentle lapping of the waves, silence all around."

Adam was quiet for a second. "So there's something of the mermaid about you then," he said.

Kate laughed gently, thinking of her fondness for swimming. "I suppose so."

"Well, you've certainly got the hair for it," he told her.

"I have, haven't I?"

"Come on. I've got a table booked for seven-fifteen and I need to go home and change before we go out. I've come straight from work. You don't mind, do you?"

Adam left her in his living room and told her to put on some music and then went off to take a shower, so Kate stood rifling through his collection looking for something that was more her style. She heard the shower turning on and tried not to imagine Adam's body naked, warm and wet and glistening with soapy water.

Opera formed a large part of the collection as she already knew, but there were a few others in there: a couple of pop CDs, some heavy metal and rock music - a strange collection, she thought - and then there was one box, over the back, looking almost gothic. She picked it out and looked at it and then put the disc in the CD player and pressed play. The music started up. It sounded depressing at first and Kate wondered what on earth Adam could see in it. But the more she listened, the more she seemed to understand it. It moved her in a way she hadn't expected. It was like a soul crying out in pain. Another track started and it was more desperate than the first. Kate picked up the box. She had never heard of them before, but was now curious enough to listen to more.

Things moved this man on a very deep level, she thought. His private life was a mystery to those around him and she began to wonder if he had vast depths that she had only just begun to scratch the surface of.

A hand rested on top of her shoulder making her jump. It was Adam, standing behind her, looking fresh and clean and ravishingly good.

"Will you please stop scaring the hell out of me," she scolded.

Adam took the CD case and put it back on the shelf.

"It's very powerful," she offered.

"It was Ali's," he said.

"I'm sorry." Kate looked at him, kicking herself for not thinking. His hair was still damp and crying out to be touched. She let her fingers spread out through the dark silky strands. He smelled so good. The tracks changed and suddenly it was a beautiful, sad, gentle song. Adam reached across and turned the music off.

"We'd better get going."

He walked out to the front door and grabbed his keys. "Come on," he called and Kate wandered out after him, acutely aware that she had done something wrong.

Outside Adam was silent. They got into his car and drove to a smart Italian restaurant in town. Not a word was said. Kate tried to think of something to say to break the silence, but everything she thought of seemed so trivial.

Before long even trivial seemed better than nothing at all, so she settled for, "It was a bit milder today, wasn't it? There wasn't even a frost when I woke up this morning."

"What? Oh. No."

"It'll soon be Christmas now. What are you doing for Christmas this year?" No sooner were the words out of her mouth than Kate realised how stupid she had been. The man had just lost his mother, his only relative left in the world. What did she think he was going to be doing? "Oh, God, I'm so sorry. I didn't think. I'm such an idiot." She put a tentative hand on his knee. "I'm really sorry, Adam. Honestly."

Adam pulled up in the car park behind the restaurant. His face was serious and his eyes were sad but he didn't seem angry. "It's all right, Kate. I do get down sometimes, but it's not your fault. It's nothing you've done. You're the one who brings me back to life."

Kate leaned toward him and taking his face gently in her hands, she kissed him, trying to let him know just how much he meant to her.

"Don't leave me for being miserable, will you, Kate?" he asked. "Just give me a hard slap if I get too maudlin."

Kate smiled. "Okay. Come on; let's get inside."

The rest of the evening went along on a much lighter note. All thoughts of dark times were pushed aside and the two of them laughed and talked together, tasting each other's food and sharing their tales.

~

At the end of the evening Adam asked for the bill. He had managed to get over the guilt that had encroached on him earlier that night and was looking forward to the rest of the evening with Kate.

The waiter brought over the bill on a little silver tray. As he took Adam's card to process the payment, he asked about their meals. "Was everything to your satisfaction, Sir?"

"Yes, very good, thank you," he said.

"And the service?"

"Superb," Adam told him.

"I'm very pleased to hear it." He handed Adam his receipt and smiled at them both. "You and your lovely wife enjoy the rest of your evening," he said and Adam was suddenly grave.

His wife. The man had said 'his wife'. But Kate wasn't his wife, was she? And that silly slip was going to cost them so much.

Adam retreated inside himself, desperate to be rid of the guilt he was carrying. He could think of nothing but wanting to be somewhere else, alone. He felt the blood drain from his skin. What the hell had he been thinking? He needed to get out of there without making a mess of things again. He had let it go too far. It was only ever meant to have been a thank you dinner. There would have been no harm in just that. He clenched his fists by his sides and manoeuvred them both outside to the car.

The evening had turned cold and foggy while they'd been inside the restaurant. Night's breath cloaked the lamps in the streets and muffled voices echoed all around. Adam didn't say a word as they left. He could see Kate looking at him, wondering what was going on, which only made matters ten times worse. The last thing he'd wanted was to hurt her, but what could he do? What could he say? How could he explain it to anyone? The way his stomach clenched at the thought of letting go of Ali for good. The way sometimes he felt her beside him, whispering comfort when times were hard, the smell of her perfume somehow near him when he was lonely. No-one would believe that. They would think he was mad. Maybe he was.

He drove Kate back home as she sat by his side, still as a statue in the uncomfortable silence.

He pulled up outside her house and shot hope down in flames. "Well that was great, thanks, Kate. We must do this again some-time," he said, barely pulling his gaze away from the road.

Kate looked at him and Adam could not bring himself to look back. He felt as low as it was possible to feel. All Kate could do was unbuckle her seatbelt and step out of the car. But she said nothing. Not a 'thanks', not a 'see you', not even a 'what do you mean, you bastard?' which was what he deserved. She just got out. At the door she turned and Adam made an effort to look her way, but he knew it wasn't convincing, and the look she returned was agony.

~

Kate walked back into the house as the car squealed away up the road.

Sophie walked into the living room and beamed. "Hello, you're back early. Everything okay?" and as Kate looked up, Sophie witnessed her features crumple and a solitary tear reached slowly over the brink and let go.

Chapter 8

Later that week, Kate passed Adam in the corridor. He was talking with Mr Cobham about a patient. Furtively, she looked across and caught his eye, but no smile was lurking, hoping to be seen. The merest hint of a quirk of his lips made a fleeting attempt to cross his face but then it was gone.

At the weekend, Kate drove over to her mum's house. They had always tried to do a big shopping trip together before Christmas and it had become a bit of a tradition. She did have to carry all the bags that year, to ease her mother's load, but her mum was walking quite well by then, only having to stop more often than usual as her ankle ached if she was on it too long.

Back at the house, Kate's mum put the kettle on to make a pot of tea. "Any nice men on the horizon, Kate?" she asked.

Kate was at a loss for what to say. She really should have expected this line of questioning and been better prepared for it, but she wasn't. "I don't know, Mum."

"What sort of an answer is that? There either are or there aren't," she said.

"There is someone, but…"

Her mum was instantly attentive. "But what?"

"I don't know. It may be nothing. We had a thing, or at least I thought we had a thing. But I did something wrong because suddenly it was all over and… I don't know."

"Can't you talk to him?" her mother asked.

"Not easily. He works at the hospital and you know what the hospital grapevine is like. I don't want it spreading."

"But you liked him?" Her mum began to pour the drinks.

"Yes. I liked him a lot."

"If it's meant to be, it'll happen," her mum said. "Chin up." She took a sip of her tea and winced. "Pass me the sugar, love."

Kate reached for something else to talk about and the rest of the time passed more easily.

She arrived home and found Sophie cuddled up on the settee with Richard.

"How's it going?" Rich asked.

"My life is a sonnet of contentment," Kate said. She put her bags down on the living room floor and slumped down into a chair.

"We've got a bit of news," Sophie told her.

Kate perked up. She could only think of one thing more exciting than getting married and by the look on her face it was an anxious type of good. "You're not…?"

Sophie quickly fell into step. "Oh, God, no! No, no, no! No, Rich's granny died."

"Oh, I'm so sorry, Rich," Kate said, confused by the mixed messages they were sending.

"No, it's okay. I didn't really know her," he added quickly. "A bit of an old witch by all accounts, but it turns out she was loaded and the long and short of it is she had a flat in the centre of town. We've got to clear it out and tart it up a bit, but it's ours if we want it. It's a good start anyway, isn't it?" He turned to face Sophie and happiness radiated from the pair of them.

Kate was weary. She tried to take it in. Letting the details percolate through her mind until the penny finally dropped. "You're moving out?"

"That's okay, isn't it? I'm paid up until the end of January and I'll help you find a replacement, but…"

"You want to go."

Sophie squirmed. "Yes." She bit her lip. "It won't be for a few weeks."

What could she say? Kate didn't want her friend to go but then again she could see that it was good for the two of them, and it was inevitable really, with the pair of them getting married, so she nodded. "Oh, go on then."

Sophie rushed over and hugged her. "Who knows, it might not be long before you don't need this place anymore either."

Kate laughed. "I rather doubt that. Anyway, I'm nowhere near as brave as you like that."

"It's not brave, falling in love," Sophie told her.

Kate looked at her. "Oh yes it is," and Sophie's face filled with sympathy.

"I'll ask around at work in the morning," Sophie offered.

"Okay. And congrats you two, but I'm afraid I'm all in. Night both."

Kate went up to her room. Having spoken to her mum, she decided that she should try again to get through to Adam. She should never have put on that stupid CD. If she hadn't, he might have been able to get past the whole 'wife' thing that happened later on. She kicked herself. She wasn't to know, it was true, but she couldn't find it in her heart to blame him. She picked up her phone and with trembling fingers, she dialled. It rang. Three times it rang and then it stopped. Nothing. She checked the number and dialled again. The same. It was no use, he wasn't answering and so with a heavy heart and nagging guilt, she made her way to bed.

Everything was changing. Her best friend was getting married, her housemate was leaving and Kate's heart was breaking. She was being left behind.

~~~

"I know how she feels," Lena mumbled.

The woman stopped and looked at her. "Is that how you feel, Lena? Left behind?"

Lena did not reply, only shrugged a little and picked at a stray thread dangling from her dark grey top.

"Shall I tell you what I see?" the woman asked. "I can see such a bright spark inside you. It's just sitting there, waiting to burst into flame. You may not feel it. You might not know where it sits, but it's alive in every injury you battle and every tear that you shed when you think nobody's looking. These are the things that let us know we're alive. You're not left behind, Lena, not a bit, you're only sleeping. Think of this place as a waiting room, somewhere to settle your troubles and come to terms with what happened while you prepare to move on. Life isn't done with you yet. There is so much more to look forward to; so much to live for. Trust me. Given time you'll see how everything fits together."

Lena's head tilted and from under that dark mop of hair a frightened eye looked out and dared the woman to be lying. She let out a small breath. "So how did Kate get through it?"

"Oh, she had much more to experience, too. So much love to give. But if someone had told her that back then, she would never have believed them."

~~~

On Monday work was busy. Kate managed to put some feelers out to see if anyone was in need of a place to live. A couple of people knew someone who might be looking to find a new housemate, but nothing more optimistic was forthcoming.

Christmas was approaching and a get-together had been arranged for those who could make it. It was at The Railwayman, the closest pub to the hospital.

It was heaving by the time Kate got there. Sophie had arranged to meet her, but as yet she had not arrived. Kate looked around.

Every department seemed to be represented, from consultants down to the most junior nurse.

Kate spotted Mr Cobham. "Hello Mr C. Who's holding the fort tonight then?" she asked.

Mr Cobham pointed to his pager on his belt. "I've left Carl in charge," he said. "It was pretty quiet when I left, so he shouldn't have much trouble. Have you spotted any orthopods yet?"

Kate faltered for a second, wondering if Mr Cobham's question had any particular significance for her. "Em, nurses, yes, not doctors."

"Here comes one. Adam!" he called. "Excuse me, Kate."

Suddenly Kate's body lost all fluidity. She didn't know where to look, so she stayed where she was, pretending to be studying a picture on the wall, but really listening as they talked together behind her. After a few minutes Kate summoned up the courage to turn around and there he was, only a few feet away, chatting quite easily with those around him. He had lost his jacket and tie, but he was still as smart as ever, even with his rolled up sleeves and theatre-cap hair. Kate longed to go to him, to slide her arm through his and see him smiling down at her, but it was obvious now that these were just pipe dreams and she would have to make do with so much less. She hovered at the edge of the circle for a few minutes, while he talked to some others in the group and then she walked away and looked for someone to distract her.

Flis arrived and she walked over to Kate. They hadn't seen each other outside work for several weeks and there was plenty that Flis had to talk about, even if Kate was finding it harder to know what to say.

"Don't look now, but Peter Florin is coming this way," Flis hissed as her posture lengthened out and she started to smile.

"Hello, ladies." The famous stud of Theatre wandered across to see them. As if by magic, Flis melted into a puddle on the floor, smiling from ear to ear and giggling inanely. Kate raised an eyebrow and smiled. "Pete, to what do we owe the pleasure?"

Pete gave her a hug and kissed her on the cheek. "A little birdie tells me that you're in need of a man about the house."

"I am?" Kate asked.

"A housemate." He put his arm around her neck and grinned at her.

"Oh."

"And as it happens I'm coming to the end of my rental agreement in a month's time and I might be on the lookout for somewhere else to bunk down. What do you say, Kate? You and me? We get along all right, don't we?"

Now it was Kate's turn to be lost for words, but Flis suddenly seemed to find the power of speech. "Wow, that would work out just right, wouldn't it, Kate?"

"Timing wise, yes," she said, "but I was actually looking for another *girl* to lodge with, preferably one who can cook." No way was she intending to 'bunk down' with a guy.

"I'm not a bad chef, even if I do say so myself," he told her.

"And he can help out with all those things that you need a bloke for, like spiders."

"I can get rid of my own spiders, thank you, Flis," Kate told her.

"What about getting things down off high shelves?"

"Stepladders," Kate said.

"And protecting you if something goes wrong."

"I am also very house-trained," Pete added. "I don't leave dirty socks around the place, I put the seat down on the toilet and I'll be at work longer hours than you."

"He sounds perfect," Flis added. "And you haven't got anyone else lined up yet, have you?"

Kate was in a tight spot. Pete looked at her, grinning and daring her to turn him down.

"Let me get you a drink while you think about it," he said. He looked at what Kate had in her hand. "What is that?" he asked, a look of distaste hovering in his eyes.

"Bitter lemon," Kate said.

"Oh yes. The girl with peculiar tastes." He smiled. "How could I forget?"

As Pete strode off in the direction of the bar, Kate spotted Adam looking across at her over the top of people's heads and *he* was *not* smiling. She turned back to Flis trying to blot out his disapproval.

"What are you up to?" she asked her. "I don't want some philandering Romeo to share a house with. Who knows who I'll bump into over breakfast in the mornings? You know how often he gets someone new."

"But he's gorgeous."

"Flis, you're a lost cause."

"And then I could come over and I'd get to see him more often and he could get to know me. I never get to see him at work stuck over on Goodwood Ward. It's the back of beyond, socially speaking."

"Poor old Flis. I'll tell you what, you give me Jenny and you can have him."

"Oh, I wish," Flis said. "But you know, you may not have any other option." And Kate realised this might be true.

Pete returned with her drink.

"Pete."

"Yes? Decided to take me on already?"

"No. It's very kind of you, really, but I've got a few other people interested outside of the hospital," she fibbed, "So I'll have to get back to you on that. If that's okay?"

Pete leaned in. "Take all the time you want, Kate. I'm a very patient man." He winked and Kate laughed at him.

Adam appeared behind him slapping a hand on his shoulder.

"Pete, how are things?" His voice was pleasant, but edgy.

"Adam. Just doing a little negotiating over terms with Kate here. You know Kate, don't you?" He winked at Kate so that only she could see.

"Yes. Hello, Kate." His tone changed to gruff, like the consultant who had torn into her that day on the ward.

Pete continued. "And…? Sorry, I didn't catch your name," he said, turning to Flis.

Flis' face lit up. "Felicity. Flis."

"This is Felicity." He turned immediately back to Kate and poor Flis' face fell. "Kate was just trying to work out how quickly she could get me into her house and settled in."

Adam's jaw clenched. "I'm afraid that slot's already taken. Didn't she tell you one of the consultants' daughters needs a place to stay? I'm sure I overheard her promising to let Kate know by the end of the day." He turned to Kate. "Hasn't she rung you yet? If you like, I could drive you over right now and you could sort it all out?"

Kate looked into his dark fiery eyes. She didn't know whether to be angry with him or grateful. What on earth was he playing at? But if the choice was staying there or leaving with him, it was easy. "I'll just get my coat," she said.

Adam stood by as Kate found her coat and she kissed Flis on the cheek. "Sorry," she said. "Tell Soph, won't you?" She laid a hand on Pete's shoulder and he winked affectionately.

"Have fun," he called.

Outside, Adam took Kate by the hand and strode off round the corner of the building, dragging her briskly behind him. In the dimly lit car park he turned sharply to face her and hot sparks flew from his eyes. "What the hell do you think you're playing at flirting around with a man like that?"

Kate was furious. Who the hell was he to tell her what to do? "I beg your pardon?" she said.

"I was watching you. He's bad news, Kate, and you just let him fawn all over you."

"I did no such thing! He barely touched me," Kate snapped back.

"But he wanted to, that was obvious enough."

"We were just talking," she said. "Until *you* came along."

"And arranging for him to move in with you?" Adam was beside himself.

"And what if I was? I need a new housemate, Adam. Sophie's moving out in a matter of weeks and I can't afford to live there on my own." Her voice softened as defeat sidled in. "I need a new housemate, and sadly Pete might just be my only option."

Adam was still seething, but he let his voice gentle just a little. "He's a womaniser, Kate. He's in bed with a different woman every night."

Who did he think he was? He didn't want her, but he was going to make damned sure no-one else could have her either. "So what?" she said in a voice that challenged. "I like him."

"But you're too good for him, Kate."

"But not good enough for you!" Kate stiffened for a moment in defiance, and then wilted. Why did everything have to be so complicated? She searched his deep dark eyes for the truth before diverting her gaze to a nearby tree, unwilling for Adam to see the tears that were starting to collect in her own. The tree billowed in the night wind, buffeted around against its will. She looked back.

Suddenly Adam was upon her, grasping her face in his hands and kissing her as if it was all he had ever wanted to do, as if he couldn't live another minute without it. "I couldn't bear seeing you in there with him," he said. "It was agony." He leant his forehead against hers. "I wanted to rip his throat out for just looking at you like that."

A glimmer of hope ignited inside Kate's heart as she basked momentarily in the warmth of his attention. "Well, at least you hid that well," she said.

Her sarcasm hit true to its mark. "Okay, you've got me. I don't share my toys well."

Kate pulled back and looked up at him, her eyebrows raised in question.

"Okay, at all." He pulled her against him again.

Kate smiled as she rested her cheek against his chest, but then she thought about the words he had used. "Is that all I am to you, Adam? A toy? To be picked up and dropped when you feel like it, because that's what it feels like."

He pulled back. "No."

"I don't want to be shared, Adam, but I can't be your toy either. It's too hard. You like me one day and then you don't the next. I'm always worried whether I've said or done something I shouldn't have; never knowing if you'll even acknowledge me the following day at work."

Adam let out a deep sigh and held her at arms' length, demanding her full attention. "You could never hurt me that way, Kate. Look at me. I'm no good without you." He shook his head in disbelief. "I can't help it, I'm crazy about you."

"But-"

"No," he insisted. "Be quiet and listen to me. I know I've been a fool not spending every minute I can with you. I thought I could manage without you, Lord knows I tried, but I can't, Kate. I can't."

Kate was uneasy with why he had tried so hard to be without her and so his words did little to settle her gnawing doubt.

"Nothing makes sense when I'm not with you." His strong arms wrapped tightly around her, crushing her to his chest.

Kate could feel his heart beating against her as the smell of him teased her senses, weakening her resolve. Awareness of his body against hers made molten her sense of yearning, growing more powerful with every second that passed. She reached up and their lonely mouths met, tasting and learning. Desire built, ever more powerful and as necessary as the air that they breathed. Adam pulled back and looked at her. "Let's get out of here," he rasped and Kate just nodded.

They drove back to Adam's in silence. No words were needed now. A physical charge clung between them as the realisation sank in: They wanted each other and they both knew it. The sleek black Audi careered through the streets and back to the road where Adam lived.

In the car park they stopped, Kate's breath coming hard as she waited for what was next. Adam got out and walked around to meet her. Her heart was hammering like a speeding train as she stepped out of the car and closed the door behind her. She was terrified by the power this man held over her. No–one had ever got to her like this before and it scared her. Her body trembled at the thought of his touch. She looked up at him in the light of the street lamp and for a moment they were lost in each other's eyes and then, like two poles of a magnet, they collided.

Adam's lips quenched her thirst as he pulled her body against him. They were a rollercoaster out of control and neither of them had the will to get off. They crashed back against the side of the car, knocking Kate's elbow and setting off the alarm. Adam burst out laughing as he fumbled for the keys and then he took Kate's hand and they hurried up to the front door like a couple of teenagers trying to escape. Behind them the car blipped as it shut down, and the night wind stilled to listen.

Inside the warmth of his apartment Adam took Kate's coat and she could feel his eyes watching her as it slowly fell away from her shoulders. He kissed the side of her neck and she trembled. His hands moved around her, his palms pressed against her aching body. She turned to face him and his lips found hers. Lost without breath, the two entwined, hungrily tasting each other. Adam picked her up and carried her into the living room, their eyes locked together in anticipation. At the door to his bedroom he paused. "I want you, Katherine," he breathed hotly. "I need you," and Kate nodded. She wanted this too. She needed him. He walked into his sanctuary and put her down.

Moving quickly, he turned on a bedside lamp, lit the smaller log burner set into the bedroom wall and then more patiently, he walked back across to meet her, leaving her nerves jangling.

Adam picked up her arm and pushed back her sleeve, kissing the elbow he had just injured and it was like diamond caresses; heavenly fire branding her skin with every touch of his lips. He let his mouth trail a damp path down her forearm to her wrist before he kissed the tip of each finger in turn and she was mesmerised. Then he moved a little closer and placed her hand against his chest and let his mouth discover hers. It lingered there briefly, filling Kate's body with exquisite pleasure as her fingers roamed his body.

Adam traced a dance down her other arm to her wrist where he placed hot little kisses before taking both hands in his and holding them above her head. His hands slid down and gathered up the edge of her top, and slowly pulled it up and over her head.

He looked at her and Kate felt both exposed and decadently attractive. He kissed the freckles on the top of each shoulder, working his way along her collar bone to the base of her throat. His hands moved back down to the skirt at her hips and pressing flat against her, he pushed her skirt down and it fell to the floor and she was standing before him in her underwear.

"You take my breath away, Katherine," he whispered.

Kate moved closer to the fire, pulling him gently with her. She started to unbutton the front of his shirt, undressing him slowly, making him wait for her touch. She looked up into his worshipping eyes as inch by inch she removed the clothes from his body and let her fingers glide over the hot skin beneath. He was beautiful.

Standing opposite each other, their gazes met in awe and as hands melted with flesh and lips dared to explore, their breath sprang ragged and uneven. The fever picked up and Adam turned her around and lay her down on the bed behind them and then moved himself above her and paused. His breath was fanning Kate's sensitive neck as she ached for the feel of his body against hers. She reached up and pulled him down on top of her, and he was hers. The smell of him, the taste of him, Kate was consumed by her senses and her soul surrendered.

Later, as she lay in Adam's arms, Kate knew that more had happened there that night than a uniting of the flesh. She wondered how she had managed to live the rest of her life without ever knowing such contentment. She felt safe in Adam's arms, and certain that he wanted her every bit as much as she wanted him.

They lay for some time, saying little, with Adam's fingers stroking gently up and down Kate's back and her cheek resting softly against his chest.

I'm sorry if I'm a bit rusty," he said when at last they had breath enough to speak. "It's been a bit of a while."

Well if that was rusty, Kate was definitely willing to hang in there and see how much better things could get. She looked up at his face and then back down again to his stomach, where her fingers were toying with his warm, taut skin. She shrugged. "Maybe you just need a bit more practice?" she teased.

The next thing Kate knew she was lying on her back, pinned down, with Adam's face millimetres away from her own. She gasped and then giggled. "I was joking. I was joking," she pleaded. "It was fantastic."

Adam looked at her sternly.

"Honestly!"

His eyebrow twitched. "No. I'm pretty sure you said I needed more practice," and he lowered his face to hers and started kissing her again.

Kate playfully begged him to stop, giggling and wriggling to escape. "I've got to get a drink," she said. "I'm so thirsty. You've worn me out." She managed to slip out of bed and grabbing his shirt from the fireside, she wrapped herself in it.

Adam propped himself up on one elbow and looked at her from the bed. "I doubt that very much," he said, his eyes twinkling. He was studying her, standing there, wrapped only in one of his shirts. Her soft freckled cheeks were flushed and her eyes were sparkling in the fire light. Behind her head, a halo of light from the fireplace spread out its golden glow over her bound-up hair. He got up and walked across to the door and her eyes followed him, appreciatively. He pulled on his dressing gown and walked over and then, reaching around to the back of her hair, he pulled at the pins, releasing it and it fell around her shoulders and down

159

her back like a shining cloak. "There," he said. "Much better." And he kissed her on the lips. "My goddess of fire… then a drink it shall be."

Adam settled Kate into the living room with some still lemonade he found in the kitchen and wrapped a blanket around her shoulders while he lit the living room fire. They cuddled up on the settee and watched the flames flicker as the logs hissed and crackled beneath them.

"So what will you be doing for Christmas?" Adam asked her.

"The usual, I suppose. Christmas lunch with Mum and Dad."

"And your brothers?"

"Probably not," she told him. "Marcus is off saving the planet in some remote back-water somewhere - Indonesia, I think it is at the moment - and Jimmy has got three kids, so it's normally easier to go to him on Boxing Day, instead of dragging them all across here."

"What about the other one? You said there were three, didn't you?"

Kate was silent for a moment trying to recollect when she would have told him that. "How…?"

"At the pub out in the sticks. The Monk or something?"

She nodded remembering the meal at the inn. "Oh yes. Jacob. He died when I was twelve," she said.

"I'm sorry. I didn't-"

"No, it's fine." She pulled in a deep breath.

"How old was he when he died?"

"Five. It's no great innings, is it?"

Adam moved a lock of stray hair across her face and shook his head. "No."

"He had Downs, with lots of complications. He didn't respond well to treatment. He was always in and out of hospital and one day… it just wasn't enough. I guess he was the reason I went into nursing really. I wanted to help other people who might be going through the same thing I was. Maybe try and stop someone

160

else's brother dying."

"It must have been tough for you, losing a brother so young?"

Kate nodded. "For all of us. I was in my first year at High School. He was such a sweet little boy too, full to the brim with hugs and cuddles. Jimmy took it the hardest of the three of us, or so it seemed at the time. He retreated into his shell for months on end, while my parents fell slowly apart. Marcus threw himself into books, reading about anything and everything, fact or fiction, he just soaked it all up in a bid to escape. We all had to come to terms with it in our own different ways."

"But that's not something a twelve-year-old girl can easily understand," Adam said.

"No. I think that's maybe why I've struggled to let anyone in… until you."

Adam was quiet for a minute and then he gave a big sigh. "It isn't easy, is it?"

"How about you? You've had more than your fair share of that sort of thing, haven't you? How are you doing?"

"I'm… okay. I mean, I'm not saying that losing my mum on top of everything hasn't been a killer." He tried to smile, but not convincingly. "But I'll get there. She was a wonderful woman, you know. She always kept my feet on the ground. Made me want to be a better person: more giving and compassionate, to be more like her."

Kate turned round to face him, resting her folded arms across his chest. She took a deep breath. "And what about your dad? I've never heard you mention him."

"Oh, he's been gone a long time. Since I was little."

Adam ran his finger down the centre of Kate's face. "How is it that you are with me?" he asked. "I don't deserve someone like you. You should be happily married off to some handsome young chap by now. Someone who can give you everything you deserve, not a worn out old grump like me."

Kate looked long and hard into his adoring eyes. "But I want you."

The next morning they were woken by Adam's alarm clock. Kate opened her eyes, startled by the piercing din. She looked around and Adam rolled over towards her and smiled. "Hello, gorgeous. I'm sorry, but some of us have got to work this morning."

"I don't," she told him and rolled back away, pretending to go back to sleep.

Adam nudged her. "No, but unless you're planning on walking home later, I suggest you get up too," and Kate groaned playfully and hauled herself to her feet.

Kate was on a late that day and so Adam decided to stay behind at work to catch up on his paperwork, giving them a small time at the end of the day to be together. The following day Kate was on an early and she decided to spend the afternoon trying to find a Christmas present for Adam. But what was she to buy?

She pulled up in the car park in town and spotted Pete on the next level down buying his ticket. She called out. "Pete. I thought you were meant to be on holiday?"

"I am. Exotic, isn't it? You coming or going?"

"I'm off to town. Got to buy a Christmas present." She walked down the steps to meet him. "In fact, you couldn't help me, could you? I've got to think of something for Adam."

"About time!"

Kate smiled. "Yes, I think we're actually happening now. Thanks in no small part to you."

Pete bowed. "Always glad to be of service." He held up his ticket, ran and popped it in his car and returned. "Shall we walk?"

They went into town and Kate tried to think of what Adam might like for Christmas. "Men are so tricky to buy for," she told him. "If you were Adam, what would *you* like from a girl for Christmas?"

Pete grinned. "A see-through negligée and a thong," he replied.

Kate held a straight face. "I'm not sure that would suit him."

She grinned and he nudged her.

"I don't know. He always used to like rock music. He still seems to have a nice car and I'm pretty sure he used to like a bottle of posh wine."

"Were you two friends?" she asked.

"A long time ago."

"Not anymore?"

"No. I think he's learned to mix with a better class of person these days."

Kate looked at him, trying to decide for herself what he meant by that. "Well, I like you," she said. "I wouldn't take it too personally. He's had a lot to deal with lately."

Pete smiled. "So, what do you usually get a boyfriend for Christmas?"

"I don't. This is my first time."

He stopped. "Really? Wow. Okay then… What about something to wear and a nice bottle of wine?"

"Sounds good to me. Do you know much about wine?"

"Not a lot, but I'm sure the guys in the wine shop will be able to help us."

With an expensive bottle of red in a bag, the two walked out into the darkening sky. Rain began to patter overhead and they quickly agreed on a stop in a coffee shop to regroup.

"So, how goes it with you and your harem?" Kate asked, sipping her hot cup of tea.

Pete smiled. "A little disappointing, now you mention it."

"Oh, you poor thing."

"I think I've been fishing in the same pond for too long. Time to be moving on."

"You've only been here five minutes!" Kate said.

"Yeah, well."

"You know you could always try and stick around in the morning, get to know a girl. They may not be all as bad as you think."

"What sort of bizarre notion is that, you strange woman?" He winked.

"Well, what's stopping you? Are you afraid?" Kate was teasing him now, trying to goad him into submission, so she was quite taken aback when he actually said, 'Yes'.

Kate's phone rang and he laughed. "Saved by the bell!"

She pinned him with a stern look that told him he wasn't going to get away with it that easily and answered.

"Kate, it's Adam. I've managed to wangle a couple of hours off to whizz around town and I was wondering if you were free to meet me?"

Kate mouthed, 'It's Adam' to Pete. "Um, sure, okay. I'm in town too at the moment as it happens. Where would you like to meet?"

Kate ended the call and turned back to Pete. "If I leave the bag with you, could we meet back here in say… twenty minutes and we can carry on with this conversation then?" Pete agreed and Kate headed off to meet with Adam.

The rain had stopped and Adam smiled as she approached him, but he wasn't as open as he usually was and Kate wondered what was wrong. "You okay?" she asked.

"Absolutely. What have you been up to, then?"

"Oh, just some Christmas shopping," she told him.

Adam looked around. "Where is it?"

"Er… I haven't bought anything yet. I only just got here."

"Right. So, tell me, what am I supposed to get you for Christmas?"

Hell. What was she supposed to say to that? She could hardly reel off a list for him; she didn't want to look like a money grabber. "You don't have to get me anything. It's enough that I've got you."

Adam smiled. "Well if you're going to be no use, I'll have to love you and leave you, because I've not got a clue. Go on, hop it. I'll ring you tonight." He reached down and gave her a peck on the cheek and then he left, leaving her standing there.

Odd, Kate thought, not quite sure what the purpose of that

~

Adam stood in a shop doorway and watched as Kate picked out her phone. Light twinkled in her turquoise-blue eyes and she smiled. *He* had not done that to her, it was whoever she was calling that made her feel that way. Adam felt compelled to seek out this torture by some invisible force that lured him on. Why had she lied to him? He had to know the reason.

She walked out of view and Adam stepped into the street. He followed her back to the coffee shop, where he'd seen her before. He moved closer. He could see her now, back at the table. Back with him.

Adam was standing in the middle of the high street, oblivious to the world. Only Kate existed now, with him watching her, and Pete. Light rain started to drizzle down as he stood outside, looking in. As if pulling a splinter, he watched as Peter took her hands in his, stroking them gently and smiling. Kate looked so happy, as she playfully took his scarf from around his neck and wrapped it around under her chin.

Adam's gaze fell to the pavement. He shrugged his collar up against the wind and walked slowly back to work, where there was always something he could immerse himself in.

Memories of his mother stifling tears crept in through the pathways of his childhood mind. He was not going to suffer as she had: cheated on over and over again by a partner that claimed to be true. No, he had been foolish to hope he was enough. He had failed one woman gravely; there would be no second chances in this lifetime.

That night Kate rang him, but he couldn't bring himself to pick up. He couldn't do it. What could he say? She had turned away from him. So easily led astray. And Pete had done it. Taken away the woman that meant the most to him. Again.

The following morning Adam knew he was being far too abrupt to the patients in his clinic. He decided to forego lunch to avoid having to talk to anyone in the canteen and now, just a few metres in front of him, was Peter Florin. He was dressed in civvies and looking as happy as Kate had been, the last time she was with him.

Pete looked up, and for the first time since he'd arrived there, Adam was appalled to see that he actually had the nerve to smile at him.

"Adam. Hi. I was just dropping off some chocolates for the nurses. Have a good Christmas and don't work too hard. I'll see you in a couple of weeks."

The hell he would.

Chapter 9

Adam couldn't let it pass. It was boiling up inside him. "Done all your Christmas shopping have you?" he asked in clipped tones that had the effect of stopping Pete in his tracks. He turned around.

"God, no. Just going to rush out and do it now. You know me."

"Maybe you shouldn't spend so much time with women, then," Adam seethed.

"Chance would be a fine thing. It's been like rats leaving a sinking ship recently," he said laughing at himself.

Adam wasn't smiling. "So what were you doing in town yesterday? I'm sure I saw you in there."

Anxiety lined the corners of Pete's face and he hesitated. His eyes scanned Adam's for censure and must have guessed what was lurking there. "Ah. No. It's not what you're thinking, Adam."

"And what *am* I thinking?" He shook his head. "It had to be you, didn't it?"

"What? No!"

"You hadn't done enough damage. You had to follow me here and do it all over again."

"That's not fair. I had no idea *where* you were working when I arrived here. It was as much a shock to me as it was to you."

"Well, it's over. Are you happy now?"

Adam stormed away, with Pete calling up the corridor after

him. Time to seal the wound.

He rounded the corner in front of him and buzzed on to the ward to meet his team. "I just need five minutes," he said to his registrar. Make sure everyone's ready. I'll be right back."

Adam waded through the casualties into A&E, looking around for Kate. He asked Gloria and she directed him down to Cubicle Three. He strode in and came face to face with Kate. She was with *him*. They were obviously getting their stories straight. Pete had his back to Adam, but Kate was looking straight at him.

"Adam."

Pete turned. He went to speak, but Adam held up a hand, silencing him, never once removing his eyes from Kate.

"This is between Kate and me."

"But-"

"Leave."

Pete looked back at Kate and she nodded her agreement and so he left.

Kate started to approach. "You've got it all wrong-"

"I don't want to hear it, Kate. I just had to look you in the eye. The eyes never lie, you know? And *yours* are screaming with guilt."

She was trying her hardest to look innocent, he had to give her credit for that, but he was nobody's fool. "Happy are you?" he said. "Laughing behind my back, I bet. Swore blind you had just got into town, when all the time you'd been with him."

"No. It wasn't like that. We-"

"We? Oh? And don't think I didn't spot you running back to him afterwards as well, because I did. Do you think I'm blind, Kate? Do you think I'm that stupid?"

"Well, now you mention it, yes. You're making yourself look a complete fool right now."

She was angry. He was pleased for it. At least he wasn't going to suffer this alone. "So you don't deny it, then?"

"Yes! No! God, you've got it all wrong."

"Oh, *I've* got it all wrong? You're damned right there. I wouldn't

169

take you back now if you begged me to."

"If you keep acting like this I'm not sure I'd want to. I thought you were different. I thought you were decent."

"*You* thought I was gullible. I don't need you anymore, Kate. I'm done with you." Kate's mouth moved but no words came out. He let out a huff of derision and turned to walk away.

"So you've decided already, have you?" she said. "Without even giving me a chance to explain?" She shook her head. "Then you obviously are *not* the man I thought you were."

"I guess disappointment is something we're both going to have to live with. My love obviously wasn't enough for you. I'd say that makes us pretty even, wouldn't you?" His anger was subsiding and the cool consultant's exterior was settling back in. "Don't go neglecting your patients, Kate. We wouldn't want any of them to suffer because of your failings, would we?"

"At least I'm not withering away, still pining after a dead wife!" Kate spat and Adam felt those words like a slap across the face.

Mark Cobham marched in, shouting their names down the corridor and Adam briefly turned to make him out. He stepped between them, separating them physically. "Kate, get back to your duties, now! I'll speak with you later. Adam, come with me," and he was frog-marched through the department and into Mark's office.

Mark slammed his office door. "What the hell do you think you're doing, storming into my department and having a slanging match with one of my nurses? Have you taken leave of your senses? Now sit down, calm down and talk to me, and this better be good."

~

Kate's heart was smashing a path right through her body, her hands were shaking and she was in absolutely no state to be doing fine needlework.

Gloria appeared at her side, like a guardian angel. "Give me that," she said, taking the suture tray still dangling in Kate's hand. "I can put a stitch in your young man. I've got a drunk down there who's not in any state to remember if you give him a gob full or not. Go on." Kate thanked her and wandered shakily down to Resus Two.

She should never have said those words to him. Guilt plagued her keenly. It had been cruel. Unthinkable. But there was no chance now to take them back. It had been said. But his eyes when she'd said them. The pain. He would never forgive her and she couldn't even blame him. But he had accused her. Unfaithful? How dare he? And he hadn't even given her a chance to explain.

This was madness. She shook her head. She was through with men. She couldn't play their games. The next time a guy made a pass at her he'd better be wearing protection, because she was going to knee him in the groin and run for the hills.

She started tending to the drunken man. "I bet you're no better," she muttered to him. How could he have done this to her? And it had all seemed so perfect, so right, just the other night.

~~~

A look of understanding passed from Lena to the woman at her side and Lena pulled her hair back over one ear and lifted her head a little higher.

"Your mother was brilliant," the woman said. "She went looking for Kate later on too, as soon as her shift was over."

~~~

Gloria found Kate, frozen in thought with a blood sugar stick in her hand. "Go home, love. Shifts over," she said and gently took the stick and dirty gloves out of Kate's hands. She offered to drive Kate home, or make her a cup of tea, but Kate assured her she'd be okay and so Gloria could only watch as Kate walked slowly away.

That night Kate's heart weighed too heavy. She tried to ring Adam to apologise for what she'd said, but he wouldn't pick up. Sophie wasn't home, so she just sat in silence with her turbulent thoughts and when she could take that no longer, she got up and went to bed. Curling up with her knees under her chin, Kate finally let the tears flow. For she had believed that he loved her. He loved her and she loved him. But loving was no longer enough. Kate needed trust. A man who was faithful to her and no other, who loved her above all else and believed in their love, and in her... if such a man existed.

~

Adam eventually gave up trying to make sense of it. It was useless. Life had kicked him in the guts again and it was his own fault for trying. He walked into his living room and dropped his keys on the side. He shivered. The cold had got through to his bones, so he ran himself a hot shower and stepped in.

Heat soaked into him as he stood, torturing himself with how he had managed to ruin everything again. He had obviously taken too long to find the strength to admit that he was falling for her, Ali always being so apparent in his mind, preventing him. She had been gone almost three years now and still he found it hard to let go. He didn't blame Kate for not wanting him. He didn't want himself. His thoughts turned to Ali as his anger began to fade. He felt her presence beside him, holding onto his hand. He missed her. He leant his forehead against the steam-clouded glass of the shower door and let out a sigh.

After he had dressed, Adam rang Mark Cobham. "Mark. It's me."

"Adam. How did it go? Have you kissed and made up yet?"

"What's the use?" he said.

"Have you at least spoken to her?" Mark asked.

"There's not a lot to say."

There was a brief pause on the other end of the line. "I think you've got it all wrong, you know. Kate was a mess after you left."

"Well that could be guilt."

"And she's not one who normally shows it. I'm sure it's all just a misunderstanding."

"I don't think so," Adam said. "Besides, she's happier with Pete. I saw them. I saw her."

There was silence on the other end of the line again. "Tell you what, it's Christmas. Give her some space for a couple of days. Give yourself a bit of space too and when it's all back to normal, *then* talk to her."

"No."

"Or I can?"

"I said no, Mark. Just let it go. I want your word on this."

Mark let out a deep sigh. "I think you're making a big mistake, but… you're the boss. Are you going to be okay? Only I'm meant to be taking the kids out to-"

"No. Sure. Sorry. I'm fine. Have a nice Christmas."

"Yeah, you too, mate. I'll ring you."

Adam put the phone back in his pocket and sat there, staring at the wall.

~

Christmas Day, Kate was round at her parents', earlier than expected.

"I'm afraid we're not dressed yet," her mum began as she walked in the front door at half past eight in the morning. "We were just opening our presents in bed. I'll make us a pot of tea, shall I? Come on through."

Kate walked in, carefully circling the mistletoe hanging ominously overhead.

"Everything all right?" her mum asked.

"Yes, fine," Kate said.

173

"You're early. Still too eager to open your presents?"

Kate grinned, though it was an effort to do so. If she were honest, Kate would have told her that she was hiding out of Adam's reach, but she was also hiding from herself, so she decided to let it slide. "Something like that."

Kate's mum looked at her thoughtfully, in that uncanny way mums have when they know there's something wrong but you're not telling them.

"Mum, would it be all right if I crashed here tonight and then we could all go off to Jimmy's together tomorrow. Would that be okay?" she asked.

"Of course. You know we always love having you here. Grab the cups will you, love, and we'll go upstairs and see your dad."

Kate followed her mother upstairs, putting a brave face on for the festivities. She laughed and smiled and joined in with all the traditions of Christmas, but in the quieter times, between the laughter, she was in a sad world of her own making, where only heartache and recriminations were allowed entry and Kate was weary.

Even the Christmas meal seemed to be laughing at her. She won the wishbone from her dad and struggled to think of something worth wishing for. "You have it, Dad," she said. "Maybe you should wish for some new slippers for Mum."

Her dad laughed. "What do you think I bought her? I'm not giving her another excuse to throw herself down the stairs on me. No, you have it, Kate," and he passed it back. Kate thought. And then she silently wished she'd never said those words to Adam.

The afternoon passed easily enough with phone calls from Marcus and various uncles and aunts and, as the day went on, Kate managed to build a cocoon around herself, keeping all thoughts of Adam at the back of her mind, helped in no small part by the copious quantities of wine her dad kept offering.

That evening she brought her overnight bag in from the car and carried it up to her old room. It was still there, just as it had ever been, as it always was whenever she needed it. And for once Kate took the time to look around at her old life. Her childhood books were still lined up along the shelf beside her bed. Cuddly toys lay against her pillow and, pulling open the bedside drawer, she found her drawing pad still lying there.

She pulled it out and flipped through the drawings. Page after page of watery themes lay open before her with gradually increasing skill. Mermaids and seahorses occupied a lot of her earlier work and she was reminded of the day Adam had first seen her room.

As she had grown older, her mind had obviously turned more to the surface of the ocean and desert islands.

A page fell out and dropped to the ground and Kate picked it up and unfolded it. It was a picture cut out of a magazine and strangely it seemed to be almost identical to the picture she now had on her wall at home, even down to the flip-flops. She tucked it back inside the book and placed it carefully back into the drawer. Further back she found her old worry dolls. She picked them out and looked at them. "I might have need of you tonight," she said and placed them on the surface.

Her old diaries were lurking in the next drawer down. She took one out and began to read it. It was mortifying. Kate cringed with embarrassment at her teenage self and popped it quickly back into the drawer.

She looked around the walls. Some of her better drawings were still up there, faded a little now, but still visible and she realised how drawing had been *her* escape back then, when so much sadness had clung around.

She reached further back into the drawer and felt around for what she knew should be there. Reverently, she pulled out a small silver picture frame holding Jacob's happy smiling face and somehow her own troubles managed to take on perspective. He had had to endure so much in his little life and all Kate had was a bit of heartache. She smiled sadly and kissed him. Time to pull yourself together, she thought, and placed it on the surface next to her bed.

The next day they were off to her brother's to visit the clan. Kate left her things back at her mum's house as she planned to drive home from there later that evening. They packed their presents and set off on their journey, with her parents in the front seats listening to Kenny Rogers and Kiki Dee, while in the back seat, settled down with her MP3 player, Kate found her escape with the voice of Rihanna.

The moment they arrived a horde of squealing girls descended on them, full of Christmas excitement and sweeties. To Kate they were a breath of fresh air. She played with them all day long, dressing dolls and racing toy horses around the rooms. Pink and sparkles littered everywhere, all brought by Father Christmas. She was 'favourite aunt', who got to tuck the exhausted little princesses into bed at the end of the day and read them their bedtime story.

When the story had ended Kate walked quietly back downstairs but as she approached the bottom, she overheard her mother talking to the others about her.

"I'm worried, Jimmy. She's not herself at the moment and she won't tell me what's wrong."

"Well, she's hardly going to tell *me*. I'm her brother," Jimmy's voice piped up. "What do you think is up?"

"I don't know."

"Have you asked her?"

"Not in so many words, but I don't normally have to."

Jimmy sighed and then her dad's voice butted in. "I'm sure she'll tell us when she's good and ready."

Kate cleared her throat and rounded the corner as four guilty faces smiled back at her. "They're ready for you now, Becca," she said.

Rebecca went hastily up the stairs, past Kate, to kiss her darlings goodnight and immediately Kate's mum started searching for something to say.

"I don't think I'll need to eat anything more for a month. What about you, love?"

"No, not a bean," her dad replied. "And I should think we'd better be making tracks soon. Kate's got to get back home tonight, haven't you, sweetheart?"

"She could always kip over with us again. Would you like to do that?" her mum asked.

Kate smiled. "No, I can't, Mum. I need to get back tonight. I've got work tomorrow. Sorry."

"Right then." Her dad gently patted his wife on the leg. "Come on, old girl, we'd better make a move."

The drive back home was quiet and it was late by the time they got back to her parents' house.

"You could have asked me, Mum," Kate said as they were getting her things together ready to go. Her mum looked up. "I thought I had found someone. The man I told you about."

"You managed to talk to him?"

"I even told him about Jacob."

"But he wasn't the right one?" her mum asked.

"It seems not."

Kate's mum squeezed her hand and finding nothing that ought to be said, she just pulled her against her in an embrace.

The following morning Kate was back at work. She rang the switchboard to ask which consultant was on duty for orthopaedics that day and was informed it was Mr Barker. She let out a sigh of relief. At least now she could be pretty sure that unless he was deliberately going out of his way to create another scene in A&E, Adam was unlikely to bother her that day.

Work was busy. Cloud had settled low on the roads, keeping a frostiness in the air that crept all around. Patients were coming in with their wrists and ankles broken from falling on the slippery ground. Asthmatics were wheezing and the overindulgent of Christmas were suffering too.

Kate spotted Adam at the top of A&E at one point in the evening. He looked at her with eyes quiet and dulled, but Mr Cobham was soon on hand escorting him carefully away. *He* returned not long after and Kate was sure she caught him sighing at her, but then he too was gone.

Mr Cobham sent a message that he wanted to speak to Kate after her shift, but Kate was in no mood for a lecture, so she pretended to forget and escaped from the hospital as fast as she could.

Kate knew then that she had to speak to Anna. She rang her from a layby a short distance away from town and fortunately she was in.

"Anna, it's Kate. I know it's late and it will be even more so by the time I get to you," she said, "but I really need to talk. Can I come over?"

Anna seemed a little alarmed by Kate's request. "Er… yes, of course. I'll be here. Are you going to stay?"

"No. I can't. I'm on an early in the morning. It'll only be a quick visit, but there's something I need to talk to you about."

"Okay. I'll be waiting. I'll get the kettle on. Drive carefully."

Kate put the car back into gear and turned around, heading west, in the direction of Brisely.

As she left the lights of the city behind her, mists were closing in and she flicked on her fog lamp and peered at the road ahead, determined that she would soon be seeing things more clearly.

Winding country roads spread out before her and the radio chatted away in the background as the miles ticked steadily by.

~

Back in A&E Mark Cobham had been wandering around the department, frustrated by Kate's disappearance. He checked that everyone was happy for him to head off for the night and told the registrar to call him if he was needed. Gloria was last to finish that evening and before she left the department she handed over to the night shift and they settled in.

About twenty minutes into the shift there was a call from ambulance control that a crew was on its way in. Their passenger was a young man, he had been a driver involved in a collision with another car. There was a second ambulance following soon after with the driver of the other vehicle and they would be arriving in A&E in less than fifteen minutes. Both were in a serious condition.

Angela, the senior nurse on duty that night, put out the call for the trauma team and before long, Mr Barker, Mr Cobham and Clare Nightingale, the anaesthetist, were all arriving. Their teams hurried in and they got ready to receive the casualties.

The first ambulance arrived and the team sprang into action, stripping away the clothing, assessing for injuries and organising lines up and fluids run in. It was a young lad, possibly in his late teens and he was shouting and thrashing around; very difficult to handle. Mark took the details from the paramedics about how the crash had happened and in what condition the casualty had been found. Orders were called out for bloods and X-rays and then the consultants stood back, making sure everything was being done.

The police walked in and approached Mark. They told him about the conditions of both vehicles and then they were directed to go and get a cup of coffee as the patient was still too unstable to be seen.

The second ambulance arrived, with a female thought to be in her twenties. Unlike the first casualty, although semi-conscious at the scene, this woman was now unrousable. They brought her swiftly into the other bed of Resus One and Mark, happy with the management of the lad, moved over to work on the young woman instead.

There was blood all over her face and her injuries were most obvious down her right-hand side. The receptionist hurried down to take the second lot of details from the crew, but so far no-one had found any means of ID and so she asked the policemen to see if they could be of any help.

179

The nurses cut away the clothing on the injured woman so the doctors could locate her injuries and then cleaned the blood from her face to see where it was coming from. Mark approached and looked at the patient.

"This is a nurse's uniform," one of the nurses suddenly noticed.

Mark looked at her. "It's Kate!"

In that moment, the whole of A&E seemed to forget how to breathe and an instant later they were running around frantically, doing whatever they thought they needed to do. Mark called everyone to a stop. "Listen," he said. "I need everyone to calm down. Right now Kate is just another patient. We need to give her our best efforts, just like we do for everyone else. Now I want you all to take a deep breath and concentrate. I don't want to miss anything."

The department kicked back into action and a minute or two later he retreated into the office to make a call.

Chapter 10

Kate's body was bleeding from somewhere inside. Her scalp wound had been found and bandaged but her breathing was still less secure. Keith Hammond, the surgeon, came hurrying in and Mr Cobham brought him quickly up to speed. Clare, the anaesthetist, voiced her concerns. She wanted Kate intubated to try and correct her oxygen level and protect her airway. Her blood pressure was still dropping. Bags of fluids and blood were put up and the surgeons were anxious to get her into Theatre as soon as possible.

Adam charged into A&E rolling up his sleeves but Mr Barker headed him off.

"Adam, what the hell are you doing here? I'm on-call tonight."

"I don't care," Adam said. "This one has to be mine."

John Barker tried to block his way, standing between Adam and the patient he needed to see.

"Don't get in my way, John," Adam warned, straining to see what was going on over John's shoulder. "She needs me. I've got to get in there. You're wasting precious time."

Mark walked over, leaving the surgeon and anaesthetist to look after Kate. "I called him, John," he said.

"What the hell were you thinking?" John snapped back.

"He had a right to know."

"It's unethical. He's too close to her to be any use."

Adam was getting angry.

Mark put a hand on John's shoulder. "If it was your wife in there, John," he said calmly, "who would you trust more than yourself to save her?"

From behind the huddle of arguing consultants the anaesthetist called out. "We're losing her."

Adam charged in and got to work, calling out for immediate answers to all of his questions. Major injuries: Chest wound, right arm fractures - many, all pulses intact - open wounds to legs, suspected internal bleeding in the abdomen. Spine? Nothing obvious, but still waiting on films.

"There's no breath sounds on the right. We've got tracheal shift," she told him. "She's got a tension."

"Someone get me a cannula," Adam called out in a voice that belied his tension. "Biggest one you've got. Now!"

"Her pressure's still dropping," Clare said.

Adam plunged the needle straight through the chest wall and a rush of air hissed out allowing the chest to sink back into a symmetrical rhythm. "I need a chest drain."

Within seconds a drain pack appeared on a trolley and Adam pulled on some fresh gloves and got stuck in.

"How are her sats?" he asked as he worked at the chest wall to gain entrance.

"Up to 75 per cent and rising," she told him.

Adam's concentration never flickered. "Blood pressure?"

"Not good."

Before long he had a drain in position and had stitched it in securely.

The phone rang and Mark answered it. "Theatre's ready for you," he called.

The X-rays came through and Mark checked them. "Spines clear," he said. "Adam, you need to see these."

Adam nodded over. "Okay everyone, we need to get her up there fast. Clare. Happy?"

Clare nodded.

"Keith, you get in there and open her up and I'll join you as soon as I can. I need to have a look at her X-rays first. Come on everyone, let's move."

Adam studied the X-rays and made a plan for all the work he had to do. Focus and determination were controlling the panic as he tried hard to forget who was lying on the table in front of him. Staff swapped meaningful glances as Adam turned the department upside down in an effort to give her the best chance possible of pulling through.

When he was satisfied he knew what needed to be done, Adam grabbed his jacket and marched down the corridor, out of A&E and up to Theatre. He scrubbed up, almost shredding the skin from his fingers in his hurry to get in.

At the doorway he paused and closed his eyes. "Just let her pull through," he silently whispered. "Let this one live and I'll never ask for anything ever again."

A nurse met him inside and tied his gown. He went over to Clare. "How's she holding up?"

"She's hanging in there, just about, but they still haven't got a handle on the bleeding. We've got some more blood on its way up, but she's certainly not out of the woods yet."

He appeared at the surgeon's side. "Keith. What's happening? Why haven't you managed to stop the bleeding yet?"

"Give us a chance. We've only had her open a few minutes and there's blood everywhere in here. I'm doing my best. Now give me some space and let me do my job."

Adam took a step back, pacing around like a caged tiger, watching the minutes and seconds tick by on a clock on the bare white walls. The porter arrived with more blood from Blood Bank and Clare was happier for a while.

"Got you!" the surgeon said after what seemed to Adam like an age. He asked his registrar to use the sucker in a particular place and called for a second clamp. Swabs were packed inside the abdomen and he looked up at Clare with relief. "I think we've got it."

A short while later a kidney was delivered up into a silver dish and taken away from Theatre. The surgeon called across to Adam. "Had to take out the kidney, I'm afraid. It was too badly damaged. But fingers crossed we've got control of the bleeding now."

Adam remembered how to breathe and he slowed his pace just a little.

The packs were removed and the abdomen was closed. The surgeons finished up and handed over, and Adam approached the table, with John's registrar standing by.

There was a lot to be done and it was already past midnight. Plates and screws were fixed to all the major bones in Kate's right arm and a nail was sunk into her femur down her right thigh, found to be cracked on the X-rays. All the many wounds down her right side and scalp were painstakingly cleaned, explored and closed, as the noise from the ventilator hushed rhythmically beside them and the chest drain bubbled steadily away.

It was well past four in the morning by the time they were finished. Adam sent the registrar to bed to try and get some rest before the ward round. The nurses bandaged the wounds and cleaned up the blood spilled by the operation and when he was done, Adam binned his mask, hat and gloves and dropped his dirty gown in the laundry.

He picked up his things and met the others in recovery. Clare was busy writing in the notes, so Adam gingerly approached the trolley and looked into the barely recognisable face of the woman he loved. He touched Kate's left hand and squeezed it in his own, unable to take his eyes off the pale skin and matted hair before him.

Shortly after, Clare walked over and handed Adam the notes and he thanked her for her help.

"Is ITU ready for her?" he asked a nurse.

"Yes. They phoned through earlier, while you were in there. Which one of you is she coming in under?"

Adam thought for a moment. "You'd better put her under Keith, I think."

"Right you are. I'll make sure ITU is up to speed by the time you get out of CT."

"Thank you." He sat down beside the trolley and started to write in the notes. He completed his operation notes and then made detailed plans for her treatment and recovery.

When he'd finished, Adam rubbed his face with his hands and looked at his watch. A hot mug of coffee was handed to him and he took it gratefully.

When Clare was happy with all Kate's observations, she gave them the nod and Adam accompanied them down to the scanner to check for any signs of brain injury. Clare stayed with her inside the room, while next door, behind the glass, Adam held his breath. "Come on; come on," he muttered, willing the pictures into existence.

He looked through the partition and saw her lying there, pale and almost unrecognisable, surrounded by wires and tubing, half-obscured by bandages and only the ends of her strawberry blonde hair giving any clue to the girl who was lying beneath.

The radiologist studied the pictures. "No. There's no bleeding."

Adam visibly sagged with the relief. The final hurdle of the night was over.

"We'll be off then," Clare said.

Adam nodded. "Right, let's get her settled in," and the team headed down the long corridor to the bed waiting for her on ITU.

By the time they got there it was nearly six: the silent time, just before the wards wake up, when the last vestiges of calm linger on in the quiet corridors of the hospital sleeping.

Adam greeted Katrina, the nurse in charge, and told her what had been happening. He checked that everything that might be needed was written up on the drug chart and that the staff knew what to expect from his side of things and when they should be calling him, and then he returned to the bedside letting the anaesthetist take control.

Adam pulled up a chair and settled down by Kate's side, holding on to her hand. "Hang in there," he quietly pleaded. "I'm here with you. I'm not going anywhere." He softly stroked the back of her wrist but of course she did not respond. "Keep fighting, Katherine. You've had a bad night, but you'll get there. I know you can do this. You have to do this… for me."

But morning wasn't far around the corner and what with Kate's need for frequent observations, the nurses' drug round and the changing of the shifts, Adam had little time alone just to sit.

When the hand-over reached Kate's bed, Adam stood up, letting go of her hand and the sudden loss of security shook him. But the staff seemed happy and then Adam looked at his watch. The dawn was rising outside. He needed to freshen up before he could face another day. "I'm around, if you need anything," he said. "Anything at all."

Katrina nodded. "We'll call if we're worried. I'm sure she'll be fine now."

Adam hovered for a moment, uncertain if he had the strength to pull away.

"We'll take good care of her, Mr Elliott," Katrina said. "Dr Lambert's on his way and Mr Hammond will be round to check on her in an hour."

Adam blinked. "Yes, of course. Good."

He walked along the hospital corridors to his office and sat down with his head in his hands. He checked his watch again. There was an hour to go before clinic started, so he sat back in his chair and stared at the walls. He'd almost lost her. He may do yet and he had never let her explain. As soon as she was better he would clutch her to his heart and, if she would still have him, he'd never let her go. But it was her decision.

A noise outside his office made Adam sit up. It was five to nine. He quickly splashed some water over his face and used the deodorant he kept in his desk drawer. He tidied himself up and rang his registrar, telling him to take the ward round without him and to meet him up in clinic to report when he was done.

At lunchtime Adam stopped off at ITU to see how Kate was doing and then again around six. He could think of no reason to go home. He couldn't bring himself to leave. How could he, when the woman he loved needed him there? He tried to catch up with some paperwork, but his concentration was shot. He was weary from the anxiety, his lack of sleep and from holding on to such overwhelming regret.

Later that night, when the hospital was sleeping, Adam snuck back on to ITU. The nurses welcomed him and tried to give him some space, so he sat in the chair at the side of the bed begging Kate to fight. She meant more to him now than he could have ever imagined, but he had been there before.

Pictures of Alison rigged up to tubing riddled his thoughts as little by little he began to feel her with them. It was like a presence at his shoulder that he couldn't see. He knew it was all in his mind, it had to be, but still he believed it was true. She was with him, standing beside him, waiting and willing Kate to pull through; he felt it as surely as he felt the ground beneath his feet. She wanted it, and with a heart filled with gratitude for everything that she had once meant to him, he now knew that he was free.

Six o'clock the next morning the nurses woke him up. His neck hurt as he dragged himself back to reality. He had fallen asleep over Kate's bed and his body was complaining. Adam sat back and stretched, apologising, and he asked if anything had changed. The nurses assured him that all was well, but that he should probably tidy himself up before his team saw him that day.

Adam went back to his office, arranging to be back a couple of hours later to ask the doctors about their plans for taking her off the machines.

Dr Lambert met him as he strode eagerly on to the ward. "Ah,

Adam, come on in, we're just about to remove her tube." Adam stood behind the others around the bed as the machine was switched off and silence lingered over them. Adam began willing Kate to breathe as seconds weighed like hours and he held his breath and waited. Machines around him hissed and ticked. And then Kate spluttered into life, the tube was removed and her chest drain started to bubble again and Adam let out a sigh. 'Good girl,' he thought. 'Keep fighting'.

He asked when she would be likely to move to a general ward and, as if reacting to his voice, Kate awoke. She was startled. Her hoarse voice cried out as she thrashed what parts of her she could. The nursing staff rushed to her side. "No," she croaked looking straight through Adam as if he wasn't there. Had she seen him? Did she still hate him? Adam backed away as the nurses tried to calm her, but her panic-ridden eyes scanned the room and spotted him. Pitifully, Kate tried to yell, but nothing came out and she winced with the pain. Adam could do little but watch as *his* face echoed the pain in her own and then he knew, without a shadow of a doubt, that he had to walk away.

Katrina came out a minute or two later and found him leant up against a wall. She looked at him. "You know it's just disorientation," she told him kindly. "She had quite a bump on the head remember. And then there's the anaesthetic and the sedation." She touched his arm for reassurance and Adam looked at her for a moment and nodded and she walked back inside.

The nurses in clinic said nothing about the state of their consultant that morning, but he was well aware of the looks passing between them. He closed the door and sat down in his room and a nurse knocked and walked in.

"Just give me a few minutes," he said, sharper than he should have, and the nurse backed away. Adam hung his head in his hands and leaned on his elbows over the battered old desk. He looked up as he remembered something he had to do. Reaching out he picked up the phone. "John? It's Adam."

"Adam. How did it go?"

"Okay. She's on ITU at the moment, but hopefully she'll be going to a ward later today. I've put her under Keith. She's just started coming round."

"What about her head?"

"CT was clear and they've just taken her tube out, so she's off the vent now too."

"I'm glad. So what was it that was bleeding?"

"Her kidney. Keith had to remove it. Now I've fixed her radius, ulna, humerus and femur on the right side and her chest drain is working well. I wondered if you'd do me a favour and look after her? I mean, I'll keep an eye on her of course, but… I think things may go a bit more smoothly if she doesn't know I'm involved."

"You want me to be the front man?"

"Yes. If you put it like that?"

"Oh, what tangled webs we weave."

Adam was silent.

"Go on then. If you think it will help," Mr Barker offered. "On ITU, you said?"

"Thanks, John. I owe you one."

"A bottle of Laphroigh should just about cover it. Did you manage to get any sleep?"

"No."

"Bad luck. Did you hear what happened to the lad?"

Adam had completely forgotten about the other casualty involved. "No. I…"

"I had to airlift him to the neurosurgeons. Nasty bleed."

"What happened? Do you know?" Adam asked.

"Sorry. I think Mark was speaking to the police after you went up to Theatre, though. I'm afraid I was too busy with the boy."

"I'll talk to Mark. Thanks, John."

"No problem."

Adam sat back in his chair and rubbed his face with his hands.

He rolled his head around and rubbed his sore neck.

Half way through clinic Adam got a call back. "She's awake, Adam, and doing fine, considering everything she's been through, just a bit groggy. We'll keep a close eye on her; I just thought you'd like to know she's off to Aintree Ward this afternoon. She's heading in the right direction."

Adam thanked him and carried on with his work, trying hard to be sympathetic to all the relatively minor ailments he had to see.

At lunch time, Adam went looking for Mark. He found him in the doctor's mess, chatting with one of the medics. Mark looked up.

"Adam. How is she?" he asked.

Adam nodded a few times. "Okay."

He got up. "Sit down. You look fit to drop. Let me grab you something to eat."

Mark Cobham came back soon after carrying a tray with pie and chips, a cup of coffee and an apple balanced on top. "Get your chops around that lot," he told him, plonking the tray down in Adam's lap.

Adam looked at the tray and then back up at his friend. "I'm really not that hungry," he said.

"Don't be a bloody fool, man. You've got to eat. When was the last time you had a decent meal? Too long, I'd wager."

Adam looked back at the tray and picking up the knife and fork, reluctantly, he tucked in.

"Mark, John said you might know what happened with Kate."

"What, about the crash, you mean?"

Adam took a mouthful and nodded.

"You really want to know? It was just your typical winter's night crash, apparently," he said. "Kate was driving out on the back road. Lord knows why at that time of night? She'd only finished at nine and she was down for an early the next morning. And it was a hell of a night too. Still, it seems she was turning right towards Brisely when the lad in the other car came steaming round the corner far too fast. He couldn't brake in time and went slap bang into the side of her.

"They found her car on its top in the ditch by the side of the road. The lad's car – if it *was* his car, of course - was spun around, facing the other way. His bloods came back well over the limit, so…"

Adam's jaw stopped chewing.

"But Kate's okay, Adam. You said so yourself."

Adam slowly started chewing again. He swallowed.

"You look awful. Are you sure you're okay? This has got to be… horrendous for you." They exchanged looks.

Adam took a swig of coffee. "Yes. I'll be fine. Do me a favour. I know you'll go up and see her some time. Don't tell her I was involved, will you?"

"Why ever not?"

"I just think she'd rather not know. John's agreed to babysit her for me. It's just easier this way."

Mark shook his head. "For who? I think you're wrong and I won't lie to her, Adam, but if you want, I'll try and avoid mentioning your name."

"I'd be obliged."

"The main thing is she's all right though, or at least she's going to be, right?"

After work that evening Adam walked up to Aintree Ward and quietly slipped inside, making sure to stand out of view. He asked the nurse how Kate was doing and then crept up to the window of her room and peeped inside. She was sleeping. Adam watched as her rhythmic breathing forced bubbles into her chest drain and he peered around at the lines bringing her pain relief and fluids. She looked comfortable. A nurse approached him asking if he wanted to go in. Adam thanked her and said he was happy to let her sleep for now, but he would look back in on her later that evening and he left the ward as quietly as he'd arrived.

It was the following morning before the police located Kate's phone, flung clear at the site of the crash. Her identity had been gathered from the staff at the hospital. They had left messages for her parents on her father's mobile phone and someone had gone round to their house, but with no luck. It was only after finding a message from her mum and dad on Kate's phone that they managed to track them down.

Kate woke up to find her mum and dad at her bedside. When she saw them, she burst into tears. The relief of seeing them after such an ordeal was overwhelming. Her mother held her gently.

"I'm so sorry we weren't here when you came in, my darling. We were staying with your Auntie Ann. We should have been back last night, but it got so late, and with all the drinks, the chatting and mince pies, she asked us to stay over. We didn't realise that your Dad had forgotten his mobile, either," her mum said, her eyes full of worry and concern.

Kate sniffled. It was too uncomfortable to cry for long. Her chest felt like a knife was sawing through it and her body ached all over. She reached up with her good hand to touch her head, but her mother caught it first.

"It's bandaged, my love. Try not to touch it," she said.

Kate rested her arm back down again. "What happened?" she asked, even though she felt she must have been told this several times before. Everything was still a bit hazy for her.

"You were hit by another car out on the Brisely road. What on earth were you doing driving all the way out there at that time of night?" her mum asked.

"Going to see Anna, I think," she told her.

Her dad joined in, his voice gentle. "At ten o'clock at night? What was so important that you would drive at night at the end of a long shift?"

Kate looked at her mum and her forehead began to quiver.

"Oh, no. It doesn't matter now. You just concentrate on getting better," her mum said. "The nurse told us how... To think we might have lost you." And her eyes began to fill with tears.

Kate's dad placed his hands on either side of his wife's shoulders. "But she's going to be all right now. Aren't you, love?"

To be honest, Kate felt pretty dreadful, but not quite at death's door yet. "I'll be fine," she said, wearily. "A bit bionic, by all accounts. I might set off the odd security alarm at the airport, but I'm not done for yet."

"Quite right too," her dad said.

"How are you feeling?" her mum asked. "Are you in a lot of pain?"

Kate tried to move and regretted it. Her face twisted.

"I'll get the nurse."

Kate was a little surprised that Adam had not been up to see her. Even though they hadn't parted on great terms, after such a nasty crash, she would have hoped that he'd have at least called in to make sure she was okay. Nurses and doctors from half the hospital had been up to check on her, but from Adam there had been nothing. In fact, she felt it was a relief she had been put on the surgical ward instead of orthopaedics. How had she been so wrong about him? Her choices in men hadn't been great so far in life, but this one certainly took the biscuit.

Gloria had popped in at one point, but Kate was a little too drowsy to remember much. *She* had assumed *Adam* had been treating her and Kate had almost laughed, except that it wasn't funny.

When visiting time ended Kate was actually relieved. It had been wonderful to have her mum and dad back again, but she was hurting and exhausted. Up until then Kate had never realised just how exhausting it could be, being injured. All she had to do was lie in bed all day long and get better and yet she could hardly open her eyes. She longed to be better and she longed to go home.

Adam walked onto the ward in the early hours of the morning. He said hello to the nurses and asked how Kate had been. "What about her parents?" he asked.

"They've been in, at last, poor things. They were staying with family. They only found out when they got home."

"But she's seen them?"

"Yes."

"I'll just pop my head round the door," he told her.

"Okay."

Adam slipped into Kate's room and stood at the foot of the bed and stared at her, tears springing to his eyes. She stirred in her sleep and Adam stilled. Kate tried to shift in all her bandages and her discomfort showed on her face. He stepped closer and carefully soothed her hair away from her lips. Very gently, he held on to her hand, speaking softly to her as she tried to settle. "I love you, Kate," he said. "I love you so much it hurts. You're all that matters to me. I need you to know that. That, and I'm sorry." He looked at her lovely long hair all bloody and matted and he leaned down and kissed the back of her hand.

Kate turned her head and appeared to open her eyes. Adam froze, preparing to make a swift exit, but she looked right through him, smiled and closed her eyes again. Adam lifted her hand to his cheek and silently prayed to God to keep her safe. Then he gently laid it back down again and walked away.

~

The following day Kate had more aches and pains than the one before, but the wounds from her injuries and operations were doing well. The physio came in to see her to discuss her breathing and limb movements. Kate felt useless. The reality of her predicament was sinking in and she was beginning to feel low and tearful, managing to put a brave face on when anyone came in to see her.

Mark Cobham dropped by at lunchtime with a huge bunch of flowers. "You'd better get well soon," he said. "You made an awful mess of my department. And you know we're going to leave it for you to clean up when you get back."

At this Kate managed a small laugh as she held on to her chest. "How are they treating you up here?"

"I have to keep an eye on them," she told him, "but they're not too bad."

"Glad you're keeping them on their toes, Kate. Gloria said to tell you she'll be up later on. She's made you a cake."

"I'm not sure if I'm up to eating cake just yet," Kate said, smiling weakly.

He chuckled. "I did try to warn her. But you know what she's like?" he said with a wink.

Kate tried hard to stifle a yawn that silently crept up on her, but Mr Cobham noticed and stood up.

"I'll let you get some rest," he said. "I'll pop by in a couple of days and see how you're doing."

"Thank you," she said. "And thank you for the flowers; they're beautiful."

Kate watched as Mark Cobham walked back up the ward and thought for a moment that she saw Adam, but she blinked and looked back and he was gone.

Her mum and dad were back at visiting time and Anna had driven over with a bouquet and a cuddly toy and was waiting outside to come in. It was a close call to say which one of them started crying first.

"Anna, I'm so sorry-"

"What are you sorry about? I should have known you wouldn't just change your mind without telling me. I feel awful. I should have checked earlier."

"It wouldn't have made any difference. Anyway, you're here now."

Anna sat down and held on to Kate's good hand.

"What was it you needed to talk to me about, Kate? It's been driving me mad not knowing."

Kate rested her head back. "It doesn't matter now."

"The hell it doesn't. You phone me up late at night wanting to drive all the way over to my place to talk to me about something just for an hour. It's got to be pretty bloomin' important for that."

"I thought it was," Kate said in her defence.

"And?"

She shrugged and her mum and dad left them alone to talk.

"Was it about Adam?"

Kate nodded sadly.

"I bet all this has given him something to think about, hasn't it?" she said pointing to all Kate's injuries.

"You'd think so, wouldn't you?" she said.

"You mean…?"

"I've not seen hide nor hair of him since it happened," Kate told her, attempting to mask the pain in her voice.

Anna shook her head. "You can't mend everyone, Kate," she said. "However much you might want to," and she smiled sympathetically. "Some people just refuse to be helped."

Kate raised a solitary eyebrow. "I guess I should be grateful he wasn't on call the night I was brought in," she said.

~

Adam was awoken at 7.30am by a call from switchboard. He lifted his head from the wing of his chair and croaked out his thanks down the telephone. He yawned and stretched and looked at his watch. Shrugging out of his old, stained shirt he threw it in the bin and picked up the new shirt his secretary had been good enough to pop out and buy for him the day before.

Adam walked down the quiet corridor to the hospital canteen and bought himself some breakfast. He was due back on call that evening and had been unable to sleep in more than short bursts since the night Kate had been brought in. Only time would tell how much sleep he would get over the weekend.

He finished his cereal and made his way back up the hospital, stopping off at Aintree Ward to check with the staff before meeting his team.

Chapter 11

Kate's pain was more bearable. Her chest and abdominal drains had been removed and she no longer had a catheter. She was now free to move around the bed and get up a little when she could. The bandages on her head had gone and they had been lightened on her limbs. Instead of a drip and pump for pain relief, she was able to take tablets and try a little more with her meals. The down side of this was that although she felt more comfortable at rest, moving her body was exhausting and it hurt, and the physios weren't big on sympathy.

It occurred to Kate then that it must be the forgotten time between Christmas and New Year and Adam may of course know nothing of her accident as he might be on holiday. She tried hard to recall any mention of his plans over Christmas, but could think of none. His absence was preoccupying her more than she wanted, as there was little else to do but think, laid up in a hospital bed, especially when you weren't very good at crosswords.

John Barker stopped by to check on her and she asked him which of them had closed the wounds on her leg, as she had been very impressed with the stitching. He hesitated and then made a vague comment about how many wounds there had been and not being able to remember exactly who had done what.

Sophie came to visit, mortified at having been away when it all happened, but brought with her some good news. She had heard about a doctor coming to join the hospital at the end of January who needed a place to live. She had been given their number and had already made contact.

"So it's all sorted," she told her. "How are you doing?"

"I'm much more comfortable now," Kate told her. "All my tubes are out, but it kills to get up and go for a wee."

Sophie laughed.

"I pleaded with them not to take my catheter away, but they wouldn't have it. They're making me use a commode."

Sophie pulled a face. "I think I'd put up with the pain and get myself to the toilet," she said.

"I know," Kate told her. "But it kills just to get there and sit down. Let alone to get back to bed again."

"Well, you need more pain relief then, you silly cow. What do you think you're doing suffering in silence? Let me get one of them in here to sort you out."

"No. I'm all right. Don't make a fuss, please. I've got to try. And if I don't feel the pain then I won't know when I'm making things worse, will I?"

Sophie shook her head. "Are you sure your CT scan came back okay?"

"Don't be so rude!" Kate scolded but then she smiled.

When the physios came in, they got Kate up and out of bed. She began to shuffle, but suddenly her body rocked with pain as she coughed and almost collapsed. A quick thinking nurse grabbed a wheelchair and whisked Kate back into bed. They ran some obs and called a doctor to come and see her.

The doctor examined Kate and found crackles in the right side of her lungs. Her obs showed a raised temperature and her pulse was racing. He looked at her notes and drug chart and asked Kate why she hadn't been asking for pain relief when she'd needed it, because it was obviously stopping her from doing her breathing exercises. Kate realised he was irritated by her stupidity and she couldn't exactly blame him.

She held her chest and coughed and then paled with the pain again. The doctor reviewed her charts and altered the doses accordingly and with a last lecture about the importance of looking after herself and being sensible, he marched back out to continue his work.

Kate felt awful. It was like having a bad dose of flu while someone repeatedly stabbed you in the chest with a knife. She was just resting her head back on the pillows when a porter arrived to take her down to X-ray.

An hour later she was back in her bed with the pain killers starting to kick in and another course of antibiotics added to the list. She had little energy for visitors that day and apart from her mum and dad, Kate asked to be left alone to sleep.

A while later she became aware of somebody moving around her room. She opened her eyes. Pete had snuck in and was looking guilty at having woken her.

"I'm sorry," he said. I had to make sure you were okay. I only just heard you were in here. I'm so sorry. I feel awful now."

"*You* feel awful?" Kate teased. "I think I have got dibs on that one."

"You know what I mean," he scolded. "I bumped into one of the theatre nurses in town. She told me what happened."

Kate reached to take a sip of her water. "How did you get past my guards?" she asked.

"Stealth and cunning. Have you had a chance to talk to Adam?" he asked, a more serious expression settling on his face.

Kate shook her head, but couldn't bring herself to speak.

"Have you tried?"

She made a frustrated gesture to indicate she was laid up in bed. "I think it's *his* move, don't you?" she said, as tears began to spring to her eyes. "Although I'm not even sure I *want* to speak to him now."

"He's a good guy," Pete said. "He's been through a lot."

"I know. I told you that. Why are you so good to him, when he seems determined to hate you?" Kate asked.

"Adam and I go back a long way. He wasn't always so prickly. It's partly my fault that he is."

"Why? What happened?" she asked.

There was a long pause. "I was the one driving the night of the crash," he said, and suddenly it all made sense. The butterfly effect. So many more people had been affected by Ali's death than just Adam. Sympathy overwhelmed her as every interaction she had witnessed between the two of them played out again in her mind, with meaning.

"He blames you, doesn't he?"

Pete just shook his head. "I don't know. Perhaps. Maybe there *was* something I could have done differently?" His breath hitched as he was forced to remember the terrible night and then he straightened. "I'm sorry I messed it all up for the two of you."

"It's not your fault," Kate said as her chin began to quiver. Her fragile emotions overtook her and Pete wrapped her in his arms and held her while she sobbed.

~

John Barker ran into Adam in the corridor late on Saturday afternoon and looked at him. "Adam, you look fit to drop," he said. "You're in no condition to take on the rest of the weekend. Finish off this afternoon and get yourself home to bed. I'll cover for you tonight. You can take over in the morning again when you've had a decent night's sleep."

"No, it's fine, John. I have to be here, besides, it's New Year's Eve; you don't want to be hanging around here."

"She's on the mend, Adam. Go home," he said. "I don't mind, honestly. The mother-in-law's up. Why do you think I'm in here in the first place? You'll be doing me a favour. Come on. You know I'll call you if anything drastic happens. I'm not taking no for an answer."

Adam looked at him.

"You're really not safe like this," John added.

"Okay. Thanks. I owe you one."

"You owe me two now," he reminded him. "I haven't seen that bottle of whisky you promised me last time yet."

Adam smiled and nodded. "Right."

He managed to get through the rest of his work soon enough and then quickly popped up to Aintree Ward to make sure Kate was okay before knocking off.

Buzzed onto the ward, Adam made a bee-line for the nurses' desk, but his gaze caught sight of Peter just coming out of Kate's room. Pete spotted him. He went to walk away, but must have thought better of it, because he turned and walked straight toward Adam, and Adam braced for a battle he had no energy to fight.

"Adam."

Adam looked at him through weary eyes.

"I know you'd rather not speak to me. I understand that. But I can't stand by and let you punish Kate for something she didn't do."

Adam stiffened.

"She loves you, Adam. She doesn't want me. She never has. Go and talk to her. Listen. You two would be so good together. Please, Adam. Do it for her."

Adam made no move to thank him. He made no gesture to show that he would and so Pete walked off, leaving Adam to wallow in confusion as he made his way slowly home.

How could he know what to think? Kate hadn't denied having feelings for Pete, but had she ever admitted it? Was this true? That he had jumped the gun and pushed her away, rebuilding his walls as fast as he could when nothing had even happened between her and Florin? Had he been so blinded by his past? This couldn't be happening. Pete had certainly had the look of honesty about him. He had faced him, openly, with nothing to gain. Was it possible that this time he *himself* would have to be the one to take the blame?

He poured a large brandy and downed it. He needed to sleep. Things would look clearer in the morning.

Sunday morning Adam was feeling much more human. He put on fresh clothes, ate a good breakfast and drove back into work. He rang John to see if there was anything he needed to know from the night before, and then called the team together for a quick ward round of the new admissions.

A little later, Adam walked up to Aintree Ward to check in. He knew he had to speak to Kate. He should have done it days ago. He should have let her explain. Hell, he should have trusted her in the first place. He would go to her and tell her he was sorry. Beg her to forgive him and make amends.

He walked on to the ward and pulled out Kate's notes. He read the entry from the previous day and was horrified to find she had collapsed with a chest infection and he hadn't known. Peter, he thought. With the wind being so knocked out of his sails as he'd arrived, he had completely forgotten to check on her. She had been suffering.

He searched for someone to spear with his ire, but neither of the senior nurses on that morning had been on duty the day before. He paged the surgical houseman and told him to meet him on Aintree Ward and then paced up and down until he arrived, ten minutes later.

~

Kate was awoken by the sound of raised voices on the ward. She couldn't see anything, but rapidly came to realise that one of the voices was Adam's. He was grilling someone, just outside her room, about why they hadn't made sure she was comfortable. Kate had heard him like this before and slunk further under her sheets.

Suddenly he stormed in and grabbed her charts, storming

straight back out again. Kate listened to what was being said. He was ranting at the other doctor about inadequate pain relief, about neglecting her and the need for more intensive observations. Kate felt the doctor's pain. She knew he was already wishing he hadn't bothered getting out of bed that day.

A nurse came hurrying in with a machine to measure the oxygen in Kate's blood. He ran a set of obs and Kate noticed her oxygen level was low, but nothing to get het-up about. The nurse smiled and then hurried back outside to report.

A minute or two later he was back in, hooking Kate up to the oxygen on the wall. He fitted her with nasal specs and then handed her a couple of tablets.

"Am I in trouble?" Kate asked quietly.

"No, I don't think so, but I'm glad I'm not Dr Danby right now," he said and walked back out.

Kate felt incredibly uncomfortable. She knew she was really the one to blame for her chest getting infected. She had tried to be stoical and not make a fuss, but she'd only ended up doing more harm than good. But as much as she had been spoiling for a fight with Adam, she really did not have it in her that day.

Adam walked in. He stood in the doorway and scowled at her. Kate had only had bed baths and washes since her arrival in A&E the week before. She realised she must have looked a wreck and *this* was the first time Adam had seen her. She dropped her gaze to her fingers, watching them twist together on top of the sheet.

"Why didn't you ask for pain relief?" he asked abruptly.

A timid voice, no more than a whisper, escaped Kate's lips. "I don't know," she said.

Adam stared at her. She could feel his eyes assessing her, but dared not meet his gaze. "You've got to look after yourself, Kate," he said. "Your body's been through a huge ordeal. It's going to take a lot of work on your part to put it right. This is not the time to be stubborn and insist on doing things your way."

"Please don't," she asked him. "I've already had it in the neck from the houseman and I'm really not up to a fight today."

"I don't want to fight with you, Kate. I'm just concerned."

"Concerned?" Kate couldn't believe her ears. "So concerned that you waited a week before even coming to see me? And then you come storming in here, with your bullish manner and think you can tell everyone what to do. Well I seem to have managed pretty well without you so far." She coughed with the exertion of raising her voice, the pain causing her to stop in her tracks and blanch.

Adam took a step closer, but she held out a hand to stop him. He glared at her as she struggled to regain her breath. His forehead furrowed and his lips pursed. "I'm sorry," he said.

"It's too late for sorry," she snapped.

Adam's features seemed to lose their strength. His voice was defeated as he stood in silence for a moment and then started to speak. "Well, you won't have to put up with me much longer," he said. "I'm on holiday from tomorrow, so you only have to get through the rest of the day and I'll be out of your hair."

"Good," Kate said, as brusquely as she could manage.

Adam looked at her sadly, unsettling her a little. He opened his mouth to say something more, but seemed to think better of it and closed it again and walked out.

Still reeling from the confrontation, Kate held her breath, in case he came back in, but he didn't. Slowly, she let it out and a tear fell away from the corner of her eye.

She didn't see Adam again after that and although it had been traumatic seeing him that way, at least now Kate believed she had faced up to her demons. She had *yearned* for him just to sweep in there and hold her in his arms, telling her how wrong he had been and how much he loved her. And the more she thought about that, the more she realised the significance of the loss she had suffered, and how much she must have loved him.

~

Adam did not return until the early hours of Monday morning, just before he went off duty. He walked quietly onto the ward and looked around for a nurse. He asked if Kate was sleeping and how she'd been and then carefully crept inside her room.

Kate was lying there, just the same, with the dim light on over her head, but peaceful again now. He spotted the earphones still hanging from her ears and traced them back to the edge of her pillow. Easing it up gently, he found her little MP3 player tucked up underneath, still playing away merrily. He looked at the screen to see what was playing – Rihanna, of course - and then he turned it off and ever so carefully, lifted the earpieces out of her ears and put them down on the side. He looked at her and his heart plunged down to new depths. "Happy New Year, Katherine," he whispered and then he kissed her softly on the top of her head and left.

~

With the increase in pain relief and the infection she was battling, Kate remained on the sleepy side over the next few days. But on Wednesday she was starting to mend and Mark Cobham came back up to see her. Her arm and leg were definitely much better and her head had almost stopped pounding. Getting up and about was still slow, but more manageable. It was her chest that was the worst of it now. Kate hated to cough, because of the pain it caused her but her fever was down and she was brighter in herself.

Mark sat down next to her bed. "How are you doing?" he asked.

Kate smiled brightly. "Better, thank you."

"You've been through the mill a bit, I hear," he said and Kate let out a soft chuckle.

"Well, a few days ago I would have gladly taken a dose of something highly toxic, but I'm not too bad today."

"Has Adam been up?"

Kate was a little taken aback. How did he know she had been on first name terms with Adam? Then she remembered their fight in the middle of A&E. "Er… Yes." She grimaced.

"And?"

Kate looked at him, reluctant to share any further.

"Look I know you two were close, Kate. You can't expect me not to have gathered that much at least. What happened?" he asked.

Kate was struggling to see how any of this was his business. "He came storming in here shouting at all and sundry," she said.

Mark looked at her sternly.

Kate frowned. "What? He was being a thug."

He shook his head. "You have no idea what that man's been through this past week, have you?"

Kate asked him, but even as the words were leaving her mouth, an ominous fear was creeping across her.

Mark Cobham frowned. "You did know his wife was killed in a car crash?" he said.

With everything that had happened, Kate had completely forgotten. "Shit."

"Yes, well. Now you see why it has been so hard for him?"

"He could have still come in to see me." Her voice was feeble now and she heard it. How could she have forgotten? "Could you tell him I'm sorry?"

"Absolutely not. The man would kill me if he knew I had been up here talking about him and I wouldn't want to get on the wrong side of Adam when he's angry. He's almost as big a force to be reckoned with as you are in that respect. Besides, he's in Scotland, fishing with an old friend at the moment. I'm sure he'll get in touch when he comes home. You're both great, you are, infuriatingly rubbish at communication; how on earth either of you ever made it into this game I have no idea, but…" He winked at Kate's shocked expression. "You'll get there," he said. He smiled at her then, patted the back of her hand and left her alone to think.

Kate knew she needed time to heal. If she was going to face what was coming with Adam, she was going to have to be in a bit better shape to do so or at least have had a proper shower before facing him again. But what good could come of it? She had to apologise, but would it really make a difference? Would there be a future for the two of them after all that had gone before? Or was he just getting her hopes up again for no reason?

The following week, Kate was allowed home, home to her parents' house anyway. She was facing six weeks off work at least, being looked after by her mother.

In the first week Kate was grateful for the haven of her parents' home. By the second, she was feeling a lot brighter, although the frustration of not being able to do things for herself was beginning to take its toll and in the third week, Sophie brought Collette over, the doctor who had taken over at the house.

Kate was looking more respectable by then. Her hair had been washed several times since arriving home and her stitches were out. She had physio appointments every week and she was absolutely determined to be diligent.

Another week passed and Kate finally got to go home. She sat down with Collette on her first evening back and they found out about each other and what they liked to do. Kate asked Collette how she had heard about their place and Collette mentioned a word that sent pain through Kate's heart: Elliott. Kate immediately excused herself, pulled out her phone and rang Sophie.

"Rich, I know it's late, but is Soph there?" she asked.

"No, I'm afraid she's not back yet," he told her. "She shouldn't be long though. Is anything wrong?"

"No," Kate said. "I just needed to ask her about how she found out about Collette." Kate held up a soothing hand to silence her suddenly agitated housemate.

Rich was stalling. "I think you need to talk to Soph about that."

Kate realised what this meant. "Was it Adam?"

Rich cleared his throat. "Look, she thought it was for the best,

210

Kate. She really did."

After a short while reassuring Rich that she wasn't angry with Sophie, Kate finished the call and settled again to continue chatting with a now very uncomfortable Collette.

Kate's orthopaedic out-patient appointment arrived. It was the day she had been waiting for and dreading in equal measure. She would have to go back into the hospital and risk bumping into Adam, but hopefully Mr Barker would give her the all clear and she could finally get back to work. She had heard nothing from Adam the whole time she had been off and she was increasingly suspicious that she only had herself to blame. If he had only shown some level of concern for her after the accident. Just a hug or a bunch of flowers. Some sort of sign that he cared.

Kate felt nervous as she got dressed that morning. She was looking forward to being able to drive again, once she bought a new car that was. The surgeons had already discharged her, but she had been with her mother that time and had been lucky enough to get in and out quickly. Today's appointment was near the end of the day. Kate had decided to take this one alone and now she had almost seven hours to be nervous in and then it was likely to be running late and she'd have to wait around even longer to get the deed done.

She cleaned the house, as best she could. By the time the afternoon arrived Kate's whole body was aching. She sat down and held out her hands. Her fingers were shaking. There were still two hours to go and Kate was already a nervous wreck. What if she saw him? What should she say? She was tormented by the possibility of seeing him ignore her, or worse, being polite. But then not seeing him might be more shattering still. And according to Mr Cobham, she had been far too tough on him. They needed to talk, yes... maybe; Kate was very afraid her courage might desert her there.

The clock on the kitchen wall ticked slower and slower. She

toyed with the idea of ringing to cancel but she needed to be discharged to get back to work.

Walking steadily up to the end of her road, Kate caught the bus into town and got off at the hospital. She looked up at it. It was like coming home. Kate had missed being there and she hadn't even realised it. She checked her watch. Half an hour to go.

Wandering over to A&E, Kate peered inside, hoping to be spotted, but the staff were too busy to notice her and so she headed over to Outpatients.

A lady appeared at the reception desk and Kate checked in.

"Katherine Heath? Mr Elliott's clinic. Down the corridor and on your right. Just hand this slip to the nurse when you get there and wait to be called."

Kate's blood ran cold. "No. I'm meant to be seeing Mr Barker," she said. "It says so on my card. There, see?"

The lady examined her records. "Miss Katherine Heath, Hospital number: 1083466?"

"Yes."

"Mr Elliott's clinic 4.25pm."

Kate fell silent. Of course. She had to face him. He had made it so. Kate took the slip and quietly said thank you and then walked slowly down to the clinic to await her fate.

Three quarters of an hour passed as she sat there with nurses and doctors calling patients all around her, sending them off for X-rays or for casts to be removed. Kate found herself summoned to the X-ray department for what felt like half her body to be checked and then she got dressed again and walked back round to clinic. She saw the back of Adam at one point as he walked over to see a patient in the plaster room, but he didn't notice her.

By the time Kate's name was finally called, her nerves were frayed and she felt sick to her stomach. Her palms were cold and sweating and her mouth was dry. She stood up, took a deep breath and walked in.

Chapter 12

Kate walked inside and stood in the doorway. Adam was sitting there, his face lined in concentration, a computer screen in front of him and a medical student by his side.

"Take a seat," he said, without looking up and Kate walked over to the desk and sat on the plastic chair beside it.

He was studying her films, scanning each one and Kate watched him closely as he did so. His hair looked freshly cut. His suit was smart and clean, if a little crumpled in places and his eyes were grey.

He turned and looked at her, his elbows on the desk and his hands folded in front of his chin.

"Mr Barker sends his apologies," he said, "but he needed to free up a few clinic spaces and he hoped, being staff, you would understand if I reviewed you for discharge instead of him."

Oh, Kate understood. She knew she had no say in the matter. She just had to grin and bear it until it was over. Her only consolation was the awareness that Adam seemed to be enjoying this even less than she. Kate nodded.

Adam looked across at the student and beckoned him over to look at the screen and then turned to speak to Kate. "If I might just...?"

Kate nodded.

"This lady came in to A&E from an RTA with a chest injury,

tension pneumothorax, fractured neck of femur, ruptured kidney, comminuted fractures of both radius and ulna and a fractured humerus." The student seemed impressed. Adam pointed to the X-rays on the screen. "Here you can see how we managed her injuries." He clicked on the mouse button. "And here. And here. And... here. But which injury was the most life threatening?"

The student paled. "Em..."

Adam gave him a minute.

"The kidney?"

"Close. Kate?"

Kate looked across at the student and then back to Adam, uneasily. "The tension pneumothorax."

"Correct." He turned to his student. "Kate here is an experienced A&E nurse." He turned back to look at her. "If she'd have been conscious when she was admitted she probably would have been telling us all exactly what to do."

Kate smiled awkwardly, unsure if this was his idea of fun, or if he was actually having a dig at her. His face was giving nothing away.

"So, how have you been? Are you doing your exercises?" His questioning was courteous and entirely professional.

"Yes, three times a day," she said.

"Are you still requiring pain relief?"

"Not much. Just now and again."

"Any stiffness?"

Kate shook her head.

Adam stood up. "Would you mind if I take a look?"

Kate's heart rate quickened. Oh God, she thought. She had known an examination was coming, but now it was Adam who was doing it and she was going to have to let him touch her and still have the concentration to respond appropriately. He pointed to Kate's arm and she slipped off her baggy jumper, revealing a vest top strategically worn beneath. Kate held out her arm and Adam took it and examined the scars. His fingertips skimmed over the surface of her arm, stirring the rhythm of her heart with

215

their gentle confidence. He put her arm through its paces as Kate struggled hard to focus on his instructions.

"Not bad. Could you slip off your jeans and pop up onto the couch for me, please?"

At least she had been wise enough to wear shorts underneath. Adam examined her hip. Then he asked to see her chest site and so she lifted up the right side of her top and he examined that too.

"Breathe," he said coolly and Kate flushed with embarrassment, realising she had been holding her breath all the while he'd been touching her. "That's fine."

Kate could feel her cheeks burning and quickly pulled her clothes back on. She re-joined the pair back at the desk and played with her finger nails until they were ready.

"I think we can let you go," he said without looking up. He raised his head. "Continue with your physio and I see no reason why you shouldn't make a full recovery." He scribbled a note on a slip of paper and handed it to her.

Kate took the slip. Only one word had been written on it: Discharged. She folded it up and put it in her pocket.

Standing to leave, Kate noticed Adam was busy writing in the notes. "Thank you," she said.

He finished off what he was writing and looked up; his face unreadable. "You're welcome." And for a second Kate thought she could see something inside him, some sign of affection, but then he lowered his gaze back to the notes and it was gone.

Kate couldn't wait to be out of there. The guarded expression on Adam's face and the detached way in which he had spoken to her made her realise there was little point in attempting to speak to him now. He wasn't interested. She took the bus back home and sat for an hour staring into nothing.

But in the end, life had to go on. Rich had sorted out her insurance while Kate had been ill and now she had a cheque lying on her bedside table waiting to buy a new car. She reached across the table and grabbed the local paper and turning to the motoring section, she began to read. Most of them were too expensive but one dealer, a short distance outside town, was a little cheaper than the rest, and they had a car that just might suit. She tore out the advertisement and rang her dad to see if he would go along and see it with her.

That weekend Kate and her dad paid a visit to the dealer and tested out the car. They looked at a couple of others too while they were out there but ended up buying the first one they tried. Sophie arranged to drive her over to collect it the following Friday afternoon, after she'd finished work and Kate was beginning to feel a bit better.

Kate arrived at the dealer's that day and signed for the car, taking hold of the keys. She was anxious about getting behind the wheel again, but excited at the return of her liberty.

She sat inside the car and started it up. She was okay. Pulling out onto the main road, she felt a little apprehensive, but she was all right; she could do this.

Kate decided to drop into A&E to say hello before she started back at work the following week, not only to break up the journey but she still needed to thank everyone for all they had done for her the day she was brought in.

She walked in to A&E as Mark Cobham was walking out. "Kate! You look a hundred times better," he said. "I was just wondering how you were getting on. Have you been in to clinic?"

Kate took a second to fall in. "No. That was last week. I've just been to pick up my new car."

"So? How did it go?"

"Great. It's lovely and very smooth."

"I meant the clinic, Kate."

Kate looked around. "You mean with Mr Elliott?" She thought she might as well say it; it was obvious he knew.

"Yes."

"Discharged," she said and smiled.

"And?"

"I'll be back next week."

"Excellent. Make sure you're fully recovered first. We don't want you wrecking yourself up again. Adam would have my guts for garters if I let you come back here before you were ready."

Kate frowned at him.

"Tell me you got everything sorted out between the two of you?" Mr Cobham's expression was suddenly less fun.

Kate sighed. "Not really. I mean, he had a student with him, but... Oh, who am I kidding? He wasn't interested in talking to me. He could barely look at me. I really don't think there's much point."

Mark Cobham huffed and grabbing Kate by the wrist, he hauled her back into his office and sat her down. "Now what I'm about to tell you may get me into a lot of trouble with our Adam," he said, "but the pair of you are just about driving me demented, so sit there for a minute and listen to what I have to tell you. Then, if you still want to walk out of here afterwards that's fine, but first you need to know the facts."

Kate swallowed. She looked into Mark Cobham's face and realised he knew something that was about to devastate her and she had no other choice but to sit there and listen.

He sat and adjusted his chair. "I told you Adam's wife died in a car crash, didn't I? Well in the end he had to make the decision to turn the machines off. He had to do that, Kate, for the woman he loved. Move three years on and once again he is devastated by the discovery that the woman he loves... Yes, I said *loves*, Kate, has been seriously injured in a car crash."

Kate forgot how to breathe. If this was just the beginning, she was never going to survive.

"He wasn't on duty the night you came in, you've probably worked that one out by now. But I rang him. I had to. If it was your friend, wouldn't you? He found me in A&E, forced John to let go of the case and took over your care, down to the last detail."

"But-"

"Your sign said Hammond and Barker? Yes, I know. That was the way he wanted it. But it was Adam who got you sorted out and into Theatre. He didn't give us any choice really. I almost had to stop a fight breaking out between the two of them, arguing in the middle of A&E about who would take care of you. He saved your life, Kate, no two ways about it. Oh, we all did our part, of course, but Adam was the driving force behind it. He wanted the responsibility for everything. If he could have managed without the surgeons, anaesthetists and everyone in Theatre, I'm convinced he would have done it. He wanted to make sure everything was done perfectly. Even down to stitching up all your tiny little wounds, which he could have easily left to any number of others to sort out for him."

A light bulb went on in Kate's mind, as her brain slowly imploded. "So that's why Mr Barker couldn't tell me who had stitched up my leg."

"He wouldn't have been allowed to say anything."

"But why all the secrecy? Why not just tell me?" Kate asked.

"For you, Kate. You were so angry with him before the crash and when you came round on ITU, you didn't want him anywhere near you."

Mortified, Kate covered her face with her hands.

"It wasn't your fault, Kate. He understood that. But to help you through it, he kept out of your way. He checked in on you with the nursing staff and the surgeons all through the days that followed and crept in to see you every night. In fact, I think the surgeons were quite glad when he went on holiday." He smiled. "He was pretty terrifying."

"But he was so cross with me?"

Mark Cobham shook his head. "He wasn't cross with you, Kate, he was scared. He didn't go home for days in case you needed him. Mr Barker had to send him home on the Saturday after you came in, to make him get some sleep or he wouldn't have been fit to carry on. You know he stayed with you the whole night you were admitted. He barely left your side through everything you went through. It was only when the nurses kicked him out of ITU in the morning that he left you and got himself together enough to go and do his day's work. He killed himself to make sure you were okay."

Kate was floating in that ocean she had always dreamed of, but this time she was alone, on a life-raft and slipping further and further out to sea. "And I sent him away without so much as a kind word." She was the lowest of the low. She looked into Mark's eyes, searching for some sense of forgiveness. So that was it. Everything that had happened to help her: the night of the crash, the operations, her care after and even her new housemate, it had all been down to him; the tireless, thankless efforts of Adam.

A moment passed in silence as she tried to comprehend what had really gone on.

"So what are you going to do about it, Kate?" Mr Cobham said at last.

Kate looked up. "Do you think he will still speak to me?" she asked.

"Kate, he loves you. Now get yourself back up there before you miss him altogether; he's leaving for Italy in the morning."

"Italy?"

"Yes. He's got a job out there; didn't you know? He refused to stay on with us, although they did ask him. He's fluent, you know."

It was like she'd been hit with a sledgehammer. Now Kate remembered: Adam had only been filling in while they advertised the post for a permanent replacement. He was only ever meant to be a locum. "Is-?"

"It's his last day, Kate. What are you waiting for? Get yourself up there." He looked at his watch. "He should just about have finished in Theatre by now."

Kate leapt up out of her seat and ran as fast as her aching leg would carry her, along the corridors to Theatre. She searched for him everywhere, but in the end, a nurse clearing up told her that he had already gone. She ran back through the hospital to Adam's office, in a last ditch attempt to reach for salvation, but it was locked, and he was gone.

~~~

There the woman stopped as she felt the drawing of the hour.

"So what happened?" Lena asked her. "He didn't really go to Italy, did he? 'Cause I have to tell you, if he did, this is the worst story I've ever heard."

"Yes, he went."

"No! I thought you were trying to cheer me up? Isn't that what everyone's trying to do these days? Cheer up the unhappy girl?"

"Is that what you think?" the woman asked.

Time was marching on and the woman felt the moment slipping away from her.

~~~

Kate pulled up outside her house and parked her car. It was bright red and shiny. She knew the shine wouldn't last, but at least it was nice for now.

In less than a week she would be a useful member of society again. She would have been excited, but for the burden of guilt hanging over her. She was dwelling at the bottom of a shadowy pit and the moment weighed heavily upon her.

Kate hated having left everything so cold between them. He had to know she understood now what had happened, both to him and to her and that she regretted everything.

It was plain to Kate that there would be no coming back from this, despite what Mr Cobham had said, but she would not be happy in herself until she had at least tried to make amends. It wasn't going to be easy, facing Adam again, but in some way Kate thought that would help. There was something unfinished between them, an apology to be made, and to be able to move on, she felt she had to know that pain.

But she was terrified. What if he wasn't there? What if he wouldn't listen? Or maybe he would listen, but no longer cared? There were so many possible outcomes and few of them were good.

She tried to rehearse what she was going to say, but words alone seemed inadequate. Kate decided to just tell him the truth. She had to lay it all out for him, everything that had happened, if he would listen, and then grit her teeth and take whatever he flung at her. She threw on something smart and brushed out her hair and prepared to go back out.

Collette came in then. "You look nice," she said. "Off anywhere exciting?"

Kate didn't like to say. "There's something I've got to do," she said. "If it all goes well, I'll tell you about it when I get back." She took a deep breath, grabbed her keys and marched out into the half-light, looking neither left, nor right but straight ahead and without so much as a coat around her.

It was a twenty minute drive from Kate's house to his and several times along the way she thought of turning back. But she was not a coward. Kate knew it was going to be tough. He was unlikely to make it easy for her after everything she'd put him through but she had to face him, and it had to be now, before he was gone and there were no more chances to explain.

She pulled up in the parking bay outside the smart building. Adam's car was sitting patiently in its parking spot. Kate took a deep breath and looked up. There were a few lights on in the apartments above, but from outside, she wasn't sure which one of them was his. She got out of the car with her limbs trembling, walked up to the entrance and pressed the buzzer. There was no answer. She waited for a minute and pressed it again, clutching her arms around her and rocking on the spot to keep warm. Still nobody answered.

Cars passed by behind her, up on the main road, but in the apartment building in front of her everything was still. Kate's breath was starting to form clouds around her head. She tried one last time and then walked slowly back across the car park to her car.

A figure approached down the long sloping driveway. He was carrying a bag and was wrapped up tightly in a long dark coat. Kate slowed her pace and squinted to make out the features in the fading light. Adam.

"Kate?"

Kate walked out into the open and stood there, shivering, waiting for him to join her.

Adam approached and stopped a short way off, as if silently waiting for Kate to explain.

She looked down at the ground and then up at his face, but there was no way she could hold onto his gaze. "I just needed to see you, to say thank you... and to say sorry... for everything. Mr Cobham told me what you did and... and I was so awful to you. If I'd only known... if I'd known half of it..." She looked up, desperate for understanding.

Adam shifted his weight and looked at her intensely, his face giving away nothing of what he was feeling inside and Kate was forced to look back down at the floor.

"I had no idea," she said. "I never thought..." Oh, how was she meant to find the words to tell him how truly sorry she was? "I was just so hurt." She rubbed her neck nervously. She tried to speak but she couldn't think of the words to say. Her mouth opened to say something, but nothing came out.

Adam took a step closer and Kate looked up again, hoping for some sort of softness in his eyes. Instead, they were burning, scrambling her brain and making her body shake more than ever. Her gaze fell to his lips. They were moving now, freed from the deathly grip that had made them so cold. They creased a little at one side, as if he might be considering a smile. He stepped closer still. He put down his bag and his hands reached for her face. Kate's heart stilled as his breath mingled with hers in one heart-stopping moment when anything seemed possible, and then he kissed her.

Kate's body was melting. All the fear and regret that had built up inside was washed away as he pulled her into him, almost sweeping her off her feet and crushing her in the strength of his hold. His aftershave lingered around her, whispering temptation and there they stood, locked in an embrace, and lost in the extraordinary depths of their love.

Kate's body shuddered as a sharp gust of wind whirled around them and Adam opened his coat and wrapped her inside it.

"What have you done with your coat?" he murmured, as his warm breath fanned across her cheeks and curled beneath her hair.

"I didn't think," she said. "I just knew I had to see you."

Adam kissed the top of her head as her fragile body trembled against his. "Come on, let's get you inside. There's someone I need to speak to."

Kate walked with him, sharing his warmth, up the stairs to his apartment.

With the key, he let himself in and offered Kate his hand. She took it willingly and walked inside and there, sat on the settee, was Mark.

Adam didn't let go of Kate's hand. He put the bag down and walked over to greet him. "Look what I found, freezing to death outside in the cold," he said.

"Kate. If I'd known it was you I would have let you in," said Mark.

Adam cleared his throat and looked at Mark. "A little birdie tells me that you might have mentioned something that you know you shouldn't have." His eyes were scolding, though his mouth couldn't help but smile and his hand was holding tight on to Kate's.

"Thanks for the head's up, Kate," Mark sighed. "I thought you were on my team?"

"Mark?"

Mark Cobham put his hands in the air. "Okay, I admit it, I cracked, but the pair of you were bloody hopeless on your own. Someone had to knock some sense into you."

Kate smiled at her boss and then looked back up at Adam. "He was only trying to help," she said.

"Don't you start," Adam scolded. "I've got enough to deal with with *him* running his mouth off when he shouldn't have. Don't get me started on you."

The pit of Kate's stomach clenched as she saw the fire of passion igniting in his eyes. "Sorry," she said, mocking him with the glint in her own and risking a grin as delicious thoughts blazed across her mind.

"Well, I hope you like Chinese, because I think this is my cue to go," Mark said.

"No. Not because of me, please," Kate told him. "I just came round to-"

"No. I must be going. Adam won't thank me for hanging around now. Have fun in Italy, Adam. Keep in touch." He turned to Kate. "And I'll see *you* on Monday."

The front door clicked shut and Kate's smile was lost. "You're really going then?" she said, suddenly devastated by the news.

"I have to," Adam told her. "They're expecting me." But that night was theirs, and in the morning, Kate went with him to the airport and struggled to let go as they parted at the gate.

"Will you wait for me?" he asked her at the final time his flight was called.

"Till the end of time," she said and her eyes became the sea.

"Marry me, Kate. When I get back from here. Marry me and never let go," and Kate hugged him to her.

"Of course," she told him. "I love you. Come back to me. Quickly."

And six weeks later Adam was back in Kate's arms, having served his notice the moment he arrived, and carrying a ring.

~~~

She had tried her hardest to reach out to the girl, the rest would have to be up to her now, and she looked at Lena with worldly eyes, willing her to take the next step.

"So it *was* happily-ever-after in the end?" Lena asked her.

The woman looked fondly at her charge, and a curious haze fell upon her. "That is for *you* to decide."

A hand come to rest lightly on the woman's shoulder and Lena saw a dark-haired, handsome man lean down and kiss the top of her head. "Come along, sweetheart, it's time to go."

She touched his hand and turned back to Lena. "One day someone will stop and look at you, Lena, and they will see you for the wonderful, brilliant, beautiful woman you really are. You'll see. And it will all have been worth it. And it will probably happen sooner than you think." She smiled and lifted her hand away and Lena shivered at the loss of her touch.

The woman stood up. "Don't stop kissing those frogs, Lena; you never know when one of them is going to turn out to be your prince."

The sound of cars pulling up outside stirred the room into life and Lena looked for her mother among the dark jostling throng. One woman peered out through the curtains to see the sad procession arriving, letting in the brilliant light of the day. Lena looked at the white china clock on the mantelpiece and then back to the woman, but the woman was already gone.

"Lee, come on love. The cars are here," Gloria called across the room. Lena stood up and looked out of the window just in time to see the woman, radiant despite the sombre turn of the

226

day, walking hand in hand across the front lawn, with her adoring man by her side. They stopped half way and Lena saw a little girl, no more than a few years old, skip merrily up beside them. The woman turned and leaning down, she held out her other hand. Happiness was shining out of her like rays of the sun. And as the little girl took hold of the woman's hand, she smiled and they carried on together.

"Lee," her mother called again.

Lena picked up her coat and wandered over to her mother's side.

Out in the sun, the cars lined up along the side of the road. Lena and her mum walked up the driveway, solemnly admiring the flowers there. At the end of the drive, waiting in all soberness, were three black hearses, already carrying their precious loads.

The men, dressed in mourning suits, were carefully lifting the wreaths into the back of each hearse and placing them around the coffins. Behind them was the family's car. The driver of this last car was young, not much older than herself, Lena thought. He had a kind face, with warm eyes and a composure that whispered of quiet confidence. The lad gave her a respectful, friendly nod and Lena accepted it without expression and looked away.

They sat in their car, waiting for the off and Lena watched as a middle-aged couple, dressed all in black, were seated in the family car along with another, younger couple, standing supportively by them.

Lena's mum asked her if she had been okay, sat all alone in the living room, and Lena told her it had been fine actually, because someone *she* had worked with had sat down next to her and told her a story about a woman called Kate who had met the love of her life after a funeral. Gloria turned to look at her daughter.

"Did she tell you her name?" she asked.

Lena shook her head. "No, but I've got a feeling it might have been her."

"Who?" her mum asked.

"Kate."

227

Gloria's voice became thin, as if she suddenly found difficulty in speaking. "What makes you say that, love?"

"She just looked like the Kate she was describing. And she knew an *awful* lot about her," Lena said.

Gloria shivered. She studied her daughter for a minute and then blinked and settled back in her seat.

The procession set off and Gloria started the engine, shaking her head a little as she waited in line to pull away.

At the church on the hill, Lena and her mum found a pew on the left side, near the back and Lena looked around the congregation. Organ music played as the church filled up to standing room only.

Gloria opened up the order of service and looked inside to see which hymns they were going to be singing. The music stopped and the congregation stood. One by one the three coffins were reverently carried in and settled down, side by side, at the front of the church, two big and one small.

The vicar asked everyone to sit and spoke a few words before the first hymn was announced and they all stood once again. Lena mumbled the words to a song she had never known and looked around the church at the sculptures and plaques along the walls. As the hymn came to an end, the congregation retook their seats and Gloria closed the order of service and laid it carefully in her lap.

A man took his place at the front of the church and addressed the congregation.

"I was lucky enough to work with Kate for a number of years and I was a friend to Adam throughout, which had its moments, I can assure you."

Suddenly he had Lena's attention.

"So when I was asked to say a few words about the two of them today I began by thinking about all that they had achieved. I listed their various accomplishments and tried hard to think of a few anecdotes to string it all together. But the more I thought about it, the more I realised that what they did in life wasn't important, it was who they were, or rather who they were when they were together that mattered."

"I had the privilege of knowing them both quite well in their short time on this earth and what struck me most about the pair of them was how much more they were together than apart. It was as if their just being together created something special, something shared by those around them and so in the end I decided just to tell you about their love in my own words."

"It really began five and a half years ago, on an icy cold evening in January; the day that Kate finally understood how much Adam really loved her."

Lena's heart shuddered. She looked across at the order of service sitting on her mother's lap and started to shiver. She quietly touched the folded sheet of paper and her mother passed it across and there, on the front, was a picture of the woman, the man and the little girl.

Lena felt her stomach heave. Her breathing became rapid and her heart beat hammered inside her. She looked around, frantically trying to spot the woman who should have been there, but she was nowhere to be seen.

Black hats and suits swam in front of her eyes and then her mind focussed in on the words the man was saying.

"I was sitting on the couch at Adam's place one night, the night before he took a brief trip to Italy, for a job he had, by then, lost all passion for."

"We were having a final farewell meal, the man way, a few beers and a Chinese from up the road, when he walked back in with Kate, his hand locked firmly in hers. 'Look what I found freezing to death outside,' he said. I could see Adam was trying hard to remain stern and disapproving, but from the look in his eyes, he had never been happier. I was in trouble, of course, for telling Kate about everything he'd done for her: saving her life after the crash and turning the world upside down to help her, but he seemed to manage not to hold that against me."

He paused for a moment to steady his voice and clear his

throat. "And the two of them never looked back," he said. "Kate came back to work a couple of days later with happiness shining right through her. She was the most caring, most compassionate, most capable nurse any of us had ever seen and when the two of them were on together, well, that was a good day to be at work."

"Adam had seen so much tragedy in his life, and he felt deeply that he wanted to do some good and Kate wanted to share that with him. After their wedding, a beautiful occasion as a lot of you will remember, Adam had planned on taking Kate on an exotic honeymoon before dedicating a year of their lives to the Red Cross, but a disaster happened and so they selflessly put their life on hold for a while to fly out and help. And so it began. Their first year of marriage, traveling the world and helping out wherever crisis needed them, be it earthquake or hurricane, landslide or tsunami, keeping in touch with the people they met along the way. And when they came back home, they worked tirelessly, sending out much needed supplies donated by anyone and everyone they could persuade to help them."

He glanced sideways at the coffins, blinking back the tears that threatened to escape and shaking his head. And then he stilled himself for a moment to settle his voice.

"Adam told me once that Kate was like a breath of fresh air; she was the best thing that ever happened to him. He said he might have regretted many things along the way, but never a single moment that he spent with her. When he had her by his side, he said, he felt invincible."

The man paused. "There is a saying that the candle that burns twice as brightly, burns half as long. Well their candle could have mirrored the sun." He looked down for a moment and steadied his breathing. "Theirs was a love most people can only dream of. Poets could not write words as beautiful as the happiness they shared. And it ended far too quickly, on the dream holiday he had always wanted to take her on, in the clear blue waters of the Caribbean. All I can add now is at least they died as I know they would have lived, together."

White handkerchiefs dabbed at watery eyes all around as the story of their tragic passing unfolded.

Gloria placed a handkerchief in her daughter's hand and looked at her with concern. Tears were pouring down Lena's face and Lena hadn't even noticed. She dried her eyes and looked back at the photo in her lap. They looked so happy together, so perfect, just like they had…

A draught blew in from behind her and Lena turned round to see who had walked in, but the door was closed. She noticed the young lad watching her from the back of the church, standing solemn and still beside the door. His eyes searched hers and made a connection.

Music started up again and Lena turned back and pretended to sing.

At the end of the service 'The Prayer' was played, a song that had apparently come to mean so much to them. It wasn't a song Lena knew well, a duet by a man and a woman, sung in English and Italian, but it suited the occasion perfectly.

Men in mourning suits – family from the pews and the undertakers - walked with great purpose up to the front of the church and lifted the coffins high up onto their shoulders. The music swelled and rose inside Lena's crippled heart, moving her with its melody.

The story of two people, so in love and so tragically lost together. And now Lena knew how it ended. And as the congregation filed outside for the interment, a small piece of paper fluttered over in a gust of wind and landed on the floor at her feet. Lena looked down and picked it up. It was the business card for the funeral director, Thompson, Thompson and Sons, and it had fallen from a pile on the table beside her. She slipped the card into her pocket and carried on.

Outside they gathered at the grave side as the coffins were

lowered into the ground and the vicar muttered the words that comforted few.

They were at peace now at least, Lena knew that. Kate, floating upon that eternal sea, with Adam and her daughter by her side. The three of them, tucked up under the ground, together forever, in heavenly seclusion.

When it was over, Lena wandered past the row of wreaths reading the words written by those who loved them. Adam had no family left to miss him, but Kate's family had taken him to their hearts and there seemed to be no shortage of mourners. They may be gone now, but Lena doubted they would ever be forgotten and certainly not by her.

Clusters of people began to form again as the congregation broke up and started to leave. It was back to the house now for more cups of tea, and Lena almost wished she was going with them. But her mum had promised her they wouldn't have to go, so they were leaving straight after. It had all been arranged.

Lena understood now all that had happened to her that day, but she had to search around one last time, just to make sure.

"I'll meet you at the car in a minute," she said to her mum and left her to say her goodbyes to the family and wandered slowly round the graveyard, searching through the sea of faces for the ones she did not expect to find. They were gone. Only the picture in her hand was left to remind her of what she had learned that day, and who would believe that?

She started walking back down the slope, away from the crowd, to the car, parked at the bottom of the hill, and standing by the family's car, patiently awaiting his charge, was the lad she had noticed from before. He smiled at her.

"It's a beautiful day, isn't it?" he said.

Lena looked up at the sky and then back to him. "Yes. I suppose it is."

"Did you know them well?" he asked.

"Better than I thought," she said, and the lad looked at her

232

curiously. A breeze danced a wisp of hair about her face and Lena smiled. It was the first time in many months that her face had looked so at ease. She caught the errant strands and tucked them back behind her ear.

At that moment, Gloria walked around the side of the church and saw her troubled daughter smiling at the boy beside the car. And as she watched the scene unfolding, new tears of joy began to trail wearily down her sodden cheeks, as Lena held out her hand and spoke to him.

"I'm Lena," she said. "What's your name?"

The End